THE MIRACLES OF ORDINARY MEN

THE MIRACLES OF ORDINARY MEN

Amanda Leduc

ECW PRESS

Published by ECW Press
2120 Queen Street East, Suite 200, Toronto, Ontario, Canada M4E 1E2
416-694-3348 / info@ecwpress.com

Library and Archives Canada Cataloguing in Publication

Leduc, Amanda
The miracles of ordinary men / Amanda Leduc.

ISBN 978-1-77041-111-1
Also issued as: 978-1-77090-393-7 (PDF); 978-1-77090-394-4 (ePUB)

I. Title.

PS8623.E426M57 2013 C813'.6 C2012-907516-7

Editor for the press: Michael Holmes / a misFit book
Cover and text design: Natalie Olsen, Kisscut Design
Cover image: (Feather) Miss X / photocase.com
Author photo: Trevor Cole
Printing: Edwards Brothers Malloy 1 2 3 4 5

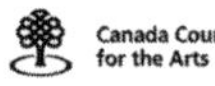

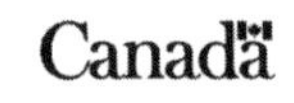

The publication of *The Miracles of Ordinary Men* has been generously supported by the Canada Council for the Arts which last year invested $20.1 million in writing and publishing throughout Canada, and by the Ontario Arts Council, an agency of the Government of Ontario. We also acknowledge the financial support of the Government of Canada through the Canada Book Fund for our publishing activities, and the contribution of the Government of Ontario through the Ontario Book Publishing Tax Credit. The marketing of this book was made possible with the support of the Ontario Media Development Corporation.

Printed and bound in the United States.

For my family, who never stopped believing in this story.

And is it not true in this instance also that one whom God blesses he curses in the same breath?

SØREN KIERKEGAARD

TEN

SUNDAY

Sam's cat crumpled like paper under the truck's wheel. He knelt down to touch her and then something like heat, some sudden shock of air, surged through his hands.

Suddenly she was breathing, blinking up at him through a mass of matted fur. Dead, and then not-dead, and his were the hands that had done it.

A car door slammed; he cradled the cat, heard footsteps. When he looked up he saw a boy, standing white and terrified in the same spot where the truck had crushed the cat against the curb. Moments ago, only just. The boy's mother stood close to the truck, her eyes large and dark with guilt.

"It's fine," he said, when he could speak. He avoided the mother and spoke instead to the boy, his hands around

Chickenhead, his fingers throbbing with alien power. The wings ached in the chill of the early evening air. "I know it didn't look like it, but she's fine."

"I saw . . . blood," said the boy. He had stubborn hair. He looked like the kind of boy who would grow up to argue with Sam in one of his classes. One day, if he was still teaching.

"It was a mistake." He couldn't think of any other way to say it. "I thought so too, but look." He let Chickenhead go and clenched his hands to stop the shaking. The cat dropped lightly to the ground and sauntered over to the boy. Sam could hear her purr from five feet away.

"She's okay," said the boy. Like Sam, he sounded as though he couldn't quite believe it. When he knelt and held out his hand, the cat rubbed against his fingers. "What's her name?"

"Chickenhead," said Sam. The mother laughed—a high laugh, edged with hysteria—and the boy made a face.

"Chickenhead?" he repeated. If he could see the wings, he wasn't letting on. "What kind of a name is that?"

"I don't know," Sam said, perfectly honest. "I was—" he almost said *high*, and then thought better of it. "It seemed like a good idea at the time."

The boy's mother rolled her eyes. "Aidan," she said, "we should go."

The boy nodded, but he didn't get up. "What're those rips in your shirt for?"

"Those?" Sam shrugged and pointed a lazy hand, careful not to touch the wings. There was his answer, right there. "It's just an old shirt."

"Aidan," his mother said again. "You're going to be late."

He was tempted to ask what the boy would be late for, just to keep the two of them there and talking. Instead he whistled, and Chickenhead jumped out of the boy's arms and sauntered back to him. Aidan gave a small wave and climbed into the truck. And off they went—piano lessons, karate, soccer practice, whatever.

Still clutching the cat, he leaned forward and vomited into the gutter. There was blood on the asphalt. A few clumps of dark fur. The wind flapped against the holes in the back of his shirt.

"Well," he said. "What happens now?"

Chickenhead, bathed in light, began to purr. She turned on her back and stretched her legs so that her claws caught the wings, which were white now, the feathers long and soft. Sam stood at the end of his drive and let them unfurl—six feet across, maybe more. When he flexed his shoulders, they beat hard against air. He rocked slowly on the balls of his feet and watched the clouds. The sky waited above him. It was almost night. The air was cold. The only light on the street came from him.

SATURDAY

In the morning he gave in, finally, and cut holes in all of his shirts. Chickenhead watched from the bed as he moved the scissors through the blue plaid shirt from Julie and the cream silk one he'd bought at the overpriced suit store on Robson. The rugby shirts and V-neck sweaters were next—he'd had some of his students pick these out, his finger no longer quite on the pulse of the fashion world. A system that had suited them all—his cash, their amused fashion expertise. Wasted now, with every thrust of his scissors.

He stopped when he got to the linen shirt that would have seen him through the wedding. Time for coffee, maybe even a morning stroll.

No one used the garden this early on a Saturday, so he took Chickenhead out with him and watched her stalk bugs in the grass. The wings were long enough to touch the ground and bounced softly in the air with each step of his slippered feet. He walked around the pond and watched them unfurl in his reflection. *A gift*, the priest had said. A gift, and it wasn't even Christmas.

When he got back inside he picked up the phone and dialed Julie, even though he wasn't drunk. He moved to hang up when a male voice answered the phone, but then he coughed and his anonymity was gone.

"Sam," said the voice on the phone.

"Derek. Can I talk to Julie?"

"It's pretty early," he said, as though Sam didn't know. "She's still sleeping. I can give her a message, if you want."

"Sure." He thought for a moment. "Tell her the church still smells the same."

"Okay." If Derek found this strange, he didn't let on. "You have a good day, Sam." Then he hung up the phone.

Sam was supposed to be the one hanging up. Sam, in point of fact, was supposed to be the one sleeping beside Julie. He listened to the air for a moment. Chickenhead, who had adjusted quite happily to the tuna juice—he was now the only person in this household losing weight—glared at him from where she sat, concentrated on her food.

"I am *trying*," he told her, and he shook the phone for emphasis. But his threats, as they both knew well, were laughable at best. She remained impassive, bored, infinitely superior. She licked a paw as Sam watched. Her eyes said *pussy*, as plain as day.

FRIDAY

School ended in a one-on-one conference, Sam on one side of the desk, Emma on the other.

"You're not going to tell anybody?" she said.

"There's nothing to tell. No one will believe me." He paused. "Are you going to tell anybody?"

This made her laugh. "What makes you think anyone will believe me if they're not going to believe you?" She ran her fingers over the faded wood of his desk. Her face held a deference he didn't like. "Are you going to leave?"

"I'm thinking about it," he said. Which was a lie; he hadn't thought about anything until right then. "Maybe I'll go on a road trip." Suddenly the idea shone in his mind. Sam and Chickenhead and the dying Jetta, Joni Mitchell on the open road. "A pilgrimage."

"Where would you go?"

"I have no idea." The word *pilgrimage* made him think of two things: Mecca and Memphis. Hot sun and fervour and praying five times a day—and Elvis. But he didn't have the cash for Saudi Arabia, and he wasn't really a Graceland kind of guy. Besides, a road trip along the Sunshine Coast? With his cat? Taking God's gift for a spin, that's all it would be. "You shouldn't be here," he said. "You're always staying after class. I'm getting looks."

"I have something for you," Emma said. She reached into her bag and pulled out a twisted loop of metal. There was a circle of string around one end. "It's an infinity puzzle," she said. "You're supposed to get the string off."

"Thank you." His hands went automatically to the string and started working it through. "Is this supposed to drive me completely over the edge?"

She laughed. "I was hoping it would save you, actually."

"Too late," and his tone was light, even though the words were not. "I don't think I have that much further to go."

THURSDAY

"Bless me, Father, for I have sinned."

Like riding a bike, the old cliché. The church felt the same, which shouldn't have surprised him but did—it had been two years, only that, and somehow it felt as though he'd been gone forever. Worn floorboards and the same threadbare cushions in every pew.

But it wasn't the same, not really, because Father Jim wasn't there. Instead, a small dark-haired man shook Sam's hand and directed him into a pew. His name, he said, was Father Mario. His voice was also small—Sam had to still himself completely to hear him, which was probably the point.

"Bless me, Father, for I have sinned," he repeated. Though he hadn't come to confess and didn't believe in sin anyway. But there—that was how he started.

"How long has it been since your last confession?" The priest's accent was soft and unobtrusive. Filipino, maybe—a roly-poly young boy who'd grown up with the light of God in his eyes.

"I don't know," and he shifted in his pew. He'd eschewed the anonymity of the confessional on the chance that Father Mario might have noticed the wings, like Emma, but so far he hadn't said anything. "I'm not a fan of confession, actually."

The priest smiled. "Most people aren't."

"I'm," he felt restless now, "not here to confess. I need... some advice?"

Father Mario smiled again. "Most people do."

If this were Father Jim, he would have taken Sam into the rectory and offered him a glass of Scotch. Father Jim, who went way back. He'd taught catechism until Sam switched schools and was famous in the diocese for going sober at Lent. Once upon a time, he was going to marry them, with Bryan there to act as best man and Julie's mother ready to outdo the town florist on dahlias.

Today, there was only Father Mario, small and stooped in a pew before the altar. He raised a hand and patted the cross at his neck. "What do you need?"

"I'm afraid," said Sam.

"Afraid of what?"

What, indeed. "I think I'm . . . changing."

"Change isn't always bad," the priest said instantly. "Especially when it draws you out of yourself."

Sam snickered before he could help it. "I suppose it's doing that, yes."

"Not all change seems natural, either," said the priest. "It is natural, for example, for a man to doubt. The growth to believing is what is so hard."

Jesus. They actually still said these kinds of things. Sam longed, suddenly, for Father Jim and the Scotch. *Advice?* Julie probably doled out crap like this to her patients. He stifled another snicker, then ruffled his wings and stood. He offered Father Mario an apologetic smile, even though he wasn't sorry. "Thank you. I'll try and remember." There was, he reflected, a bottle of Scotch at home in the cupboard.

The priest stood with him. Before they exited the pew, Father Mario reached out a hand and patted the right wing. When he drew his hand away, there was down on his fingers.

"No one can know what His gifts are for," the priest said.

He grinned, suddenly boyish in the dark light of the church. "I am a man of God," he said. "Nothing surprises me anymore."

WEDNESDAY

He decided to skip school again, and drove to Julie's studio. This time he managed to tuck the wings in so that they didn't block the rear-view mirror. He parked the Jetta in the old spot, the corner by the rhododendron bush, and walked into the studio with a mat rolled under his arm. Just another patient, that's all. The receptionist was new, and fell for it. He smiled at his luck and watched her blush. She couldn't see the wings, obviously—otherwise, there'd be no welcoming grin. The thought took his own smile away, even as the blush deepened down her neck and spread across her collarbones like a flush of poison ivy.

Once upon a time, he might have asked for her number. Asked in spite of Julie. Asked *because* of Julie, just to make her mad. But once upon a time was long ago. Back when wings weren't sprouting out of him, back when the world made sense.

Instead he asked for Julie. The receptionist was instantly all business.

"She's just finishing a class," she said, and she ushered Sam into the office. "She shouldn't be long."

Julie was over twenty minutes. Sam walked around the office and looked at the pictures on her desk—Julie and Derek at the Capilano Bridge, Julie in her gear, doing yoga on the beach. The dogs. The big, slobbering German shepherd—Max, how original—and Einstein, the tiny, slobbering Shih Tzu. They had to be leashed all the time, or God knew what would happen.

Chickenhead had no trouble walking alongside him, even without a leash.

He peeked through the files on her desk because he was bored, because he wanted to make her angry but didn't know why. The top file was red tab, which meant a hard case, a lot of work. Thirty-four-year-old female with advanced scoliosis and mild cerebral palsy, significant depression, significant suicidal tendencies. *Significant.* Was that even doctor-speak?

"Sam."

He looked up and put down the files in one fluid motion. Julie pulled the office door closed and went to the other side of the desk. She took the file and placed her arms around it, a dare, her anger evident in the thrust of her chin, the stiff angle of her legs and feet. Her hair was darker than he remembered.

"Nosing around, I see. Should I be surprised?"

"I was waiting," he said. "I didn't make an appointment."

She had pit stains, which annoyed him. Great gaping circles of dark blue beneath each arm. "I have another class in five minutes."

"I won't stay long."

"Fine," she said. "What do you want?"

Sam retreated, gripped the back of the patient's chair, the wings enormous and white and still. "I wanted to ask you something."

Julie swept an arm out and then back as if to say she had all the time in the world.

"Do you still go to the cathedral?"

She blinked and shook her head. "No."

"Just that church? Or any others?"

"I haven't been," she said, and she flushed. He knew, then, that she hadn't said anything to her mother. "Derek and I are taking a Buddhism class."

"I didn't know they had classes for that type of thing."

This, of all things, made her angry. "They have catechism—why not this?"

He shrugged. The wings ruffled against his back. They were heavy. Why hadn't he noticed that before? "I just wondered. I was thinking about Father Jim. Thought I might go and see him, and I wondered if you knew whether he was still at the church. That's all."

"Oh." She shook her head. "No. I don't know. I could ask my mother, if you want."

"Don't bother." He could ask his own mother, but that would get her excited. Not as excited as she would be to find out that her son was sprouting the wings of seraphim—if, indeed, she could see them at all—but there were plenty of things that Carol didn't need to know.

"Is that really all?" Julie asked.

He fought the urge to snap. *If anyone has a right to be edgy here, it's me.* Instead he picked up his mat and ignored the rolling eyes this earned him. "Thanks for letting me stop by."

"No problem." Her voice was dry and hesitant at the same time. "Any time."

He nodded, then turned and took three steps to the door.

"Sam?"

"Hmm?" The sudden thumping of his heart, the clammy slick of his hands. *Rocks*, his best friend had said. And still, here he was, hoping for the confession, the terrible mistake.

"Are you all right? You look . . . not well."

"I'm fine," he said. "Just tired."

She nodded. "All right. If you see Father Jim, tell him I said hello."

TUESDAY

He called in sick, and went to see the doctor. Chickenhead, who hadn't been eating, came with him in the car—they could stop at the vet on the way home, make it a family affair.

The wings made driving difficult; they were larger than yesterday and pushed against the roof of the car. The brightness of the feathers sent beams of reflected light into his eyes whenever he glanced in the rear-view mirror. Twice, he almost ran into oncoming traffic. Chickenhead and her claws were the only thing that saved him.

In the doctor's office, he sat quietly in a corner and leafed through a stack of trashy magazines. The wings draped over each side of his chair, terribly unmistakable, terribly invisible. No one glanced his way or said anything. But people avoided the chairs beside him all the same. He sat and turned the pages and wondered what the doctor would say.

But when the doctor called his name, she said nothing. He put down the magazine and followed her through to the examination room, ducking slightly to fit the wings under the door. That, oddly enough, got him a look. But she covered it quickly and ushered him into the third room on the left. He ducked under the doorframe again and turned to face her. She couldn't see the wings, he was sure of it.

The doctor was short and very pretty. She wore a yellow shirt under her lab coat and her hair was brown, like Julie's. "Mr. Connor," she said. Her voice, if it had a colour, would be yellow too. "What can we help you with today?"

Help. No one could help him here. "I have a growth," he said lamely. "It's hard to explain."

"All right," she said. "Where is it?"

"On my back." He choked back a bout of hysterical laughter. *Five feet of wingspan, lady.*

The doctor nodded, made a note in her file—*psych consult* wouldn't surprise him—and asked him to remove his shirt. He wiggled each wing through the haphazard holes he'd torn in the back and then, when it was off, folded the shirt so that the rips weren't showing. Here he was, in front of a pretty doctor in all of his soft, greyish glory. He turned his back to her eye and stifled a shout when her hand went right through the wing and pressed against his skin.

"These scars have healed well," she said. "Who was your doctor?"

What? Scars? "Ah . . . out of town," he said, making it up as he went along. "Doctor Marriner?" What the hell?

"Ah." Her hands prodded his flesh. "Sometimes," she said, "traumatic wounds like these take a long time to heal. It's not unusual for patients to develop odd sensations around extensive stitching." More prodding. Then a pause. Sam could hear the doctor shake her head. "I can't see or feel anything here, Mr. Connor. But let's book you for an x-ray, just in case."

On the x-ray table, he watched as the attendants fitted him with a protective bib, unconsciously avoiding the wings. The cartilage folded neatly against the cold leather of the table. He fought the urge to itch as a feather tickled the inside of his arm.

He was sure that the x-rays wouldn't show anything. He was right. The technician who came to take his iron bib away was young and bored. "You can change over there," he said, and he pointed to the stalls. Then he left.

He couldn't fit the wings into the changing stall, so he dressed quickly in the middle of the room. The right wing stuck in its hole and for a moment he was paralyzed. Then it pushed through and the wing flexed of its own accord, several feathers dropping to the floor. He picked them up and stuffed them into his pocket.

In the car, Chickenhead hissed as soon as he opened the door. She didn't like waiting. He ran a tired hand along her fur and then snatched it back, surprised, when she turned her head and bit him.

Julie had never liked Chickenhead. Even then, pre-Max, pre-Einstein, she'd been a dog person. Maybe it appealed to her sense of charity. He'd stopped trying to figure it out. But given the choice, he'd choose Chickenhead any day, in spite of the biting. She didn't slobber. And as long as he stayed on top of the kitty litter, no nasty smell. She had manners, his cat.

Or perhaps not so much manners as personality.

At the vet, the cat was quiet, calm, and detached. The vet and his assistant (who didn't notice the wings, but that was hardly surprising) cooed over the cat's fur and laughed when she shook herself after the exam. The air he knew so well didn't leave her face at all—if anything, she looked more disgusted with him when they left the office. She'd rung in at seventeen pounds.

Chickenhead. The fact that she wasn't eating (*try tuna juice*, said the vet) was probably a good thing.

MONDAY

In the morning there was a fine layer of down on his sheets. He showered with the door open, the wings quivering in the cooler air but dry. None of his shirts would fit—they bunched and made him look like the Hunchback of Notre Dame. He settled, finally, on an old sweatshirt, the grey one from McGill that he didn't mind destroying. He took the kitchen scissors to it, twisted and turned and bent the wings through the holes. The entire process took him almost half an hour.

Dressed, he looked in the mirror and found himself wishing, not for the first time, that Julie still lived in the house. His face was almost as grey as the sweatshirt and there were bags under his eyes. A glamour touch-up would do him so well right now. Just a smidge of cover-up, a touch of blush to bring him back from the edge of dead.

He wore a jacket—the gangster trench coat, Bryan called it—even though it wasn't that cold. The wings could fold against his back and the bulk of the coat was just enough to disguise it. He was not prepared for questions.

At the school, he slipped in through one of the back doors and looked over his shoulder every few metres, like a thief. No one said anything. In the staff room, he waved away the jokes—*Pulling the Mafia act on the kids, are we?*—and kept the coat on. Sweat that was part heat and part fear began to collect in the small of his back. Dave, who taught in the Mathematics department, poured him a coffee and then, seeing his face, added a shot of espresso.

"Rough night?" Dave asked. The pat on Sam's shoulder was briefly sympathetic.

"Rough weekend," Sam said, and left it at that.

In class he was quiet, distracted, just this side of short. He angled his chair so that his back faced the wall, and avoided the chalkboard. Some of his students shot odd looks his way—*What's with the coat, dude?*—but he ignored them and made the kids choose their own roles for *Macbeth*, instead of standing in front and reading as he normally would.

Halfway through the day, an early group of students surprised him. He'd removed the trench coat during lunch because his back was slick with sweat, and he was just about to put it back on when they tumbled through the door. For an instant he froze, terrified—the wings were longer than they'd been in the morning, and the feathers that peeked through the down were an unyielding, brilliant white.

But no one noticed. No one said anything. Just to be sure, he stood and flexed his shoulders so that the wings gave a half-hearted flap. And nothing. The students were engrossed in their conversation, and no one even looked his way. He folded the coat deliberately over the back of the chair, and then he straightened, and he taught.

His last class of the day was Modern English—Philip Roth and Martin Amis and Vladimir Nabokov, because once upon a time (when literature mattered, when he couldn't feel the weight of feathers on his back) he'd loved *Lolita*. The syllabus had enough Alice Munro and Doris Lessing to keep his female students from revolting. To date, he hadn't had any truants. Maybe that said something about him. Maybe it didn't.

His favourite student in this class was Emma, the petite redhead with journalistic aspirations. He was careful—even she didn't know. But he sought her opinion in discussions and he looked forward to her essays and he liked the sway of her hips. She had a lovely laugh.

Today, though, she walked in and looked straight at Sam, desperately nonchalant at his desk. No laughing—she looked puzzled at first, and then her face went pale. She sat at a desk in the back, as far from the front as space would allow.

He taught the class from his desk and dismissed them early. He stacked papers and watched Emma lag behind her friends. She waited until there were no students left and then came slowly to his desk.

"Hi," she said.

"Hi," he said, and swallowed. His throat was very dry.

"Is this an early Halloween?" and she forced a laugh, pointed to the wings. He felt them arch over his head and stretch as if in response to her question; two inches since lunchtime, it wouldn't surprise him at all.

"Not exactly," he said. He blinked and her face swam in and out of focus.

"I see," she said and nodded, as though that explained everything.

"I don't." His voice was sharper than he'd intended. "I don't see at all."

"Oh." The word seemed very small. "They're real?"

"Yes." Strange, the relief that rushed into his bones.

Unexpectedly, a quirk of her mouth. "You don't strike me as a particularly religious man."

"I'm not." He'd been Catholic, just as he'd believed in the Tooth Fairy. His mother still said prayers for him. They weren't helping, obviously.

"Maybe you should be," she said. "Maybe it's, you know, a sign."

This was surprising—he wouldn't have pegged her for a religious person, either. "I'll think about it," he said, another attempt at nonchalance. He tossed a hand back to the wings and tried a crooked smile, his first of the day. "Might try to get through the week, first."

"Okay." She gave him a tentative smile in return, then left. Much later, he realized that he hadn't asked her to keep it a secret.

Maybe you should be. Tomorrow, the Tooth Fairy would show up at his door with a bag of old teeth, dressed in rags and asking for change.

SUNDAY

He woke up with a stiff back, that was all. Stumbled into his bathroom and flicked on the light and there they were—greyish knobs of skin that unfurled from his shoulder blades and hung to just above his waist. He blinked and leaned in to the mirror. Close up, he could see tiny feathers, densely packed together and obscured in some areas by grey, fuzzy down. He splashed water on his face and looked again.

Wings.

He was hallucinating. He had to be hallucinating. He reached around and grasped as though expecting air, then shouted when his fingers touched a feather, all too real. A hint of cartilage lay beneath the fuzz. He followed that slight ridge up to where the growth met skin—the move from wing to flesh was seamless. His skin was both clammy and hot, fevered.

Chickenhead heard his cry and pattered into the bathroom. She hopped onto the toilet and watched him, her head tilted to the side. Her eyes grew wide and then narrowed; she batted at one wing and then licked her paw, as though it was no big deal.

"This isn't funny," he told her, almost shouting. She raised a paw again and ran her claws through the feathers. It hurt, more than he could have imagined.

Bryan. It was the only thing he could think of. He'd stumbled into his apartment alone last night, but Bryan was the craftiest jokester he knew, and he lived half a block away. His hands shook so badly he could barely dial the number.

His best friend answered on the seventh ring, sounding half asleep. "Muh?"

"Very funny. *Ha ha*."

"What?"

"I have down on my bedsheets. Extra points for getting in and getting it all done without waking me up. Now how do I get the damn things off?"

"What the hell are you talking about?"

"The wings, Bryan. Is it Super Glue?"

Pause. "I'm coming over."

"Don't bother. Just—"

"Five minutes, Sam." And *click*.

Bryan was at his house in three, pounding on Sam's door as though he'd just called 911. He'd run over in slippers and his flannels and when Sam opened the door expecting a yell, or at the very least a startled *What the fuck*, all Bryan did was grab him by the shoulders and pull him in for a brisk, hard hug.

"Sam," he said, when he pulled away, "I thought that was it."

"What?"

"I thought you'd lost it. All this stuff with Julie—I thought it had pushed you over the edge." His hair was in matted brown disarray and there were bags under his eyes.

Sam took one breath and then another. "I called because of—these." He gestured wildly behind his back. The wings fluttered, up and down. "See?"

Bryan's broad face was puzzled. "What?"

"Can't you—" waving madly "—*see* them?"

Now he looked nervous. "See what, buddy?"

Sam blinked, unsure—was he still dreaming?—and then looked back over his shoulder. There they were, the feathers limp against his spine. "You don't see anything? Anything out of the ordinary?"

Bryan snorted. "Aside from you and one hell of a hangover? No."

He felt dizzy, and slumped against the wall. "Oh. Okay." The wings bent against the wall with a sound like crumpling tissue, but Bryan didn't appear to hear it. Sam closed his eyes.

"Dude. You need to forget about this chick. Look at what it's doing to you."

That almost made him laugh. "She's not just 'some chick,' Bryan."

Bryan ignored him and padded down the hall into the kitchen. Sam listened as he opened the cupboards—out of coffee again, most likely. Then he shuffled back to the door. When Sam opened his eyes, Bryan was readjusting his slippers, coffee in hand.

"I'm telling you, Sam. It's over. She's granite. You're humping a fucking rock."

"I think," he said, "that the expression is 'beating a dead horse.'"

"Whatever. A rock is a rock is a rock, Sam—time to move on. We should go out more, introduce you to some people."

"Since when do you know people?" Sam asked. Each word felt forced, too big for his mouth.

"This might surprise you, but the whole world hasn't gone into mourning."

"I haven't gone into mourning."

Bryan snorted. "Sure," he said. "You've practically disappeared and now you're hallucinating after one night out on the town."

"I'm not—"

"Sam."

He blinked and then remembered. Pressed his hand against the wall and felt feathers, just waiting. "I'm just—old. Too old for nights like that."

"Speak for yourself, friend. What you need are *more* nights out. We should do this again soon. To hell with Julie and the accountant."

"Professor," he said. And, "Maybe." He couldn't think about Julie right now. He needed to get Bryan out of the house.

"Want me to make coffee?"

Sam shook his head. "No. Must be tired—should just go back to bed."

"Suit yourself," and Bryan clapped him on the shoulder, narrowly missing one wing. Sam bit his lip and fought to keep from crying out. "See you later in the week?"

"Sure." He closed the door as soon as it was polite, then stumbled to the bathroom and stretched out on the floor, the wings a feathery mass between his back and the tile. It hurt to breathe, and still the air pushed onward, through his lungs.

After a long moment, he dragged himself to sitting and blinked at Chickenhead, who hadn't moved from her perch on the toilet.

"I think I'm going crazy," he said. Something in his voice moved her, because she jumped down and crawled into his lap. Her purr was robust and warm against his stomach. He ran his hands through her fur and stopped just short of praying. Here he was, with his wings and his cat. Her eyes were amber slits in the soft light of the bathroom. If she could talk, give him some of her nine lives' wisdom, she might have said: this is just the beginning.

X

It’s a cold night in February 2001, and Lilah is very drunk. A party, a boy who kissed her in the bathroom, and Lilah, waking up outside. She stumbled home and now she’s trying to sneak in through the back door. But it’s locked. When she checks for the spare key, it isn’t there.

Timothy opens the door instead. “I heard you outside,” he says.

“Thanks.” She whispers from the porch—even here, the word feels too loud.

“Mom’s asleep,” and now he’s whispering as she steps past him, into the house.

“I know.” She stumbles again and the world tilts for one crazy moment. Then she’s at the kitchen counter, heaving into the sink.

“Do you want some hot chocolate?” he asks from behind her.

Hot chocolate is the last thing on her mind. "Sure," she gasps.

Timothy pads to the cupboard and takes out two mugs, then pulls the spoons from the drawer. He is trying to be quiet—the cutlery is muffled, the mugs placed so delicately on the counter it's a wonder that she can know he's done anything at all. But he has, and she knows. She always knows with Timothy. She rests her forehead against the edge of the sink and breathes in deeply. The counter is smooth beneath her hands.

"Mom waited for you," he says. "And then she got mad and locked the door."

"I noticed." She speaks the words down into the floor.

"I waited for you," he says. "I didn't want you to sleep outside. It's cold."

"Thanks, Timmy."

"That's okay." The kettle hisses. When she turns around, finally, Timothy is holding the two mugs carefully in his outstretched hands.

"I made this one with milk," he says. "Just for you."

Their mother will not do this, because milk in hot chocolate is *wasteful* and *unnecessary*. But since Lilah was small, she's been sneaking milk into her cup when Roberta isn't looking. Timothy has learned all of these habits from her. He hands over her mug. He is so young, so solemn. She places her palms around the mug and lets the heat burn her hands until they hurt.

"You look sick," he says. "Are you okay?"

She can't remember the name of the boy she kissed. She woke up with dirt in her mouth, and black spots in her memory. Whole hours she doesn't remember. "I'm fine."

"Mom says you're going to get in trouble." He sits on the

bar stool and stares at her. He is pale, as always, and too small for a ten-year-old child. His toes dangle far from the ground.

"Mom says lots of things."

"I don't want you to get in trouble, Lilah."

"I'll be fine, Timmy."

He sips his own hot chocolate. Foam clings to his lip. "Mom also says you're going to leave."

He says this every day. "I'm going to leave sometime. Yeah."

"But not right now."

"No, not right now."

"If you go," he says, "no one will talk to me anymore."

"Don't be silly."

"It's not silly. Mrs. Graham said it to Mom when she came over. When they thought I was in my room. She said, *He's such a strange little boy.*"

"Mrs. Graham is a fat, smelly pig."

He giggles. But he is serious again so quickly, so young, so small. "I don't want you to go."

"I'll die if I stay here, Timmy." Because this is honestly what she thinks—she'll die, or she'll marry that nameless boy she met at the party, and one day she'll become Roberta, which is to say worse than dead. She is twenty years old, invincible and furious, selfish in the way that only the young can be. She doesn't realize what she'll be breaking, what she'll be leaving behind. All she wants to do is disappear.

—

Now, these years later, she walks through the city and sees Timothy's face everywhere—on the posters, in the grocery line, in every other ragged heap rocking on the street. He drifts through Vancouver like fog that lies close to the ground.

She is like a detective, or an exotic birdwatcher—stalking

the streets, looking for the flash of his pale skin, the hooked nose they both share with Roberta. Some days, she wanders the streets alone. But usually she finds him. She brings him food and clothing: a hat, a jacket for the rain. Maltesers, because they are his favourite. A toothbrush from Roberta, who lies awake at night in Victoria wracked with thoughts of gum disease.

He likes Stanley Park, and the streets that line the sand of English Bay. He haunts the bakeries scattered around the West End, because the bakery women feed him leftover cupcakes and sometimes the grates pump hot, flour-filled air into the cold stretch of early morning.

"How can you see anything?" she asks him one morning at five. The air is thick with flour. Timothy, hunched up against the side of the bakery, looks like a snow-dusted child. "This can't possibly be good for you."

"It's just flour," he says. As always, she is frightened by how small his voice is, by how much he is now the one disappearing. "I think it's nice."

"Nice," Lilah echoes. She fingers the red fringes of her scarf and stares down at him. "This isn't what I would call 'nice,' Timmy."

He doesn't look at her. "That's not my name."

"Of course it is. For God's sake, Tim. Grow up."

He ignores her. He is good at ignoring her now. She makes a deep irritated sound in her throat, an impatient *hmph*, and then stops when she realizes that she sounds exactly like Roberta. "Mom's worried about you," she says. "We're all worried about you."

"Worrying will only take you so far," he says, in one of his hard, unyielding flashes of clarity. "You can't spend your life thinking about me."

"But I can," she shoots back. "I do."

"Even in Europe," he says, his voice dull. "Even when you were travelling in Thailand, when all you ever did was yell at Mom and hang up the phone."

"Yes," she says, simply. "Why do you think I came back?"

"You were meant for better things," Timothy says. He is eighteen years old now, but the sound that comes out of him belongs to a little boy. He clenches his hand into a fist and then lets his fingers unfurl. He is thin and bedraggled, so dirty. So pale.

"And you?" she asks, her voice bitter. In three hours she'll be trapped behind her computer. It is five o' clock in the morning, and the grey expanse of pavement stretches out before them both. "What were you meant for?"

"I don't know." His voice shrinks even further. The silence that sits between them is dark and practised, like a game. "That's what I'm trying to find out."

Lilah works in an office on West Georgia, typing notes and taking calls. The other receptionist, Debbie, takes the front desk, the one closest to the door. Debbie has purple hair and wears black shirts with skulls on the collar. She gets away with the skulls because of her minute-taking skills, and because her smile is brighter than one might expect from someone who listens to so much heavy metal. Penny, the office manager, likes to have her facing the front, a fresh face to greet those who might come in. Lilah does not smile as much, so her desk faces inward, toward Israel's door. Debbie has a lover and a dog and climbs mountains in her spare time. She is the only person in the office who gets Lilah's sense of humour.

Apart from the flour-dusted welcome of the morning, today is a day like any other. Lilah takes calls and schedules meetings, drafts spreadsheets, makes coffee. During lunch, she sits at her computer and looks at vacation spots. Bermuda. The Bahamas. Tenerife. This despite the fact that she is administrative sludge and can't afford bus fare, never mind a plane ticket.

Halfway through lunch, Penny catches her ogling a yoga holiday. *Namaste in Dahab, Egypt.* Beaches, Bedouins, and meditation twice a day.

"Are you on your break?"

"Lunch," Lilah says. "Actually."

Penny sniffs. Sniffing is a peculiar art, one that Penny has mastered well. She nods to the screen. "Dahab. That was lovely."

"Was it," and Lilah is already losing interest. "I'm still deciding."

Penny nods. "Good beaches." Penny dyes her hair black and is paler than the moon outside the window. Her mouth slants down to the left, and her words follow the same curve. *Penny* would speak *only in italics,* if she could.

"Hmm," Lilah says. As though it is actually something to consider. "I'll keep that in mind."

"Of course," and just the tilt of her head makes Lilah hate her, "if you *really* want a beach, Delilah, you should book a holiday in Greece." Sniff. "More expensive, yes, but *completely* worth it."

"Yes. I expect so." Lilah closes down the holiday page and opens her data sheets. She's already been to Greece—she's already been to a lot of places, not that Penny would know. But a friend's floor on Naxos is no doubt not quite what Penny has in mind.

"I'll need you to go get more coffee," Penny says. "We've run out."

"Regular?" Lilah reaches for her pen. Dictation, all types. It's the best kind of skill.

Penny frowns. "No."

Lilah pauses, pen in mid-air. *Kopi Luwak*. "Really? But I just bought—"

Penny tosses her hands out. "I *know*. Colin tells me the man drinks at least eight cups a day. Honestly, I don't know how he can sleep at night." She shrugs. "But he's *the boss*. So everything else can wait. You'll need to be back before two. Debbie has to take minutes, so you'll need to work the front desk."

"Of course," she says. Then, because Penny isn't moving, Lilah switches off her computer and pulls her coat from the chair. "Do you want me to get anything else?"

"No." Penny grimaces. It hurts her, this coffee excursion. All this money, all this manpower, and all for coffee beans that are shat out by South American cats. Not cats, though, because Lilah looked that one up. Palm civets. The things they must do for the boss. "Just get it and come back."

"Sure," and she hides her sudden rush of cheer. Coffee girl, yes, but coffee girl on the company dime. Things could be worse. She leaves the office without smiling, but as soon as she's out of the front door she can't help it—she opens her arms and breathes it in, that salty brine whiff of the world.

Inevitably, though, time spent weaving through the streets of downtown Vancouver is time spent looking for her brother. She can't help it. Timothy will disappear again now, and maybe one of her friends will be the next to see him. Like The Actor, who saw Timothy a week or so back and bought him lunch, then called Lilah to tell her about it.

"He looks good," The Actor told her with his typical sensitivity. "I mean, considering."

"Considering *what*?"

"Well, you know." Pause. "At least he's not starving, Lilah."

"You could have brought him home," she said, nearly shouting into the phone. "What good is one Happy Meal going to do?"

"You can't assume he's in trouble just because he's on the streets," he said. "For all you know, this is the life that he wants."

"Right. Begging and sleeping in doorways. Some life."

"He didn't beg, Lilah. I offered." The Actor. Conversations like this are the reason why they stopped fucking, why they don't talk anymore.

She said something in response to this that she doesn't remember, something that was mean enough to make her call later on and apologize. The Actor was out—she left a rambling message. The machine cut her off at the end.

Today, on the coffee run, Timothy is nowhere to be found. This is not surprising, not least of all because the homeless do not frequent Yaletown. Normal people can't afford the coffee they sell here. On this opposite end of Davie Street there is nothing but ocean, condos, and grocery stores that sell square watermelons and imported French baguettes. And coffee merchants who sell the longed-for Kopi Luwak, at three hundred dollars a pound.

Timothy would not show his face here. Partly because he's always hated Yaletown. And partly because he does not want to show his face anywhere—she didn't say it to The Actor, those few days ago on the phone, but Lilah knows at least this much. He is the Loch Ness Monster now, Bigfoot, Ogopogo. Disappearing into the world and leaving nothing but stories.

The new man in the office—*the boss*, yes, although Penny speaks of him as though he is temporary, a passing storm—is Mexican, but his name is Israel, like the favoured son of long ago. He has a high forehead, and dark hair that thins at the top. He may hold baldness back through force of will or he may embrace it. Either way, he is a man who makes decisions forcefully, the kind of man Roberta would be afraid to know. He likes expensive coffee, black. Penny has given grudging permission for Lilah to take this out of the stationery budget, because everyone wants to keep him happy.

But keeping him happy is not the same thing as being happy that he's around. Some of her colleagues have begun to call him the Hass Avocado. The imported boss. *Twice the price and half as nice, just to have him in season*. Penny grumbles about the budget, about the extravagantly expensive fountain pens he keeps in his lapel. But even Penny can see that things are changing. Two months ago the walls in the office trembled with talk of redundancies. Then Israel came, his hands full of promises that had less to do with milk and honey and more to do with profit, hours, and *people retention*. And milk and honey came anyway. Jobs that stayed and bonuses for everyone but her.

Instead, Lilah has been assigned to Israel, like a servant, and so when there are meetings, she is the one left to sort through his mail. He doesn't require much more than the coffee—a clean desk in the morning, someone to field his calls. *Mr. Riviera is in a meeting. I'm sorry, but Mr. Riviera is out for the day. Mr. Riviera has left the office—can I take a message?* Occasionally he asks for someone to go through his papers and re-organize his desk. Not much. Not hard. Lilah is careful and ordered, efficient, and so polite that Roberta wouldn't recognize her. Sometimes Lilah can't recognize herself. She has travelled to more countries than her mother can name, and slept with scores of men. Now she works as a secretary, and Timothy lives in the alleys of her city, and every day she waits to find his body in the street.

Today, just before she leaves, the Hass Avocado comes to her desk. Debbie flies out of his office and waves Lilah to attention, just in time, and then Israel Riviera marches through the door and up to her.

"Delilah," he says. It's the first time he's ever said her name. "Penny tells me you're the one to get my coffee. I wanted to say thank you. It has not gone unnoticed."

"Oh." Debbie is waving frantically behind Israel's back—a warning? What? Penny probably pointed the finger in the hope that Lilah would get in trouble. She shrugs. "It's no big deal, really. I like the walk."

Israel traces his fingers across her desk. His smile is, surprisingly, somewhat endearing. "That may be—but I am appreciative, all the same. I am not so foolish as to think that a person who requires an expensive drink such as that one might not be seen as a . . . a *diva*."

She would snicker if he wasn't so serious. "I think divas are usually women. So, um, no. I don't see you as a diva at all."

Unexpectedly, he laughs. Apparently the Hass Avocado has a sense of humour. "I see. That's good, then. I will be sure to remember that in the future." He runs his hand across the desk again and back. And then once more. Lilah doesn't know what to do.

He nods. "Yes." Lilah raises an eyebrow. "I would like to take you for dinner, Delilah. To show my appreciation."

She blinks. Across from her, Debbie coughs. "Lilah. Call me Lilah."

"But it is such a beautiful name," he says. "Delilah Greene." He has shining, crooked teeth. One front tooth is slightly discoloured, which gives the smile a flawed, off-kilter charm. "Yes. Delilah. I would like to take you to dinner, to thank you for my coffee."

It is not a question. "Um." Debbie, at her desk, is trying not to smile. Penny—Penny is nowhere to be found, thank fuck. "Um. Okay. That would be lovely."

"Very well," he says. "Shall we say Friday? I will pick you up at seven."

"I have plans on Friday." This is a lie, a very bad one, and for no reason other than that it irks her, being told what to do. Debbie covers another cough with her hand.

"Ah," Israel says. "Then I will pick you up on Saturday at seven."

"I can meet you." *Saturday. Seven. I will drive.*

"That's silly," and his voice is smooth, even jovial, but she can hear the thread of steel that has the office in thrall. It turns her on, just a little. "I have a driver—he will take us anywhere we wish to go."

"I like walking." Because she is stubborn. Because Roberta would definitely say yes to the car.

For a moment he stands immobile on the other side of the desk, a frown at the edges of his mouth. Then he laughs. "Fine. North American women—you are all so bold. So silly. But all right. You can meet me, and I will drive you home." This time, he does not wait for her to answer. He turns and strides back into the inner office, and then the door shuts, and the air around them is charged with the scent of man and spice.

"Well," says Debbie. "That was interesting."

"Yes," Lilah says. She draws the word slowly over her

tongue, like a kiss. She can't say anything else. The room shimmers with energy. She stares across the desk at Debbie, and remembers out of nowhere nights in Thailand, dancing small beneath the stars, the ocean loud in her ears and the air hard with possibility. *Everything starts now*, says a voice in her head. It is Timothy, so loud and so clear that she turns her head to face him, even though she knows he isn't there.

NINE

Two days after Chickenhead's unexpected resurrection, Sam's mother died. His stepfather called him at the school, his voice sounding detached and bewildered. *Collapsed. Just like that.* The paramedics had come and taken them to emergency, but Carol was gone long before they got to the hospital. There was nothing they could do.

Sam stood with his fingers locked around the phone and pictured this: a stretcher, his mother inert under a starched white sheet. They would have stepped carefully through the house, manoeuvered the stretcher around each plant, each precariously balanced vase. The house would have been disheveled and unready, as it always was in the morning. *Too bad,* he could almost hear his mother say. Too bad it hadn't happened in the afternoon, when the house would have been washed in sunlight and gracious to visitors. Even those of the unexpected, paramedic variety.

Too bad it hadn't happened on Sunday, in front of a guilty mother and her wide-eyed kid, when miracles had rung through the air.

"Sam?" His stepfather sounded impossibly old.

"Sorry, Doug. What?"

"I have to make more calls."

"Oh. Of course." His mother, the stretcher, *nothing they could do*. Of course. They were, after all, only paramedics. They did not have wings, they couldn't bring cats back from the dead. "Do you want me to come over?"

"There's nothing to do."

He'd wanted to visit them this morning. Had thought of dropping in for tea, then decided against it. Running late, not enough time. "Is anyone there with you?"

"What? Oh. Janet." Doug's sister. Janet and his mother didn't get along. Hadn't, Sam realized. Hadn't gotten along. The floor shivered under his feet and he steadied himself against a desk.

"All right," Sam said. "I'll call you later—" but Doug had already hung up. Sam fell into a chair and ran a hand across his face. He looked blankly at Lisa, the new student teacher, until she blushed and crept out of the room. The wings draped softly over either side of the chair—heavy, white, useless. *This*, said the voice in his mind. *This is what happens now.*

After a long while, during which there were whispers and the shuffle of shoes, the opening and closing of the staff room door, someone put a hand on his arm. He drew his fingers away and followed the curve of a shoulder up to a worried face, blue eyes. Stacey, the vice-principal.

"Sam," she said. She smelled of lavender, like Julie. *Close your eyes. Swallow.* "Go home. It isn't good for you to be here."

"I have a class." But he let his head fall forward, almost into her chest—Stacey was fond of low-cut blouses. The skin above her breasts was freckled, as though someone had flicked a brush of light brown paint against her flesh, one final flourish.

"Is there anything I can do?"

"No." He wanted to laugh, it sounded so awful. "My stepfather will have called everyone. There's no need." He pulled himself out of the chair and reached for his jacket.

"I'm so sorry," Stacey said. "Had she been ill?"

Now he did laugh. "No. She wasn't. Not that I knew, anyway."

"Oh." Another stumbled apology. He stared at her and felt the world contract to this room, this floor, the jacket he held in his hands. He wanted to draw the wings over his face and let her words bounce off muscle and blood and feather.

"No," he said again, his voice soft. Then he opened the door and stepped into the hall. He saw the flash of Emma's hair at the end of the corridor and turned into the stairwell before she could spot him.

Stacey followed him outside, her hand never far from his elbow. She stood patiently by his car as he crawled in and nestled the wings against his seat.

"Will you call us at the school when you get home?"

"Of course," he said, although this was silly. What was he going to do—drive the car in front of a truck? The next few kilometres would probably be the safest of his life.

"All right." She closed the car door very carefully, as though afraid that it would shatter under anything less than a delicate hand.

He bent over the wheel and started the engine, his left wing obscuring Stacey's face. He backed out of his cramped spot a little too fast, shifted into gear, and pulled out of the lot. A hundred feet past the school, he reached for the radio —something, anything to fill the silence.

A silty breeze ruffled the wings as he drove over the Fraser River. He wondered what kind of son he was, that his cat—eating more than she should be now and looking remarkably well after her return from the dead—waited to welcome him while his mother lay cold in the morgue.

When he was twelve, he'd had a dog.

Dodger, the incontinent beagle, had barked into all hours of the night and remained happily oblivious to housetraining. Sam had come home from school one afternoon to find Dodger gone and his mother weeping. A garbage truck, she'd said. The grave was a fresh pile of dirt by the back garden.

Years later, his mother got tipsy at a New Year's party and confessed that there had never been a garbage truck. She couldn't stand the barking, the smell of stale pee in the house. That long ago morning, after discovering dog shit on the couch, she loaded Dodger into the car and drove thirty kilometres out of town. She dropped him off at the side of a green country road.

"There was a farmhouse," she'd said, remembering. "A grey farmhouse with maple trees out front. It looked like a nice place." As though nice people lived there, as though they might have taken him in. As though it mattered, now.

"I was fine for a while," she said. "And then I felt terrible."

"*You* felt terrible?" he said.

"So I went back," she said, ignoring him, "and I walked up and down the road for an hour, calling his name. I went back the next day too. And the day after that."

"What if you'd found him?" he'd asked. "What would you have said?"

"I don't know," she admitted, her smile sheepish, strangely shy. "I never got that far."

Now, driving home, he found himself wondering what had become of Dodger, all those years ago. The first and last dog he'd ever had. Maybe the nice people in the grey house took him in. Or maybe he froze in the ditch—that was a cold autumn. The grave marker wouldn't stick in the dirt because the ground had frozen over.

That was the first lie she'd put in the ground. Flowers, turnips, falsehoods—his mother had planted all manner of things.

Had she known about the wings, she would have marched Sam into the church and done one of two things: prayed for deliverance or given thanks to God. A hunch told him it would have been the latter—*all my hard work paid off!* Either way, it would have been seen as an event, a signal, a forerunner of change. Maybe that's why he hadn't called her.

"This is a sign, Sam," she might have said. Perhaps she too would have patted the nearest wing, or run her hand along it, once more the mother, smoothing away his worry.

A sign for whom?

"You," she might have replied. "The rest of the world. Does it matter?"

He should have called.

When he opened his front door, he heard a thump in the kitchen. Chickenhead, jumping off the counter. He took off his shoes, put on his most menacing face, and stretched his wings as far as they would go.

"What have you been doing?"

She came into the room at the sound of his voice, all purrs and delicate paws. He curled his right wing in and brushed the lower feathers against her fur, over her eyes. She batted the feathers away and wound herself around his ankles, then followed him back into the kitchen. He opened the bottle of Scotch and poured himself a glass. Drank it straight down. He thought of Doug, blank-faced and making calls from the quiet of his mother's house, and poured himself another. And Father Jim. Father Jim would need to know about this. He hadn't the faintest idea how to get in contact—but perhaps Father Mario would know.

He trudged to the bedroom, shedding clothes as he went. Naked except for his boxers, he pulled his black dress pants out of the closet. A black button-down shirt to finish—this would impress Janet, this image of sober, sorrowful son. No doubt she'd be more impressed if she could see the wings, of course, the starkness of white against black. But Janet did not believe in God. (*Neither do you*, said that tiny voice in his head. *And look what happened.*)

Back in the kitchen, Chickenhead was mewing for water. He splashed some into her bowl and briefly considered bringing her along. But Janet, like Julie, was not a cat person. Janet wasn't an animal person at all. Doug once joked that even her plants were bound to die. She was tall and thin and Sam couldn't think of her as anything other than a shrivelled spinster in an empty apartment, husband notwithstanding.

The drive to his mother's house wasn't long, but that night he caught the tail end of rush hour. He pulled up to the gabled North Vancouver house as the sun set over the Pacific. Emma—too poetic for journalism, though he hadn't yet had the heart to tell her—would make something of that sunset. All purple and red and gold reflected off the ocean.

Carol had purchased the house for the view, back when money could buy a view in North Vancouver. Nowadays views were hereditary, passed down from parent to favourite child, new husband, whomever. The house would probably go to Doug. His mother's mind had been fixed on dahlias and the northeast trellis—he doubted there was a will. He doubted a lot of things today. Like the fact that forty-eight hours ago he'd been standing on his own curb, a resurrected cat fresh in his arms. And now he was here, with his wings and his empty hands, his mother's husband grieving on the other side of the door. Even Janet the Atheist would judge him now, if she knew all the facts.

Inside, the first thing he noticed was the light. Someone had pulled back the curtains in every room and rays from the setting sun were a shifting mass of red-gold-white over the furniture, against the hardwood floor. He could feel the wings shift, stretch, and lengthen into the golden glow of the house.

Doug sat in the kitchen, at the bar. Janet had brought Chinese food and the containers sat open on the table. She looked up as Sam entered and then back down at Doug, who was locked around a mug of tea. There. No double take, no slam of shock on her face, not that he'd expected anything less.

He said, "Traffic," as though it mattered. The water in the kettle was still hot, so he took out a mug and made himself tea. He turned to face them, the mug steady in his hands, and waited.

Doug was five years older than Sam—a musician, a composer of ridiculous radio jingles whom Sam's mother had met two years ago, on New Year's Eve. The same New Year's Eve as the dog story, in fact. The joke used to be that Doug had an instrument for every flower in the house, although he wasn't good with plants, except perhaps to sing them into growing. Usually he looked younger than Sam but today something old seeped from his skin.

"She wasn't feeling well," he said, the words directed at the counter space between his hands. "She'd had a headache the last few days, but we thought it was the weather. You know how she gets when it rains," and yes, Carol had suffered migraines since Sam was a child. "But when she came out of the shower she had this look on her face. She blinked, and she put a hand to her head," and Doug's own hand went up, remembering the story, "and she just slid down the wall until she hit the floor." He took another deep breath. "I thought she'd fainted and I went over and shook her. Then I dialed. I should have been faster."

"It wasn't your fault." Janet, quick to jump in.

"It was so quick," Doug continued, as though he hadn't heard her. "It was over before the paramedics even got here." His voice cracked, stumbled to a halt. "I don't know what to do."

"I'll take care of everything," said Janet. She rubbed a hand up and down Doug's back.

"Actually, *I'll* take care of everything." Sam ignored Janet's narrowed eyes, her pursed lips. Instead he stood, and he stretched the wings out, then pulled them in. He was so tired. "I have to find Father Jim and let him know."

"She didn't want a big funeral," Doug said. "We only talked about it once. You know—just in case." Then he looked up. "Father Jim? I thought Father Mario served at the church."

"He does," Sam said, not wanting to elaborate. "Father Jim was there while I was growing up. He should know, at least."

Doug nodded. "Where will you start?"

"I'll go to the church tomorrow." He looked over at Janet. "Will you take him back with you tonight?"

She nodded. Her face had relaxed and she looked, surprisingly, somewhat pretty, somewhat sad.

"Good." The irritation went as quickly as it had come, leaving behind the sour taste of guilt. He *could* have been here, this morning. He could have stretched time for tea, a chat, the chance to extend his hands and push Death away.

But God, it would seem, had thought Shakespeare more important.

When he got there the next morning, the church was empty save for Mrs. Glastonbury, who knelt in the front pew and whispered loudly into her hands. Mrs. Glastonbury, who had come to the church to pray for her dead husband every morning since Sam was a child. The husband (officially, according to the Church) had died while investigating a domestic dispute in the city, but (unofficially, according to Father Jim) had actually died of heart failure while screwing a whore in a seedy East Hastings hotel. At eleven the story had been thrilling, all the more because Sam had heard it via the eavesdropper's window. Stooped in the vestment closet, forgotten while putting his robes away, he heard Father Jim say the word and had to stifle a yell of delight. Whore. *Whore.*

Mrs. Glastonbury, he remembered, had given out toothpaste for Halloween. Today she muttered her rosary in a low, fanatical tone that made perfect sense—only a person who thought candy came from the Devil could sound like that.

Father Mario was behind the altar, fiddling with the tabernacle. He closed the door of the little silver box and then turned to face the entrance. He saw Sam immediately, smiled, and gestured to a pew. Sam, once more in black, the wings hunched on either side of him like extra, flashy limbs, slid into a seat.

"Samuel," said the priest. "I heard about your mother—I am so very sorry."

Had he introduced himself before? He couldn't remember. "Yes. Me too."

"How can I help you?"

Sam coughed into the left wing and felt strangely embarrassed, as though he were turning down a lover. "Can you tell me where Father Jim practises?"

"Father Jim? I believe he's on the Island now." If the other priest was surprised, he didn't show it. "In Tofino. He is teaching and writing a book."

Sam nodded. "Is there a phone number I can call?"

"Of course," said the priest. He stood and motioned to the rectory. Sam followed, the wings trailing softly in his wake.

The rectory smelled the way it had when he was eleven—incense and dust and fresh linen from the vestment closet, all resting on the weathered scent of old wood. The white cupboard in the corner had held Father Jim's supply of Scotch, once upon a time. Scotch and vodka, for those difficult pre-Easter days. He had an urge to open the cupboard and check to see what currently graced the shelves—Father Mario probably kept candles, or extra glasses for the holy wine.

The priest, oblivious, copied a name onto a small red notepad and then scribbled a number. His hands were small and square, the nails blunt-edged. "Brother Thomas receives the visitors, I believe."

"Thank you." Sam's own fingernails were dangerously short now. A childhood habit, that, come to taunt him. He took the paper and folded it once, then once again.

"Have you thought of going to see them?" Father Mario asked. "The drive is not so long."

An hour to the ferry, then the ride across the water and another three hours or so to the coast. Sam opened his mouth to disagree and then remembered: his cat, his car, Joni Mitchell on the open road. It wouldn't be Mecca or Memphis, but Cathedral Grove, that wonderful forest of ancient trees, was part of the drive. His mother had loved the green.

"Your mother and I were great friends," the priest continued. "She was a wonderful woman."

"Yes." The wings rustled with sudden energy. "I'd like," Sam cleared his throat, "to see if Father Jim could perform the service. You understand?"

"Of course." Father Mario nodded. "I will be happy to attend."

He was still so tired. He followed Father Mario back to the entrance and allowed the priest to open the door and make way for the wings. Sam blinked against the sudden sunshine and stepped across the threshold, then turned back, one hand shielding his eyes.

"Thank you," he said again.

The priest nodded. "My best for your journey." He raised a hand and made a small sign of blessing over the wings. Sam braced himself for more priestly wisdom, but Father Mario gave him a sad smile and turned back to the church, so he went quickly down the steps to hide his surprise.

—

The phone at the retreat house rang eleven times before someone picked up.

"Barnabite Fathers," said the voice. An oddly business-like, almost military voice.

"Hello," said Sam. "I was told that I could find Father Jim at this number. Father Jim McDougal?"

"Yes." The speaker cleared his throat. "One moment. May I tell him who's calling?"

"It's Sam. Sam Connor."

"Sam," said Father Jim when he came on the phone, his voice warm and familiar. "What a nice surprise."

"Hello, Father." He was at once five years old, eleven, thirty-five and about to be a jilted man. Somehow, the air smelled of incense. "I'm sorry to bother you."

"It's no bother," said the priest. "Is everything all right?"

"Mom died yesterday," he said, hating the boldness of the words. "I thought you should know."

Silence on the other end of the line. "Sam. I'm so sorry."

"Yes," he said. "I was wondering if you would mind doing the service. I know I haven't been in touch—"

"Of course," said Father Jim. "Are you still in Vancouver? Shall I leave tonight?"

And suddenly the pilgrimage coalesced, took shape. "No," he said. "The service isn't until next Tuesday—I could come and get you."

"From the ferry?"

"The retreat. I'd like the drive, if that's all right."

—

Stacey was very understanding when he made the call into work—maybe too much so. She greeted the news of his road trip with an odd enthusiasm, her voice both respectful and envious.

"I'm sure the drive will be lovely," she said. "And it will be good for you to have the time alone, no doubt."

Time alone, he wanted to tell her, was not the problem. Then he wondered if she harboured dreams of coming along. "Yes," was all he said. They'd found a supply. He could take as much time as he needed.

He called Doug at Janet's apartment. Doug's voice was low and detached—where Stacey had had too much concern, he seemed to have none at all.

"Father Jim's class finishes on Friday," Sam told him. "So we'll be back on Saturday, in the afternoon."

He paused. Doug said nothing. "Could you put Janet on the phone?"

The switch to Janet was accompanied by footsteps; she'd taken the phone into another room.

"How is he?"

"Tired," she said, her voice muffled. "I don't think he slept at all last night—I could hear him pacing."

"Hmm," he said. His turn for the non-committal grunt. They were conspirators, suddenly, he and Janet—careful and polite in the face of death. "Well, let me know if anything happens."

"I will," she said. "Have a safe journey."

Safe. He gulped down an urge to paint a picture for Janet right there on the phone: his hands locked around the wheel as he navigated hairpin turns and precarious mountain highways, the wings shining white and blocking his rear-view mirror. "Sure."

Once more in boxers he padded into the kitchen, the tiles cool against his feet. An offhand glance at the thermostat told him it was ten degrees in the house, which had to be a mistake. It felt like summertime. When he got back from Tofino, he'd have to get the heating fixed.

The next morning, he was up before the sun. He crept out into the parking lot and loaded the Jetta with water bottles, granola bars, and cat treats to keep Chickenhead calm.

A map of the Island to help with the hairpin turns, two cases of CDs to help with the quiet, and he was almost ready to go. Just before pulling Chickenhead out the door, he put on the black shirt and the black dress pants. He slid the shirt over his shoulders and started with the bottom buttons, but his fingers began to shake. He stopped and looked in the mirror.

His reflection was pale, his fingers locked and white-knuckled. His hairline was receding. The wings rose and fell behind him, in tune to his breath and yet not quite, as though sucking air on their own. He put a hand to his head and clumps of hair came away in his fingers, leaving slivers of shiny white scalp. He took a breath and reached for the buttons again but his fingers were slippery with sweat and he fumbled. The wings waited behind and on either side of him like malevolent ghosts.

Suddenly, he felt hands reach out and cover his own. His skin surged with power and his fingers moved slowly, deliberately through each button. He watched in the mirror as these hands that were not his hands finished the shirt up to the collar. The dryness in his throat wouldn't go away.

Now his reflection showed a man in a crisp black shirt,

the wings white and stiff and still. One more breath, and this time the wings moved with him, up and down, and settled behind his shoulders as though they'd been there all his life.

Chickenhead mewed in the hallway, and he went to find her, and from there to find the priest.

IX

In those years before—before the street, before the office—Lilah spent her time moving, and flying, and sleeping on strange floors all over the world. A basement floor in Dublin, a cold beach in Edinburgh, littered with seaweed and trash. A whirlwind few weeks in Madrid, where men touched her hair as though each strand were made of magic. She called home once a month, if at all. Aidan, the boy from New Zealand she met on a dance floor in Cork, thought this was hilarious.

"I've never met anyone who hates their own family so much," he said. He grew orchids back in Wellington, and had come to Europe just because.

"I don't hate all of them," she said. Careful, even then, to make the distinction. There was Roberta, and then there was Timothy. "I just—I'm just tired."

He laughed again. Aidan from New Zealand was always laughing. "You're not tired," he said. "If you were tired you wouldn't have the energy to run away."

"Maybe." She thought of Timothy, alone in his room. When Roberta wasn't yelling she spoke of doctors, psychiatrists, and disapproving parishioners. Timothy wouldn't come to the phone—he never came to the phone—but when Lilah stayed in one spot long enough he sent postcards. One found her in Amsterdam, weeks after her time in Ireland, when she was staying with Sabastian the artist. Sabastian was tall and thin and clumsy in bed, like an overgrown child. He collected plaster busts and sat them around his kitchen table, as though they were family that wouldn't go away.

"You have mail," he said. He passed the postcard across the table. Somewhere over the Atlantic it had gotten wet; the ink was smudged on the left-hand side of the card, the writing small and blurred. *Lilah,* it ran. *I miss you. I hope your well. Mom thinks we might get a dog, maybe. I told her it could sleep in my room, but she wants to put it in yours. See you when you come home. Love, Timmy.*

"I didn't know you had a brother," Sabastian said. The busts around his table were replicas, cast from the bronze torso of a woman who had drowned herself in the Seine in 1889. The night Lilah arrived, he'd told her the story in his garret bedroom and said that her body reminded him of the woman they'd pulled from the river.

"You hold teardrops in your shoulders," he said. "As though you are so sad, you have nowhere else to put them."

Now, thinking of this, she looked at the postcard and shrugged. "I have a brother, yes." She put the postcard in her backpack and carried it around like a talisman, or a child.

And three weeks later she left, early in the morning after a sleepy goodbye, like something from a film.

There were other men, other artists. Halfway through that first year away she stopped paying attention. She poured drinks in a greasy pub to make money, posed for a photographer in Oslo, and played volleyball for cash on an Anzio beach. She kept the postcard in her bag, and as she moved through Greece and Turkey it was joined by another, and another. Some of the postcards had Roberta's name dashed across the bottom beside Timothy's—a jumble of letters, an *x*, an *o*.

Sometimes the postcards came after she'd gone. Sabastian, who had left her his number, and whom she called now and again because she liked the sound of his voice, kept her last postcard on the dinner table, next to the bust he'd painted red.

"They have not gotten a dog," he said. His voice was gravelly, all angles and bones. "He says your mother has decided not to have one."

"That's because she's a bitch," Lilah said. She shivered in the phone booth and stared out across a busy Dhaka street blanketed in rain. Monsoon season in Bangladesh, and she had only one pair of shoes. "Does he say anything else? Is he okay?"

"Come home," Sabastian said.

"What?"

"No. 'Come home.' That's what he says."

"Oh." She tapped a finger against the receiver and the sound echoed through the booth.

"You're not going to go home."

"What are you, my father?"

Sabastian snorted. "No. But you're not going to go home."

"Not yet," she admitted. "Maybe never."

Now he laughed. "'Never' is a big word."

"Look. It's not—I shouldn't have to stay there. To live my life."

He was quietly, gently amused. "Did I say that?"

She closed her eyes and saw the postcard, Timothy's words haphazard and crooked over the page. "Well, whatever. Can we talk about something else now?"

"Of course," Sabastian said. "We can always talk about something else."

—

In Chiang Mai, she met a man who had left his wife for an opium den in the hills. His name was Rainer. His wife lived in Berlin, with their children, and when Lilah met him he hadn't seen his son or daughter in almost five years.

"Do you miss them?" she asked. They were sprawled on the floor of a hut that smelled of grass and mould, dark paste between them in a little earthen dish.

"All of the time," he said. "But there are more important things."

"More important things?" Even there, stoned and as far from Timothy as she could possibly be, she couldn't quite believe it.

"God," and he breathed out as he said it so that the word became silver smoke. "I have God here. Everything else is just an illusion."

She laughed. She couldn't help it. Did Roberta's arm stretch this far, this hard? Was the bad-daughter guilt going to catch up with her now, more than halfway across the world? "You're not serious."

"Of course I am." He shifted so that he was on his side, looking directly at her, drawing circles in the dirt. "You have to let go, Lilah. So much can change in a minute, or an hour, or a day. You can't let anything tie you down. God goes beyond the world."

"But," she said, not quite understanding, "it's your *family*."

"This is my family," and he spread an arm, took in the hut, the smoke, the pitter patter of mountain rain. "Only this."

She watched him, silent, and then took a turn with the pipe. "I think that's a load of shit."

"You're a child. Children don't know anything."

"Fuck off," but her words were sleepy and slow. "My mother believes in God and she's a crackpot."

"Your mother believes in fairy tales," he said. "That's different." He pushed the opium pot off to the side and rolled so that he was on top of her, grinding her into the dirt. He tasted of smoke and burning leaves. "Only idiots believe in happy endings."

In the morning, she went back to the city. She left Rainer in the hut, a week's worth of opium still beside him on the ground. God around him, in the mountains and the tress. She met a group of American tourists back at her hostel and they spent the winter months trawling the beaches on Koh Samui, fucking and sleeping and wondering where to go next.

But as that second year drew to a close she found herself thinking of them both, Timothy and Roberta, all the time. Timothy's twelfth birthday came and went—she was dancing on a beach in Pattaya and paused, just for a moment, to stare across the water. Little brother, growing up so far away.

The last postcard came to her in Bangkok, the edges soft and worn. *Lilah,* it ran. *Lilah, I'm lonely. I love you. Timmy.*

Running to them, running away from them, always away. She flew back like a boomerang, gathering strength for her next curve into the world even as she drew near to home.

Today, she finds Timothy singing. A dirty, scuffled youth, rocking away and singing nonsense to himself on the beach. Beach strollers mark a wide path around him.

"You look like a lunatic," she says, by way of hello. "You're going to scare all the children away."

"Let the little children come to me," he says, and laughs. "It's just a song, Lilah."

"I know it's just a song." Whatever that means. Lilah sits beside him and pulls food from her bag—sandwiches, apples, a hunk of sharp cheese. "Eat."

Timothy makes a face, but he doesn't run away. He reaches for the first sandwich but Lilah stops him and puts a bottle of sanitizer in his hands instead. "Wash your hands with this, first."

He rolls his eyes and opens the bottle. The sanitizer cuts lines through the dirt at the bottom of his wrists.

"When was the last time you had a shower?"

He shrugs, and this time gets the sandwich. "I don't remember. Two weeks ago?"

"Yeah, well—you smell like it."

"Thanks," he says, his mouth full of tuna. "You're always so tactful."

"It's true." She pushes another sandwich across the wood, and he takes it. "Why don't you come home with me for the night and get cleaned up? I won't tell Roberta," she adds hastily, as his face clenches in panic. "You can sleep in my room. I'll take the couch—you won't even have to talk if you don't want."

He hesitates, and she lets her heart expand with hope.

"What if I want to leave halfway through the night? What if I want to go at three in the morning?"

"Then you can go." She doesn't breathe. "I'm not taking you to a fucking prison, Tim."

"Don't swear," he says. He finishes the sandwich. "You won't have company, or anything? The boyfriend won't be there?"

"He's not my boyfriend," she says instantly.

"Mom thinks he is." Timothy reaches into her bag without asking, grabs another bun. "You're lucky Mom can even keep track. The Actor. Your Montreal men. And *Joel*. You know, that's a stupid name."

She blinks, and then remembers. Of course. They are talking about Joel, the somewhat-boyfriend, because Timothy does not know about dates with the boss at the office. "It is not."

"Sure it is. It's one of those names that people always think is so cool, so different. And then they realize—it's just *Joe*. With an *l*." Third sandwich done, he goes for an apple and bites. His hand is hard and white around the fruit.

"Well—whatever," she says. She could laugh. It would be so easy to laugh. Also easy to tell him how many times she's heard the joke before. "Are you going to come or not?"

"You can't follow me if I decide to leave."

"I won't."

"You can have showers at the Y, you know. That's where I went the last time."

"I thought you said you couldn't remember the last time."

Timothy wipes apple juice on his filthy jeans. "I just remembered." He stands. It's almost dark, and Lilah's stomach has begun to rumble. Guilt flickers over Timothy's face. "Were those for you?"

"No." She stands too. As always, she is surprised to see how much he now towers over her—how he can be so large and so small all at once. "Do you want to go now?"

"Fine." He falls in step beside her.

They don't talk. Lilah concentrates on the sidewalk in front of her and the soft *pat-pat* of Timothy's feet as he follows her along the streets. She thinks of Roberta, worrying in her house across the water, and of Joe-with-an-L, who has indeed been scheduled to make an appearance tonight. She will text him when Timothy is in the shower and tell him that she's busy.

They drift, not talking, to the other side of the city. The landlord, a skinny grey woman with yellow fingers, is there, waiting, when they enter the building.

"Good evening," the landlord says. Her name is Jemima, and she doesn't trust anybody. She sits on the couch in the front foyer with a magazine across her knees. She's probably been there for hours.

"Hello," Lilah says brightly. She thinks of Debbie and smiles with all her teeth. Then she grabs Timothy's wrist and pulls him into the elevator, jams a finger against the number 4. The doors shudder closed.

The elevator is noisy and old. Timothy wiggles out of her grasp and stares at the floor. "I hate elevators," he mumbles.

"Since when?"

"Since forever."

"You never said anything about that to me," she says, hurt. "Why didn't you tell me before?"

"Idiots are afraid of elevators," he says. When the elevator stops, he is the first one out into the hall. She's not sure if he'll remember—he's only been here once in the entire two years that she's been living in the place—but he stops directly in front of her door. When she opens it, he walks in, his shoulders stooped and his head down, like a misbehaved dog.

She shuts the door and points to the bathroom right away. "Get in." The closet to the left of the bathroom holds towels and soap—she pulls them out, folds them into his outstretched hands. "I have some of your old clothes here, if you want them." Roberta had sent them for moments such as these, but Lilah keeps her mouth shut, says nothing. "Throw those clothes outside of the door and I'll wash them now."

He nods. Once upon a time he'd been ten years old, slipping milk into her hot chocolate. Her co-conspirator in life.

He shuts the door, and she walks into the kitchen and lights a cigarette to calm her nerves. The water starts running. A moment later the bathroom door opens and closes again—when she comes back into the hall, Timothy's clothes lie in a pile on the floor. She finishes the cigarette and scoops up the clothes, then slides out of the apartment as quietly as she can and takes them down to the laundry, where she feeds coins and powder to the washing machine and then sits on one of the grubby chairs. She watches a beetle scuttle across the linoleum. The lights flicker, go out, come back on again. Timothy's clothes tumble through the quick cycle—when they are finished, she shoves them into a dryer and lights another cigarette.

Jemima, who doesn't smoke, glares at her as she passes through the foyer. Lilah smiles again and blows a ring out into the air—a most unladylike skill, that, learned courtesy of Rainer and those days in the Thai mountains. Jemima huffs in her seat and pretends to go back to her magazine, but her eyes follow Lilah as she heads for the stairs. Lilah ignores her and slides her hand along the greasy rail as she climbs the steps.

Back in the apartment, Timothy is sitting on the floor in front of the fireplace that does not work. He wears the clothes that Lilah gave him, bunched under his filthy jacket. His ears are red, as though he's scrubbed them too hard.

"Hi," she says, softly. She closes the door behind her and is careful not to lock it.

"Hi." He fidgets and then holds out his hands. "Where are my clothes?"

"They're in the dryer," she says. And then, because she can't help it, "I could keep them here. For you. If you don't want to carry so much stuff."

"No." His voice shakes with urgency. "Give them to me."

She nods. "Okay. When you want to go, we'll get them from downstairs." She tries not to stare at his hands. His wrists are thin, his arms long, so awkward. "You've grown."

He snorts. "Yeah. It's what people do."

"You need new clothes."

Timothy shakes his head. "My clothes are fine."

How many times have they said this? "Look—I can take you. Shopping. We can just get a few things—"

"I'm *fine*," he snarls.

"Just a few things," she says again. "How can you sleep if you're cold?"

"I'm not cold." He rocks forward as he sits, just as he did when he was young. "Are you leaving again? Is that it? Do you want to buy me clothes again to make yourself feel better?"

"I'm not going anywhere," she says, her voice low.

"That's what you always say. And then oh, look—you're in Europe, or you're in Thailand, or Mom's sick and you're in Montreal. Or Toronto. Or New York."

"I came home," she shoots back. "I always come home. And now *you're* sleeping by some garbage can. Mom must be so proud—some family this turned out to be."

"That's different," but already he is smaller, unsure. "That's completely different."

Lilah stares at him, watches as he rocks on the floor. Then she gives up. "Do you want something to drink? Tea? Anything else to eat?"

"Hot chocolate," he says, surprising her. She can hear the hint of a smile in his voice. "With milk."

She laughs. "I always make it with milk." She steps into the kitchen, pours milk into a pan on the stove. She pulls out the spoons and the nice mugs, the ones that Timothy gave her years ago as a birthday present. Clay mugs, rough and brown. When the hot chocolate is ready, she fills the mugs and lets the steam brush over her face.

"Are you sure you don't want anything else?"

"I'm fine," he says. And then, when she hands him his mug, "Thank you."

"You're welcome." She sits on the floor beside him and pretends not to notice when he inches himself away.

"This is good," he says, sipping. "I always forget how good it is."

Lilah snorts. "Of course it's good. It's *always* good."

"Hey—I made a pretty good cup too. Back in the day."

She sniffs. "You always left lumps."

"I did not."

"Did too." She turns to face him so that he can see her smile. He was so tiny, then, her Timothy, swinging his feet in the air. "I ate them anyway."

"Right. Because you're the greatest big sister ever."

"Naturally."

He doesn't laugh, or disagree. They sit and drink the chocolate. Lilah has opened one of the windows and they listen as two people shout at each other on the sidewalks below. *Fuck you* this, and *motherfucking* that. A quarrel, maybe, or two people falling in love.

Timothy finishes his drink first, and places the mug on the floor beside the fireplace—carefully, as though afraid the cup might break. "Thank you," he says again, once more so polite.

"You're welcome."

He fidgets again, and picks at a thread on his jeans. "I like your house," he says, finally. "Does Joe-with-an-L like it too?"

She shrugs. "I guess so. We spend all of our time here."

"Right. Because Joe-with-an-L lives with his mom."

"Is that a problem?" she asks, annoyed.

Timothy looks at her, then away, and shrugs out a laugh. "It's just—"

"Just *what*?"

"You could do better. I don't even know the guy, and I know you could do better."

"Better men, dear brother, seem to be in short supply." Then she remembers Israel, the soon-to-be-date. *Saturday. Seven. I will drive.* She opens her mouth to tell him about it but Timothy stands, suddenly, and when he glances down at her he has the street look in his eyes and that's it—he's disappearing, again, right in front of her.

"I have to go," he says. "I'm going to go."

"You can have my bed," she says, speaking slowly. "You can go in there now, Tim. I won't bother you." Please. Stay. "I promise."

"You said you wouldn't keep me," and he backs away from

her, toward the door. The whites of his eyes are showing, and his breath comes fast and shallow. "*You said.*"

"It's just a night," she says, standing, again speaking slowly. Stay. Stay. "Just—just rest for a night. I just want you to be safe."

He laughs—the high, terrified laugh of a madman. "No one can keep me safe," he says. "No one, Lilah. You least of all." He turns from her, wrenches open the door, and runs into the hallway, shoes dangling from his hand.

She stands in front of the fireplace, silent. He takes the stairs down—flying down the stairwell and back into the night. Running away from her, now, always away. The rest of her hot chocolate goes cold. She puts her mug down, beside Timothy's; she'll have to get his clothes from the laundry, but for the moment she sits back down and listens. The *motherfucking* voices are still fighting, but they're now on the move; they dwindle, fade away. For three seconds the world is heavily, achingly quiet.

Then a breeze comes in, and she stands and shuts the window.

—

In the morning, Israel leaves a message on her machine. *Delilah. I think Indian would be lovely. Don't you?*

She showers and picks her outfit, and when evening comes she makes her way to the Indian restaurant, the famous one on 11th Avenue. She shivers in the high-necked black dress, the red silk scarf from Timothy, the boots that lace up at the back. Her hair is down because she likes the way it looks, white-blonde in the light from the street. The black feathered fascinator—a guilt gift from Roberta, who has great taste when it comes to matters of the millinery world—completes everything. She feels enchanting and subdued. Greta Garbo, Marlene Dietrich. Grace Kelly in *Rear Window,* on her way to break another man.

Then she reaches the restaurant, and sees Israel at the window, and as she steps inside the door everything changes.

"Delilah," he says. He stands to greet her, and the words carry. "You're late."

She flushes to the tips of her fingers. She is five years old. "I'm sorry." She allows him to take her coat, to drape it gently over the last chair. His coat sits on the chair to her left. She can tell it's expensive just by the way it hangs.

"Not *very* late," he concedes. He pulls out her chair and she sits. "But I am not used to waiting."

"Well," she snaps, before she can stop herself, "I don't rush for anybody." She winces and tugs on her scarf. "Just so you know."

Israel laughs and sits down. "So you are not as polite outside of work. I wondered. We will overlook it, for tonight."

"Overlook what?" She wipes her hands against her thighs. "Being impolite or being late?"

"Both." He has beautiful hands, this man. Large. Long-fingered. He wears a silver ring on his right index finger, and when he motions to the waiter again the ring glimmers in the light. He orders wine for both of them and lets his menu lie open on the table. "You are young—I must remember this."

She thinks of Rainer and those long ago days in the mountains. "Why does everyone talk about my age like it's some kind of fucking handicap?"

"You watch your mouth," he says softly. There's that hint of steel. "But that's just what a young person would say. Maybe you're not ready just yet."

She blinks. The waiter brings a bottle of wine and fills her glass. What kind of date is this? "Ready for what?"

"Never mind." He shrugs and places one hand on the table, then hooks his other arm around the back of the chair. "Let us begin at the beginning, then. Tell me about you."

"But I don't know anything about you," she blurts, hating the way it sounds. The wine is cool and sharp. "I don't even know why I'm here."

"I come from Mexico City. And now I live here. What else do you want to know?"

"Do you have any brothers? Any sisters?" Or favourite foods, a favourite colour. Suddenly everything sounds so juvenile, so strange.

"I do not," he says. "And you have a brother."

"Yes," she says, surprised. "He lives here, in the city." She drinks, and suddenly her glass is empty. "Did Penny tell you that?"

"I pay attention," Israel says. His hand around the wine bottle, more wine in her glass. "It's amazing, what you learn."

Joe-with-an-L, she realizes suddenly, does not even know her brother's name.

"Mediocre men do not pay attention," he continues. "Surely you've met enough of those, by now, to know the difference. Surely you know enough to long for something better?"

She sips her wine, uneasy. "Well isn't that a lovely thing to say."

"The truth is hardly ever *lovely*, Delilah. But no doubt you know that already, as does your brother." He shrugs. "This is what you learn when you look deeply at the world."

"Is this what you do, then? 'Look deeply at the world' while we're making you expensive coffee and shuffling papers around in the foyer?"

"You could say that." The waiter arrives with poppadums and chutney, places the dishes noiselessly on the table, and then retreats, once more, into shadow. Israel cracks a poppadum between his hands. "You might call it a . . . project. Or a hobby. Most people, Delilah, pay the world no attention at all. They do not watch for opportunity. They are content to let their lives mean nothing. But you," he points a long finger at her, "you are different. I think so, anyway."

This from the man who, up until two days ago, had never spoken her name.

"I think you're crazy."

"People have said that before," he tells her, unperturbed. "But they only say it once." The waiter comes back and Israel orders for them both—jackfruit in masala, saag paneer. He finishes his own wine, refills it, and watches her. Lilah stares at the table and says nothing. She is mortified and furious, her fingers tight around the stem of her wine glass. Where is the sparkling conversationalist, or the girl who at the very least knows enough about decorum to watch her mouth in front of the boss?

"You needn't worry about being proper," Israel says. Now her wineglass is empty again; he refills it. "We are not at work anymore."

"So you read minds now?" she mutters.

"You'd be surprised how much a face can tell, Delilah. And is this a date? I am no longer so sure." She glances up, blushing, as he continues. "You are so much quieter than the women I usually entertain."

"Well, maybe you're not entertaining me."

He chuckles. "So I am not interesting, then?"

"Interesting enough."

Outright laughter this time. "Delilah, Delilah. I have never met a woman like you."

"You can't have met many women, then." She spoons chutney onto her plate and dips in a poppadum. "I'm not that special."

"If you say so." The waiter places another bottle of wine on the table. "Somehow, I don't think that is true."

They stumble on like this until the food comes, and then Israel talks for most of the meal. He tells her about a childhood in Mexico—the colour, the food, parades down the Paseo de la Reforma. A mother who prayed a hundred times a day, a struggle with numbers at school.

"You call them the *times tables*," he says. "Even now, I find them difficult."

"Yes," she says, surprised. "I know." In return, she tells him about Thailand, about the hills, about sleeping drenched in opium and rain. About the café job she took when she moved back in with Roberta, about the man she met there and the job opportunity that took her to Toronto, then Montreal. She does not tell him about Timothy, or the phone calls.

"And now you're back," he says.

"I've been back for two years. Almost three."

"Why?" Israel spoons the last of the jackfruit on his plate. "If it was so wonderful—why come back?"

"My mother got sick. I moved home for a while, to help." She laughs; she can't help it. "And it drove me crazy, so I moved here. Now there's practically an ocean between us, and I'm still only a few hours away."

"And now you are a secretary." The sentence thuds onto the table. "Do you enjoy your job?"

"Yes. I've dreamed about being a secretary since I was five. Doesn't everybody?"

"Then why are you there?" he asks.

"Why didn't I get a bonus?" she blurts. "At the end of last quarter. Everyone else got a bonus. Even Debbie."

"Debbie," Israel taps his glass before he continues, "is an exemplary worker. This is what Penny tells me."

"So—what? I'm not? Do I need a fucking degree to organize your desk?""

"I was a good son," he says idly. "Once upon a time, I *was* exemplary. But there is more to this world, Delilah, than following the rules. The Debbies of the world, exemplary or not—they will not matter. Is that what you want? Do you not want a future that reaches higher than an annual bonus?"

Five days ago, she knew nothing about this man apart from his taste for coffee. Five days ago, he was only The Boss. "What could I do that would make things any different? I make barely enough to pay my own bills."

The waiter brings them tea. Lilah crumples her napkin onto the plate and watches it unfold, slowly, like a flower. This is what she's learned, from years of travelling and searching and needing something else: that there isn't something else, that some people will forever look at the world and see broken things that they can't change. One moment of clarity, fuelled by opium and mountain rain—it's an illusion, nothing more.

"Opportunity is not about money," Israel says. "God does not mete out miracles only to the rich."

"I haven't seen much evidence of God in the last few years," she says. God. Why is it that her life always leads her here?

"Perhaps," Israel shrugs. "Or perhaps God has just been . . . waiting."

"Waiting for what?"

He reaches across the table and takes her wrist, then

turns her palm up so that the veins are illuminated in the light. "Who knows? God is very patient."

She stares at his hand, transfixed, and shivers as his thumb traces a circle at the base of her palm. She pulls away. "Well. Whatever." Suddenly desire is a hard knot in her stomach. She can't speak, she's so surprised.

Israel smiles again. "Yes," he says. "I know."

—

He gets the bill and leaves a fifty-dollar tip on the table as they ready themselves to go.

"It wasn't that great," she says as they leave the restaurant. "The service. Did you really think so?"

"The service was mediocre," he says. He places a hand on her back and guides her to one of the cars parked by the side of the street. "But they will remember the tip, and next time, the service will be better."

A bald man sits behind the wheel of the car they approach. He reads a book by the light of a dashboard lamp, and looks up as they draw near. He opens his door, slides out, and nods to them both. "Mr. Riviera. Madam."

"Emmanuel," says Israel. His hand moves in circles across the small of Lilah's back. The sudden soft rhythm in his voice says that these men speak Spanish all the time. Lilah wonders how far back they go, how much Emmanuel knows. Maybe Israel is a promised land of mystery to everyone. A man of shadows, a man who fades into the world just like her brother. "We are ready to go now."

"Of course, of course," says the driver. He opens the door and helps Lilah in. She slides across the seat. The car smells of leather and wealth. Israel climbs in beside her and lays a hand on her knee.

"Home," she says, and she tells them her address. She thinks of Timothy, hunkered down by a grate somewhere in the city.

They seem to drift down the street, and every hunched figure on the sidewalk has Timothy's face, Timothy's hands. Lilah closes her eyes, dizzy from the wine, or the man beside her, or both. She wants to go home and crawl into bed, or sink back into the city and look for her brother. Timothy Timothy Timothy, soft in her head like a song.

She almost falls asleep, lulled by the hum and Israel's hand, now against the soft skin of her neck, but when the car stops, she realizes that they're in a different part of town and blinks, suddenly unsure. "I thought we were finished."

"Did you?" Israel smiles. "But that would hardly make me a gentleman." He opens the door, pushes one foot outside. "Surely, Delilah, you can stop for one more glass of wine." He pauses and shrugs. "But of course, Emmanuel can drive you home. It is up to you."

Lilah bristles. "Fine." She follows him out of the car and steps onto the pavement. She does not wobble.

"Emmanuel," he says. "I will call for you." Here they are, the two of them, in front of one of the most expensive apartment buildings in the city. "Delilah." He takes her hand. "Come inside."

They walk through the lobby and into the elevator without speaking. This elevator is gleaming and sleek and rises soundlessly into the building. Lilah watches the two of them in the polished surface of the elevator mirror. She looks calm, composed. Classy. Her cheeks are flushed from the wine and the almost-sleep in the car. Israel is busy punching numbers into his phone.

They ride to the top floor. The elevator opens directly

into his apartment, and the first thing Lilah notices are the doilies, which are everywhere. Lace on the hall table, lace on the TV stand, a garish purple mess that hangs on the back of the door. The lampshade over the hall light is an inconceivable shade of orange.

"Does your mother live here?" she blurts before she can stop herself. Israel looks confused, and then follows her eyes to the lampshade.

"Ah. No, no, my mother died some years ago. But she made these. They are lovely, no?" He fingers the doily on the table. "A woman is not a woman until she can create works of art like this."

Lilah snorts and then hurriedly coughs. "I don't crochet."

He shrugs. "Yes, well. North American women—they are different in many ways."

"Such as?"

"You have forgotten your place here," he says. "Women. You expect too much. You need to learn." He smiles. "But that's why you're here, Delilah. This is what I will teach you." And that's when he hits her. He smacks her mouth with the back of his hand and her head snaps back. The world is blurred. He pushes her against the wall and her head cracks against the door. She focuses long enough to see Israel above her like some ancient god, lightning pulsing in his fist. He hits her again and pain blossoms along her cheekbone. She tastes blood at the corner of her mouth, hard and metallic, like fear.

EIGHT

He drove.

Chickenhead had glared at him for the first five minutes, then curled up on the passenger seat and ignored him. The sun rose slowly as he made his way across the bridge. He drove past his mother's cul-de-sac and thought about stopping to check on the plants, then decided against it and wound the window down instead. The air smelled of spruce and rain and earth. He drove, and Joni Mitchell sang of strangers and trembling bones.

The summer he turned twenty, he'd loaded the old Jeep with books and had driven across the country, just because. The cassettes thrown over the passenger seat soon outnumbered the books. He listened to The Eagles. He beat the steering wheel in time to Jethro Tull. He bought a second-hand guitar at a dilapidated music store in Kelowna and knew "House of the Rising Sun" before he was through the Rockies. By the time he got to Winnipeg he was sick of it, and stashed the guitar in the back.

He'd forgotten—maybe he'd never known—how big the country was; how seamless and yet different the landscape, sliding from mountains to flat and back again as he climbed the rocky Ontario roads. Further east, in Trois-Pistoles (a history stemming from three coins lost in the river—he stopped because he liked the name), a grizzled old boutique owner pushed *Hejira* into his hands.

"The road," he said. His name was Remy. He had a club-foot and a burn scar that stretched all the way down the left side of his face. "The road, *oui*." He wouldn't let Sam speak French, though his English was passable at best.

"You listen," he said. "*Écoutez*—you like."

He accepted the tape—the old man was a keen disciple, because he gave it away for free—and listened to two songs, then took it out and went back to Jethro Tull.

But he didn't throw it away, and when he got back to Vancouver he kept it because it reminded him of Remy. Gradually, it began to remind him of the entire trip—mountains and lakes and hot sun over the prairies. *Hejira* hadn't been meant for the prairies, of course—Joni had written it with the road from Maine to LA in mind—but it worked. Snow and pinewood trees and Benny Goodman—he'd had sunshine and cedar and seventies psychedelia, yet somehow it was all the same.

Now here he was, again, listening to Joni sing as he wound the car down to the water.

"Am I missing something?" he said. To the air, to Chickenhead. The only answer came from Joni. Wax and rolling tears—couldn't help him any.

Chickenhead spared him a glance and then went back to her catnip, holding it soft between her paws and then snapping it between small white teeth. Lately she'd taken to looking at him with a renewed glint of interest, the same look she reserved for mice and other objects of play. Not surprising, really—he was, after all, turning into a giant bird.

Scars, the doctor had said. Traumatic scars, extensive stitching. What did that mean? He couldn't begin to guess.

—

On the ferry, he sat outside on the floor, in an alcove made by a sleek silver lifeboat bin and a blank stretch of wall. He willed himself smaller, invisible. It had started to rain; hardly anyone came outside and when they did, they walked past him or away in the opposite direction, avoiding him like those in the doctor's office. The Gulf Islands passed in shifting hues of green and grey.

He went downstairs as soon as they began to near the island, and crammed into the Jetta—no one around to question the adjusting, the crazy shuffle as he settled the wings around the seat. Chickenhead, curled into a fat dark ball, woke up, blinked at him, and then turned her head and went back to sleep. A few minutes later, the opening door and the calm brown shores of Departure Bay.

He drove.

—

The island felt at once like an extension of his city and an entirely different world. The mountains that followed the road were softer here, their tips blue-green and grey and fading into clouds that hung low in the air. Farther north, they grew sharp again, were hostile, unapproachable. Four summers ago he'd hiked part of the northern park with Julie. Middle of August and they'd shivered over a nighttime bonfire, surrounded on all sides by peaks that were black against the dark of the sky.

"It's like being surrounded by giant witches' hats," she'd said. They'd laughed because it was silly, but also because it was possible, in the dark, to believe that it might just be true. In the utter blackness of a night in Strathcona Park, he could see a million things rising up to finish them—fire, water, acts of God.

But nothing had happened, and now Julie was with Derek, and Sam had woken up in his own bed with wings sprouting hard from his back. *If you're destined for trouble*, his mother would have said, *it will find you anyway.*

He did not believe in destiny—or he hadn't, until just over a week ago. How many times had they argued, he and his mother, squared off on either side of the debate?

"We make our own destiny," he'd said. "Anything else is shirking responsibility."

Carol had laughed at him. "Shirking responsibility, just because I think that some things are out of my control?"

"It's a crutch," he said. "A cushion. People can't face reality, so they make up stories and cling to belief."

"But everyone does that," she pointed out. "Some people kneel to a cross and some people get mired in quantum physics. In the end, it's all the same."

"Quantum physics is all about chance," he'd argued, aware, as ever, that she was serene and intractable. "*That* makes sense—you have to pull yourself above the chaos. But destiny? Some people are meant for greatness and others—what? They're just filler?"

He might even have argued the line on Tuesday, had he gone to the house, had he been in time. He might not have argued it well, especially if she'd been able to see the wings, but he'd have argued, all the same. *This thing, happening to me—it's nothing special. It's like a disease. I have a different set of cards now, that's all.*

Outside Parksville, just past the provincial park, he stopped the car and almost turned back. What was he doing? Why wasn't he home, helping Doug, making arrangements, seeing to it that the plants were taken care of? What could he possibly expect? He'd stopped not far from the ocean—the old highway ran for miles along the water. There was a smattering of trees to his immediate right, and beyond them, winking bits of blue and tan. *Miracle Beach*, the map reminded him.

He got back on the highway, and kept going. He rolled down his window and let the air rush in. The trees melted by in blurs of green and brown. The mountains began to sharpen. He drove, and when he saw the sign for the Tofino–Ucluelet junction, he took the right.

The retreat house, according to his map, was actually just outside of Tofino, a little farther down the highway that led to Ucluelet and the beaches of the national park. It was new, as retreat centres went, and fairly low key. The place didn't even have a webpage. Maybe it didn't have running water, either. Maybe—his sudden gasp of laughter made Chickenhead startle in her seat—the fathers marched down to a neighbouring stream two by two, yoked under heavy wooden pails. In tune with God, with nature, with Greenpeace. How very twenty-first century.

Then, all of a sudden, he was there. A nondescript brown driveway, an etched sign on a sturdy iron post. He turned into the drive and followed the path through the woods. It ended at a white house that stood in the middle of the trees like a cheerful child. When he got out of the car he noticed that the house was weathered—the paint cracked, the roof missing tiles—but the path to the front door was meticulous. He walked softly up to the house and knocked, and wondered what would happen when someone answered the door.

It opened, and the answer was immediate: nothing. The man who greeted him was small and bald and no one Sam had seen before.

"Hello," he said, in the same business-like voice that had sounded so strange over the phone. "You must be Samuel. I am Brother Thomas. Come in."

It was a house that didn't deceive: tired and plain, the walls white, the floorboards scuffed and worn. But the light increased as they walked to the back, and he saw that the south wall of the house was made entirely of glass and interlocking wooden beams, and the kitchen opened up onto a patio. The patio door was open and there were grey tree stumps sprinkled on the grass.

"Father Jim is just finishing his rotation," said the man. "If you'd like to wait here, he will be by in a few minutes." He pointed to a chair and Sam sat down. "Can I get you anything? Something to drink? Eat?"

A splash of holy water, perhaps? Sam was seized by a sudden, sinking fear. Suppose Father Jim saw a man limp with grief, nothing more? "No," he said. "But thank you."

Brother Thomas nodded and disappeared down the hall, and Sam was once again alone. He thought of Chickenhead, picking at catnip in the car. He thought of his mother. And then, as always, he thought of Julie, who still didn't know. When they got back to Vancouver, he'd have to tell her the news.

Behind him, the wings lay soft and still. They were warm with the light from the windows, a warmth altogether different from the heat that they'd given off in his mother's house —a green warmth, the long, slow heat of trees. He lifted the left wing and curled it out so that a greenish-yellow light dappled through the feathers. A sudden, strange comfort, knowing they were there.

"*Holy shit*," said a voice.

He turned and curled the wing in all at once. "Hello, Father."

There he was, six-foot-four, with his winking white collar. His beard had more grey in it now, but his hands were tanned and he still looked more like a lumberjack than a priest. He came to the table, sat across from Sam, and hooked his fingers around one knee. His eyes were shrewd and blue, and they weren't looking at the Sam that everyone else in the world could see. "I think," he said, "you have some interesting things to tell me."

The little white house in the woods had a surprising number of rooms. Sam's faced the woods, the lone window scratched and blurred. It held a single bed and dresser, and a mirror that hung lopsided on the back of the door. The floorboards were bone white beneath his feet.

That next morning, he woke with a headache, and remembered the edges of a strange dream. A view of the sea from the edge of a red-brown cliff, the waves rising to the level of his feet and then receding, slowly, under the guidance of his hand. The power in his fingertips softer than that which had woken the cat but still there—humming, unmistakable. Gone, now that he was awake. The room felt hushed and sweet. He could hear the brothers shuffling about in the rest of the house. Even the faint trickle of water from the bathroom tap sounded like a song.

He climbed out of the bed—he'd slept face down on the mattress, the wings spread over bed and floor—then stood in front of the mirror and spread his arms. The wings arched out from his shoulders. They had stopped growing, at least for the time being, which was good. He ran his index finger along the left wing, tracing from under his armpit out as far as it could go. Suddenly he was dizzy. He put a hand out to the mirror and leaned into it, the glass cool against his palm. The wings came up and whispered against the mirror. All was dark. Calm. He was and was not himself.

"Did you sleep well?" Father Jim asked, over breakfast. The dining hall had four tables, and wooden floors like the boards in Sam's room. It was still early, but there was no one else around. Everyone else, the priest said, had eaten and gone about the day.

"No," Sam said. "I mean—yes." He'd slept, after all. And dreams were just that. The ocean was not going to rise to the touch of his hand.

"Ah," said the priest. He shot Sam an odd look over his cup of tea, and resumed drinking.

"What was that look for?" How silly—here he was, eleven years old again, a sudden cheeky imp in his voice.

"Nothing." Father Jim waved the question away. His eyes narrowed, sharpened. "What are *those* for?"

"Beats me." They'd talked until the dark hours of the morning, tossing out a million things. *Sleep on it*, Father Jim had said, finally. As though that would do anything at all. He thought back to the night he rescued Chickenhead, standing alone on the drive and rocking on the balls of his feet. The empty sky above him. "They don't even work."

"The interesting thing about wings," and now the priest's voice was idly conversational, "is that they're completely unnecessary. At least from an angelic perspective."

"What?"

"The seraphim, the cherubim, the classically angelic—they're powerful messengers of God. They appear and disappear at will. Why fly somewhere to mete out the judgment of the Most High when you can appear instantly anywhere in the world? Wings—a human concept. That's all."

"So I have wings because people assume that angels have wings."

"That would be one guess."

"That still doesn't explain why they're here."

Father Jim shrugged. "In my experience, God isn't heavy on explaining."

"When people get stressed, they get hives. They don't grow feathers."

The priest chuckled. "At least you haven't lost your sense of humour." He stacked the teacups and saucers and stood. "Does anyone else know?"

Sam shrugged and heard feathers slide against the floor. "No." Emma. "Yes."

"Yes?"

"One of my students." How strange that sounded. "And Father Mario, back at the cathedral."

"Ah." Father Jim nodded. "Mario. Yes. He's a good man."

"So—what? What does that mean?"

"It might mean nothing." The priest began to stack the plates on the counter. "I certainly don't mean to suggest that he saw the wings only because he was a good person, if that's what you think."

Sam pushed his chair back. The dishes. "I can do that," he insisted.

"You think I'm actually going to wash? That's what the dishwasher's for, dear boy."

"You have a dishwasher?" Sam asked, amused. "How—"

"Modern?" said the priest. "Yes. But practical. Less time spent ministering to plates means more time ministering to people."

"The wayward souls of the universe?" Sam couldn't help himself.

"Naturally." Father Jim grinned. "Keeping in mind, of course, that my soul is more wayward than most."

"They call that the blind leading the blind, no?"

"Yes," said the priest. "That's exactly what they say."

The light that filtered through the windows of the study was green, like the trees.

"When I was in Portugal, I blessed a woman who had an arm growing out of her back—the arm could work, but the fingers had no muscle tone. She kept the arm hidden under clothes, so that it looked like a dowager's hump. *That* was strange. An unborn identical twin, that's the scientific explanation. Still, it was a fluke, no purpose. Those," and the priest pointed at Sam, "are entirely different."

"If that's true, then what the hell are they for?"

Father Jim smiled. "Playing chess with the Almighty is tiresome business, Sam." He flipped another page in the book he held and stopped. "Here. *If wings were not the essential element in determining the difference between a hawk and an airplane, they were even less so in the recognition of angels.*"

"That doesn't sound very biblical."

"It's Marquez. A short story. I thought you'd know it, being the English teacher and all."

"Oh. So I've come all the way to Tofino just to sit and talk Marquez?"

"Perhaps." The priest lit a cigar. "We could also talk about Kafka. Although your own transformation, I think, is somewhat more beautiful."

"More beautiful," Sam echoed. Wings, instead of countless tiny, waving arms. "Gregor Samsa dies at the end of that book."

"He does indeed." Father Jim offered him a cigar. "Much different from real life, you see, where everyone lives forever."

"I went to see a doctor," Sam said. "She saw scars. You see wings, and so did Emma, so did Father Mario. What does that mean?"

The priest shrugged. "People see what they want to see, Sam."

"That's not an answer."

"Isn't it?" the priest said. "Some people see magical things at every corner. And some people train themselves because they would rather see nothing. What more do you want me to say?"

Sam threw out his hand. "I don't know. Why you, then? Why Father Mario? Why Emma?"

"Or," the priest countered, "why *not* everyone else?"

"Yes. Yes, exactly." This time, he wasn't surprised when the other man shrugged, when he lifted his hands, when his shoulders said *no one can know.*

Eventually, of course, he told the priest about the cat. The surge of power through his fingers, the crackle of electricity in the air. And Chickenhead, staring up at him where before there'd been only death.

"Ah," said the priest. They stood outside in the clearing while Father Jim chopped wood, his hands rough and confident around the axe. "That's interesting."

"Interesting? That's it?"

Father Jim shrugged and split another log. "I was never really one for that story," he said. "The Lazarus episode. It always seemed a bit much."

"That's not very priestly."

"Perhaps." The other man grinned. "But then, I'm sure there are plenty of people out there who would tell you I've never been much of a priest."

Sam scuffed his shoes in the dirt and did not answer. The wings seemed to stretch of their own accord, sliding across his shoulder blades and out into the air. "So—what? You don't believe it? You don't believe me?"

"That's different," said Father Jim. "When we talk of Lazarus, that story—that's what it is. A story. I have no eyewitnesses, no one with whom to consult. And we know, historically, there were magicians at the time of Christ who went around the land performing 'miracles' just like this.

People who woke from comas. Stuff like that. Who's to say that that's not what happened?"

"So you're saying," Sam said, feeling oddly let down, "that you don't believe any of it."

"No." Father Jim rested the axe against the ground. "I'm saying, Sam, that it's more of a mystery than anyone wants to admit. God—you have no idea about God. *I* have no idea about God. All we can do is guess, and try to follow where those guesses might lead."

"But you're supposed to know," said Sam. He bent down and picked a handful of grass from the ground. The blades quivered in his hand. "I need someone to *know.* What am I supposed to do?"

Father Jim gathered the split logs and lifted them onto the woodpile before answering. When he looked back at Sam, he seemed genuinely surprised. "Why would you think to ask me that when the miracle is happening to you?"

"Tell me," the priest said at another point, "about Chickenhead."

"What about her?" Chickenhead, it seemed, was growing soft. The brothers fawned over her like grandparents, and she'd taken to Father Jim like no one else Sam had ever seen. "Surely there are more productive things to say."

"The bond between human and animal is always interesting," Father Jim said. He grinned. "And if what you say is true, then perhaps yours is a stronger bond than most."

Very well. Chickenhead. Chickenhead had come into his life six years ago this past May, a sudden surprise one morning when he'd gone to take out the trash. Something sharp in the bag had clipped her ear and she'd let out a little hiss that for some reason had reminded him of Julie. He'd looked in the can and there she was, wet and bedraggled and bleeding from the gash on her ear. After a moment's blank stare, he reached in and picked her up, all bones and air and fur.

Then she was his, and that was that. Aloof and pissy and rather heavier today than she'd been six years ago, but still his. Chickenhead. To the best of his knowledge, Father Jim was the only other person in the world who'd been able to pet her, although Sam's mother had tried. Given another six years or so, she might have been able to wear the cat down.

"And she can see the wings," said the priest.

"Yes."

Father Jim chuckled and ruffled a hand through the cat's fur. "I guess this gives new meaning to nine lives, doesn't it?"

Sam grunted, not wanting to laugh. He was tired of the jokes. "What does it mean?" he said, for the umpteenth time. "Should I—I don't know. Should I be expecting her to talk anytime soon, or something?"

"I expect, Sam," the priest said, his hands still steady, calm, "that this is less about her, and more about you."

"That doesn't make any sense."

Father Jim shrugged. "The miracle came right from your hands. You can't deny or ignore that. Wings can be chalked up to a hallucination, but bringing someone back from the dead makes you extraordinary. It means that there are amazing things in store for *you*. Not for the cat." Then he smiled—a sad smile, the light of God lurking deep in his tired face. "You don't hear much more about Lazarus, either. Even if it was only a story."

—

They left on Saturday, and hit the deer late that morning, just before they reached Cathedral Grove. Sam flicked his turn signal and moved into the oncoming lane to avoid a hunk of debris on the road, and when he moved back, the deer ran out from the trees and into the car.

He felt the thud, saw in one long, panned shot the deer's shock and the sudden blossom of its fear. The Jetta cracked and crumpled and came to a lurching halt. For an instant, only that, the world was silent. Then Chickenhead hissed and Father Jim ran a calming hand through her fur.

"Are you all right?" he said, meaning Sam.

"I'm fine."

The hood was crooked and glass from the shattered headlights shone dimly on the road. A broken moan came from in front of the car.

Then his hands began to tingle, and everything else went out of his head.

Sam got out and closed the car door. No one had stopped. The road was inky black, glistening with fresh-fallen rain.

In front of his car, the deer lay dying. It was a young doe, not quite a year old. The eyes that followed Sam were large with terror. The impact had broken the deer's collarbone—several ribs poked through its torso, the whiteness of bone gleaming stark against dark red flesh. The deer's rear legs were bent at strange angles, the outermost leg still trapped beneath the car, and its heart pumped furiously beneath a thin layer of skin and muscle, each throb adding to Sam's own rush of adrenaline and fear.

He'd watched a student die once, back in his first year of teaching. A fight in the school parking lot—always about drugs in that part of the city—had ended in gunshots. He'd rushed outside in time to see the perpetrator drive away, and had held Steve's head until the ambulance came, stroking his brow and saying three words over and over. *You'll be okay. You'll be okay.* The life had ebbed from the student's eyes like a thinning swarm of fireflies. Flicker, flicker, and nothing.

He felt the same now, crouched by the deer. Except that this time his hands tingled with fever and the air around him shone. The wings were a steady pull against his back; were he to look over his shoulder, he felt sure he'd see them glowing. The car door opened and closed. A moment later, Father Jim stood behind him.

"Do you have a knife?" he asked.

What an odd thing for a priest to say. "No." He was out of breath, as though he'd run into the deer himself. He thought of Chickenhead. He thought of his mother. He closed his eyes and touched the deer.

A warm rush of air, and then nothing. When he opened his eyes, the deer was dead.

"I take it," Father Jim said after the first moment of shock, "that this isn't quite what happened with your cat."

Sam couldn't speak for a moment. "No." The deer's eyes were still open, but the terror was gone, its eyes glassy and unfocused. It was a mess of blood and flesh and broken bones. It did not—what was it that people always said about death?—it did not look peaceful. It looked *interrupted.* It looked terrible.

Sam stood and marched into the trees. The ground beneath his feet was spongy with moss and rotting leaves. The trees blocked much of the daylight, but the wings shone milky white, showing him all of the roots and debris on the ground. He walked until the sound of traffic was muffled almost completely, and then he stopped, and put a hand against the nearest tree. His hands were cold now, the tingling gone from his fingers. He closed his eyes and saw the deer, mangled and dead. His mother, lying cold in the morgue. And Chickenhead, alive and well, who waited in the car.

He bent and picked a handful of earth from the ground—mud, rotting leaves, small stones. Then he arced his arm and let fly, and the debris thwacked against the nearest tree. Again, more stones this time. And again. By the time Father Jim came to stand beside him, minutes or hours later, it was a rhythm, almost a dance. Stoop, scoop, thwack.

"Someone stopped," said the priest. "They've called the wildlife authorities, and a tow truck for the car."

"The car will be fine." He threw another handful of dirt. "Is Chickenhead okay?"

"She's all right. Sam." Father Jim stepped forward and put a hand on his arm. "Sam. It could have gone on for hours like that."

"Still." *Thwack.* "A knife—even a gun—would have been somewhat less spectacular, wouldn't you say?" The deer could be floating in front of the trees right now. Energy particles floating in the air, just like his mother.

"They'll be here soon," Father Jim said. "We should go back. Be careful where you step."

"I can see in the dark," Sam said, mid-swing, and he choked on a bout of hysterical laughter. "Didn't I tell you?"

The priest said nothing.

"Do you *ever* crack?" Sam turned sharply to face the other man. "I just killed a deer with one touch of my hand. Don't you find that strange? Oh, but nothing surprises a man of God—I forgot."

"Plenty of things surprise me," Father Jim said. His face was lost in shadow, his voice both long-suffering and stern. "Come on, Sam."

Suddenly the anger sluiced from his bones. They trudged back to the road in silence, Father Jim cautiously picking his way through the undergrowth. Sam, less careful, followed the glow of his wings and stared into the surrounding green. The trees loomed overhead and the entire world was dank and dark and smelled of night, of old decay. His hands were filthy—too late, he realized he had no way of cleaning them up. He felt as though he were walking in circles, as though he'd been lost in the forest for days. The trees he'd hit were lost now. He'd never find them again.

When they reached the road, the ranger and the tow truck were already there. The driver of the tow truck was barely five feet tall and carried a blue-green Slurpee, from which he took noisy sips. He looked as though he couldn't hold up the drink, never mind take a hitch to the Jetta. An orange pylon sat a few yards ahead, toppled against the road like a lopsided Halloween hat.

As it turned out, though, the car started fine. A hardy little thing, his Volkswagen. He backed it up slowly and then moved it out of the path of the deer. Father Jim opened the passenger door and climbed in, and Chickenhead jumped forward into his arms. Aside from the rickety sound of the hood, the rumble of the car beneath Sam's feet was steady and strong.

"It's a pretty clean kill," said the ranger. He was young, and tall beside the tow truck driver—they looked like a sketch team, a wilderness comic duo. "Eat venison?"

"No."

He shrugged. "We'll handle this, here on in. Odd bit of luck, that," and he nodded to the car. "It shouldn't be driveable, what it did to the deer." Then he laughed—Father Jim had turned to face them and a sudden shaft of light from the sun illuminated his collar. "Or maybe not."

All Sam could manage was a watery grin. "No," he echoed. "Maybe not." Then they pulled onto the road, and in a scant few seconds they crossed the bend and left the deer behind.

They didn't speak again until the ferry terminal came into view. Sam pulled into the wait line and turned to face the priest, who sat serene, his hands buried in Chickenhead's fur.

"Do you have any idea?" he asked.

Father Jim shook his head, and Sam had the sudden impression that he'd heard the question before, too many times to count. "Everyone wants to know why," the priest admitted. "Even me."

VIII

The first time Lilah swore, she was fourteen. This was the year before mascara, that last year when she still thought nothing of wearing sweat pants to school. Roberta was still a year or so away from the Fernwood house, and Carl had left. They had moved, the three of them, into the basement apartment of an old house in Oak Bay. There were spiders. Lilah shared a room with Roberta and pretended not to notice the muffled sobs, the shaking that came from the other bed. Usually, Timothy would crawl into bed with her at some point in the night. He burned as he slept—a human furnace that smelled of snow and dirt and air.

That day, she walked home from school to the rhythm of her times tables. Eight times eight is sixty-four. Eight times nine is seventy-two. She'd always had trouble with these, and she was concentrating so hard that she missed the curb.

Her foot buckled and down went the rest of her. Her face smacked against the stone.

She lay still for a moment, and then stumbled to her feet, the copper taste of shock warm in her mouth. Raised a hand and felt it, warm beneath her nose.

"Say fuck," said a voice. She turned—slowly, still unsure of the world—and saw a boy. He was breathing hard; he'd been running. Later, Lilah would realize that he'd run to her. It had been a spectacular fall.

"Are you all right?" he said. Sixteen? Seventeen? She couldn't tell.

"I think so." Her words were slurred.

"Say fuck," he said again. "It will make you feel better, I promise."

"*Fuck*," she whispered into the air. The word took shape and danced. Not good, a word brought to life with dirt and blood. But she didn't know that then. She wouldn't know until years later. Fuck and blood, linked forever.

She dreams of light that isn't warm.

"This doesn't hurt." He hits her again.

She squirms underneath him, and uses her fingernails to scratch a white furrow in his arm. "Fuck you."

"Delilah," he says. He makes her name a benediction, a prayer. "It doesn't hurt you. It *can't* hurt you. How can I show you that you are so much more than your body?"

I don't want you to show me. It would be so easy just to say it. But she doesn't say it, because it isn't true. *Get off*. She doesn't say that, either.

"I won't." He kisses her, a lovely kiss that makes her think, for a moment, that none of this has happened. "Tell me. This doesn't hurt, no?"

She weeps. "Please, Israel." Or has she said anything at all? Maybe all of this is a dream, one small dream of a man with hands that could crush her. If he wanted, he could snap her arm, her neck. She is nothing but an extra layer of silk against the mattress.

"Let me go," she whispers. "Please."

He pulls his hands away from her wrists and sits back, then watches her in the dark. "You can go," he says. "Emmanuel will drive you home."

Her breath comes in short bursts—even her lungs hurt. Israel shifts so that he sits completely apart from her, dark at the end of the bed. Lilah doesn't move.

"Well?" Even as he says it Lilah knows what her answer will be. She raises her arms above her head and rests them against the headboard. She looks at him, and says nothing.

"I thought so," he says. She can hear the smile in his voice. He moves toward her, bringing darkness over her head like an angel, come to end the world.

And then she balls her fist and hits him, so fast it surprises them both. Her hand meets the hard curve of his cheek and keeps going, so that as Israel falls back her fist thuds into the bed. Her knuckles hit the mattress, crack. She breathes in and hunches, still. She can't see. The room is so dark she can't see.

Silence. Now—*now*—Lilah's hands start to shake. Blue-white energy shoots through her arms, through her fingers. She throws her head back and sucks in air, opens her eyes and there he is, against the bed. She imagines that she can see the imprint of her hand on his cheek, the energy from her palm glowing soft against his skin. Were she to walk outside, right now, that same hand would write her name across the sky. She's never been more certain of anything.

Israel laughs. "I *thought* so," he says again. All of a sudden his hand is around her throat, solid and strong. She closes her eyes and thinks of nothing. Everything that she is has shrunk to this bed, and she is incandescent, suddenly, with the knowledge that she could die here, in this apartment, and no one would ever know.

—

Another dream, this one of death. A darkened road that glistens with new fallen rain, and Lilah, running across. Headlights. A flash of light greater than anything she's ever known, and then she's on the ground, and her ribs poke through her skin and she can't breathe, she can't breathe.

A man swims in front of her eyes. In the shadows his face is hollow and long. It is a kind face, creased with sorrow and some twitchy, unnamed fear. She reaches out to touch his cheek but nothing moves.

He shines. She is not imagining this. He is iridescent, shimmering with some uneven power. She tries again to reach his face, but the hand that stretches up is not hers. It is not even a hand. It is a *hoof,* broken and bleeding. She screams. The man reaches out to touch her and through his fingers she sees the sky splinter into countless shards. Behind them, oblivion. Death. Hers.

She wakes with icy fingers and an abdomen that aches. In her own bed, her own home, the ride back through Vancouver a silent memory, Emmanuel at the wheel. She climbs out of bed and into her bathroom, pees and then crawls back into bed. She snuggles deep into the duvet. Then she does the unthinkable, and calls her mother.

"Delilah," Roberta says, before Lilah has even said hello. "It's Timothy, isn't it? Is he in the hospital? Have you found him? Is he sick?"

"Mom." Impossible that her heart could break any more but it does. "No. I don't know where he is. I was calling... about me."

"You?" *You. What is there to say about you?*

"I mean—I need."

"*What*, Delilah? What's wrong?"

"Nothing," she says, finally. "Never mind. It's okay, I'll deal with it."

"Are you sure?" Now she's suspicious. When Lilah calls Roberta expects disaster, as easily as she might expect absolution from her priest. But Lilah can't tell her about Israel, this man who took her for dinner last night and then beat her in his bed. This will terrify her. And then it will terrify Lilah, and who knows what happens then.

"I'm sure," she says. She hangs up, and she looks at herself in the mirror. Her mouth is swollen and her eyes are red, wounds that will fade by tomorrow.

In the afternoon, she pulls herself out of bed and heads to the diner on Nicola. She has a lunch date with Joel. An apology. She wants to cancel, but instead she washes away the smell of Israel and counts her bruises in the mirror. She *wants* to be normal. To have a normal day, to remember what exactly it is that other people do. She spends as much time dressing today as she did the night before. She does her hair. She wears long sleeves. She picks a blue scarf that hides the bruises on her neck, and a hat to match. And as she walks to the diner Lilah imagines that, yes, she could love the haphazard, messy, charmingly idiotic Joe-with-an-L. Done. She could say it. She could make it true.

But even as she thinks this, she remembers the energy in

her hands, that wild sense of freedom on the mattress. Her fingers, writing a name across the stars. And the fact that she did not die in that bed after all. So instead they dance for space in her head, the two of them. Joel, who finds her Catholic schoolgirl background a huge turn-on and thinks that the George Sand volumes on her bookshelf were written by a "homo." *Joe-with-an-L*, who manages despite all of this to be charming, to make her laugh. And Israel. Israel Riviera, the boss, who has yet to say anything funny, who took her for dinner and then held her life like a seed in his hand.

Joel is late. He is also hungover, and quite possibly high. He squeezes half a bottle of ketchup onto his burger and massages the inside of Lilah's thigh as if he thinks it's her vagina. His hands feel small and girlish. In the harsh light of the diner he looks—not unfit, exactly, but softer than a man really has any right to be.

"I really like you," he says. He talks with his mouth full and sprays hamburger onto the table.

Lilah thinks of Timothy, who had a seizure two days before he left home and vomited his dinner over Roberta's best china. "Thanks."

"I should move in," Joel says. "Don't you think so?"

"You don't call me enough."

"But if we lived together, I wouldn't have to call you."

"Maybe." She eats the rest of her salad in silence, and wonders what Israel is doing. Graphing management charts? Drinking wine? Reading in his apartment, intellectual and harmless?

"I don't love you." She blurts the words with her mouth half full. Now it is her turn—milk sprays across the table and sprinkles Joel's lap.

"Love?" he says. He is surprised. "Who said anything about love?" He wipes his mouth and misses a piece of lettuce that sticks in his stubble. For some reason, Lilah thinks of Timothy again and fights back tears. "Love is a farce, Lilah," Joel says, suddenly serious. "All you can do is find someone to hold on to—that's it."

"I don't want to hold on to you," she says. Because she's a bitch, because this is what she was meant for. Hearts broken around her like glass.

Joel is unfazed. Not for the first time, she realizes how much she's underestimated this man. "You will," he says. "I might have to wait a few years, but you will."

"Why the fuck would you think that?"

He shrugs. "You've got no one else, Lilah. Don't tell me you can't feel your life falling away. Sooner or later you'll want to do something with it. And I'll be here when you do."

"That's pathetic," she snaps, and she's up from the table fast enough to make it shake. She opens her mouth to tell him about The Actor—no one else, fuck you—and then remembers that The Actor is gone, that she sent him away.

"It's not," Joel says. "It's not pathetic at all." He wipes his face again and gets the lettuce. "You think I can't tell how much you hurt?"

"Fuck you."

He shrugs. "Fine, then. If that's what you want." He shakes his head as she reaches for the bill. "Never mind that. I'll get it."

Lilah stays bent over the bill for a moment—frozen, seething with rage. Then she straightens, and as she stalks away the clack of her shoes on the hardwood floor gives the only kind of comfort she can find.

She walks down Hastings before she goes home, as always. It is an oddly empty day—air damp, first fall leaves on the ground. She shoves her hands into too-small pockets. Main, Gore, Columbia, Abbott. Eyes open for a tousled head, a ragged heap rocking on the ground.

At one point, she sees a figure crouched in an alleyway; a flutter stays in her abdomen even after seeing a face she doesn't recognize. A man bent on his knees, his hands pressed against the wall and his forehead touching the brick. He mumbles into the wall. He might be praying. He might be mad.

She stops staring and turns. This time the sound of her shoes on the pavement is hollow, and the echoes follow her as she hurries away.

All great men are terrified—this is what Timothy told her, all those days ago. He'd been reading *The Inferno* in the months before he'd left their mother's house.

"Dante was frightened," he told her, once. "He was really frightened."

"Of what?" The two of them, a nice coffee shop in Victoria. Time away from the office job. She watched a couple at the patio table across from them laugh.

"Of failure. *It seemed to me that I had undertaken too lofty a theme for my powers, so much so that I was afraid to enter upon it, and so I remained for several days desiring to write and afraid to begin*. Even he felt it."

"But you're not failing," she said. Careful, suddenly terrified. "You're not failing at anything, Tim."

"Aren't I?" He rocked back and forth in his chair and wouldn't look at her. "I think I'm failing all the time."

"At what? We've talked about school—you can go back when you're ready—"

"School," and there it was, just for a moment, a flash of the Timothy she remembered. "I'm not talking about school."

"Then what are you talking about?"

He stared at the table and smoothed his napkin down against the wood. "But you shouldn't be afraid, Lilah. You shouldn't be afraid."

"Afraid of what?" she said, exasperated and so cold all at once. The couple looked over at their table, then away. "I don't know what you're talking about, Timmy. I don't understand."

"Don't call me that. I'm not ten years old anymore."

"Timothy." Deep breath. "I shouldn't be afraid. Of what?"

"Me," he said, and this time he did look at her. "You shouldn't be afraid, Lilah. I won't hurt you, ever."

"Of course you won't," she said. She held his hand and marvelled at how warm he was, how hot. "I know. I know that."

Two weeks later he left, and hurt her anyway.

—

When she does find him, later that day after leaving Joel, he's sitting at the western edge of Georgia, bedraggled and alone. She brings him water, and chocolate, and another goddamned hat. He lets her pull the flaps of the hat over his ears. She ties the hat strings beneath his chin, just as she did when he was a child.

"I don't have a fever," he says. He breaks the chocolate and sucks a large piece into his mouth, and speaks as though the flight from her house hasn't happened. "I'm fine."

"Timmy." She crouches beside him and rests her hands against the sidewalk. "Timmy, come home."

"That's not my name," he says. "You know that's not my name, Lilah."

"I don't understand," she says. "Tim—I don't know what to do."

She watches uncertainty flash across his face. "You're not supposed to know. It's not your life."

"But what about my life?" Israel Riviera, above her, and blue-white energy in her hands. "What if it's just... too big?"

He sucks his chocolate and stares at her for so long she feels the world recede. "We're all small, Lilah," he says. He takes another bite of chocolate and lets it melt, dribble down his chin. Her sweet maniac. "You have to know that, if you don't know anything else." He offers a bite of the bar and she takes it, hurt.

"I know plenty of things," she says. "Don't take that tone with me."

He hiccups, laughs. "Don't take that tone with *me*." Then he stares at the ground. He wipes the chocolate against his sleeve. "I'm just trying to keep you safe. You and Mom both."

"We're not the ones who need to be kept safe!" She's said this too many times. She grabs his arms and steels her heart against the sudden rush of panic in his eyes, the despair. "Tim. There are people who can help you."

He screams. "Don't touch me!" Then he hits her. *Smack*, once more in the mouth. She rocks back on her heels just as he scrambles to his feet—a slender young man made huge by the gathered shadows at his back. "No one can help me but God, Delilah. No one." Then he runs down the street like a terrified rat, quick and small.

—

Tonight, in another dream, she stands before the ocean, on a cliff that sits several hundred feet above the sea. Her palms are filled with grass and sand. Her dream-feet are bare and the shirt she wears belongs—belonged—to her mother. *Reclaim the Night!* A relic from Roberta's frog-marching days, when she was filled with rage and estrogen and Lilah was her unwilling partner in crime. The shirt disappeared years ago but tonight, as she stares out over the water, it is threadbare and soft on her shoulders. In some places the material is so thin you can almost see through it.

A man stands in front of her on the cliff. A slender man, taller than she is, who faces into the sun so that he is a silhouette, his arms stark against the sky. His shoulders remind her of Timothy. Were he to turn his head his eyes would be deepest blue.

"Timothy," she says. The wind blows her hair into her mouth and the words come out clogged.

The man does not turn around. Instead, he raises his hands until they touch, palms inward, over the top of his head. All Lilah can hear is the ocean, and she watches as the waters rise up to her feet. The man pushes his arms out and the water begins to recede. Lilah stands behind him until the tide is far away and there are rocks at the bottom of the cliffs. Now she hears the air, the faint rustle of wings. She opens her own hands and lets the grass and the sand blow away until they are nothing. Would that she could break and blow away this easily—but even in this dream, she remembers that she's made of sterner stuff. She is the rock below that breaks the water.

She wakes weeping, and she can't remember why.

—

On Monday, she wills herself invisible behind the desk, and buries her head in spreadsheets. She steadies her hands as they shake over the keyboard, and counts her times tables, slowly, as one minute moves into the next. Not sure quite what to think, what to feel. Is it fear, that twist in her stomach every time the door opens? Excitement? The flu?

"What's *with* you?" Debbie asks, exasperated, as Lilah blinks into focus for the eighteenth time that morning. "Hello?"

"I'm sorry," she says, quickly. Statistics. Figures. Absence reports. A moment on a mattress, the certainty that her life was about to explode with power. Or a daydream, and more words lost on her keyboard. That's all. "What did you say?"

Debbie has green eyes, young but shrewd; they have looked through Lilah more than once. "I said—how was your weekend?"

"Fine," Lilah says. "And yours?"

"*Fine,*" Debbie mimics. "That's all?"

"That's all."

"How was the date?"

"It was fine, Debbie."

"You know you'll have to tell me about it eventually."

"Maybe," Lilah says. She doesn't look up. "Does Penny have any errands for me today?"

Debbie's snort echoes through the front office. "Not that I know of."

"I'm sure she'll think of something," Lilah mutters.

"She wouldn't be Penny if she didn't," Debbie says, absentmindedly. She flicks her chin at Lilah and frowns. "Why is your neck all red?"

"It's nothing," Lilah pulls her scarf tight around her neck. "I'm cold. Have I told you how much I hate winter?"

"Multiple times." Debbie pinches her lips together in a gesture that reminds her of Roberta. Lilah stifles a giggle and turns back to her computer. Spreadsheets. Numbers and lines.

At a quarter to ten, Debbie gets her notepad and goes into the inner office, ready for the morning minutes. But no sooner has the door closed than she's out again, looking both perplexed and highly amused.

"Mr. Riviera wants you to take the minutes," she says. "That must have been some date."

"What?"

"He wants you to take the minutes," Debbie says patiently. "Do you need my steno pad?"

"I can't take minutes," Lilah stammers. "My shorthand is crap."

"Really?" Debbie's voice is pointed, still amused. "I thought it was okay."

Lilah shakes her head. "I don't want special treatment, Debbie. Just—tell them that I'll fuck it up. Screw it up. Whatever."

"You want me to disobey a direct order from the boss?"

"He won't be mad at you. If he gets angry about anything, he'll be angry at me."

"Right. And that's supposed to make me feel better."

"I don't want to be in there. With him. In front of everyone else."

Debbie does not move. "He can't very well ream you out in front of the entire senior management team."

"It's not that," Lilah says wearily. "Could you please just do this for me, Debbie?" She looks up into the other girl's troubled face. "Everything's fine—just tell him I don't see why anything has to change."

"All right." Debbie does not look convinced. "And if Penny says anything?"

"Oh." Right. Penny. "Well, I'll survive."

Another snort from Debbie's corner. "I'm sure." Then she goes back into the office. She doesn't come out for two hours.

Mondays are usually quiet, and today is no different. No one calls, and because Penny is in the meeting, Lilah passes the time between her spreadsheets and the Internet. For two hours, she is once more administrative sludge—unremarkable, unimportant. The kind of woman who does her time and counts down the minutes to her break. The employee who doesn't think beyond the weekend.

But it is pretending, only that. As she types she listens for the rise and fall of his voice—there's an entire wall between them and yet she can see him, clear as clear, sitting calm at the head of the table. Talking figures, talking power. The cadence of his accent holding everyone in rapt attention. If she closes her eyes she can smell him, feel his hand around her throat. He's so close that when the door opens, two hours later, and she turns to it like a flower following the sun, she isn't the least bit surprised to see his face. He marches over to her desk and stares down at her.

"Are you avoiding me?" he says.

"No." She hates the sound of her small voice. "Good morning, Mr. Riviera."

Israel laughs. "Delilah, I should think we are past that by now."

Behind him, in the doorway, Penny stands murderous. "We're at work," Lilah says, her voice low. "I don't want to lose my job."

"No?" His own voice dips. "Because it is such a wonderful job?" Then he leans against the top corner of her desk and takes her hand. His palm is rough and warm. "Your mother. How is she?"

Lilah blinks, surprised. What is there to say about Roberta? "She's fine. As fine as she could be, I guess." Her hair grown back now, her thin hands poking holes in Victoria dirt.

"Ah." His eyes are also shrewd; dark eyes, eyes that have no bottom. "Fine, but not well."

"She's fine," Lilah says again. She's confused. Where has this come from? "We're all fine."

"'We,'" he says. "You, and your mother. And Timothy."

"Yes." She sneaks a glance at Penny, still waiting. "And—Timothy."

"You are loyal, even though you're angry. Even though they frighten you."

Lilah scoffs. Debbie, who has come back to her desk, is typing furiously into her computer, her eyes cast low. "They don't *frighten* me."

"You would do anything for them," he says softly. "Even now, you are trying to protect them, to keep them happy. That is a very rare thing."

"It's not. Anyone with a family would do the same." She wants to yank her hand away. This is so much worse than taking minutes.

Israel shakes his head. "If you did not have them," he says, "you would be nothing."

She stands abruptly and pulls him with her, out through the front door. They walk a few paces away from the office windows, and she turns to face him. "What is it with you and these stupid statements?"

He laughs, clearly delighted. "It's been so long since someone has spoken to me the way you do, Delilah. I am—I am utterly enchanted."

"Well, that's just fantastic," she snaps. "And *I'm* mortified. What the fuck are you talking about? My family isn't gone."

"Not yet. But if they were? You would need something else. You would fight for it the same way, protect it just like you try to protect your brother." He touches her cheek. "Even if it threatened to break your heart. Even then."

She's suddenly dizzy—she stumbles on the sidewalk and braces herself against his arm. "I'm going back inside now," she says. Does Penny sit inside, waiting? "Let's not make a habit of this."

"A habit of little displays in the office?" he says. Has she ever heard a more beautiful voice, ever? "Or a habit of strange conversation?"

"How about both?"

He chuckles. "Are you going to avoid me?"

"Is that what this is about? One date and I'm supposed to be your office lap dog? One date and it's okay to ask me personal questions in front of the entire office?" She stares into his face and does not blink. "Well, I won't. I won't be that girl."

"I wouldn't expect you to." Now he is smooth, and just the tiniest bit smug. "It was merely a test."

She opens her mouth, and nothing comes out. She wants his face beneath her hand, the skin of his ear between her teeth. Blue-white energy pulsing swift between her fingers.

"I thought so." He nods once. "So if I say we're going to have dinner, again, this Friday night, you won't say no."

"Ah . . . no." Could she avoid this man, even if she wanted to? Even if she tried?

"Friday night," he says, again. "I will cook for you this time."

He cooks. "Friday night," she repeats slowly. "At yours."

"Yes."

She has bruises like a necklace along her collarbone. Of course she should say no. But the air around them is sharp, heightened. Everything around her is sharpened when he's around. She pauses for a moment and summons her will. "Should I bring anything?"

"No." Again, the uneven smile. How does a man this sure have a smile this crooked? "Just yourself."

"All right."

Israel nods. "Good. I will see you then." He walks back into the office. She does not see him for the rest of the day, or the day after that, or the next one. By the end of the week, if it weren't for the bruises still fading from her skin, she'd be tempted to say it was all just a dream.

When they got home, everything was different. And nothing was different. There were fifteen messages on the machine. Seven of them were from Julie.

"Sam. Sam—Doug just told me." *Doug?* "I'm so sorry. Just —call me."

"Sam? I don't know if you got my last message, but—call me. Please. I—if there's anything I can do."

"Sam. I'll understand if you don't want to talk—" this one was structured, slightly, her therapist voice "—but I just spoke to Bryan and he hasn't heard from you, either. He didn't even know. Are you all right? Please let us know that you're okay."

Julie had spoken to Bryan. That was interesting. He flipped through the next four messages—Julie, starting to get angry, and Bryan's hesitant, awkward voice—and then laughed as Stacey's voice came into the air.

"Sam." Cautious, unsure. "I'm not sure if you're there, but . . . I . . . we . . . we're all thinking about you. Our prayers are with you."

Prayers. That was funny. They didn't allow prayers at the school anymore.

"Did you tell anyone you were going away?" Father Jim. Sam started, then turned and of course, yes, the priest was there. In the hallway, the cat still in his arms. Chickenhead, who did not like being held by anyone but Sam. Her eyes were narrowed with calm, her limbs relaxed. She yawned.

"A few," he said. Doug. Janet. Not enough.

"People seem to be worried about you."

"Yes," he said, not quite sure how to take that. "They do."

Father Jim put the cat down. "Sam," he said. "Sam, what's happened to you?"

He blinked, did not understand. "I have wings." The deep, green stillness of the trees. "Didn't we go over this already?"

"Sam."

He laughed. A few hours ago he'd been a madman. Dirt. Stoop and throw. "I'm fine. As fine as one could be, I suppose." They would not discuss this now. Not now—Julie and Bryan and the great gaping hole where his life used to be. Instead he picked up the phone and dialed Janet's number. Kenneth answered the phone.

"Sam," he said. The wonders of call display. "I'm so sorry. Janet's up at the house. With Doug."

"I figured," Sam said. "I just wanted to check. We'll go up now. Do they need anything?"

"Naw." He spoke like that, Kenneth. He probably sounded different in the suit, when he spoke legalese, but every time Sam talked to him it was the same. *Naw. Nothin'.* "Janet took up some food. How was the drive?"

"Fine." He thought of the deer, broken bones on the road.

"Janet said something about arrangements next week," Kenneth said. "Did you find your priest?"

"Yes. I'll talk to Janet when we go up."

"Sure." Pause. "You take care now, Sam."

"Yeah. You too, Ken." He hung up the phone just as Father Jim emerged from the hall, his face damp from a wash.

"On to North Van?" said the priest.

"Sure," he said, echoing Ken without realizing it. He opened the front door and let the priest walk through, the cat once more in his arms. "You can leave her in the house, if you want. She likes having time by herself."

Father Jim shook his head. "It's too cold."

"Cold?" Sam asked. "But it's not cold."

Father Jim gave him another strange look. "It's freezing. It's colder here than it is outside."

"What?" And then it clicked—the wings, the constant rush of blood through his veins. That fire inside him. "Oh."

"Yes," said the priest. "Oh."

He hated funerals, almost more than he hated weddings. So did Doug. Mindful of this, and mindful of the fact that the body had already been cremated, explicitly according to Carol's wishes and explicitly against the dictates of the Church, the plan for the day was to keep everything short. A few words in the church, and sandwiches back at the house. Janet, as it happened, had sailed in to take care of everything after all.

Sam spent the next few days alternating between his house and his mother's, watering plants, making sure that Doug got out of bed. The air was cold but he was always hot.

He would have gone shirtless in the house if not for Janet, who could have had any of the guest rooms but was sleeping downstairs on the couch. He ignored her as best he could, sat on Carol and Doug's back deck and smelled the earth, the dirt. That was his mother's garden, right there. She'd been thinning out the perennials, clearing away everything that had gone grey and brown. That was her trowel, stuck in the dirt. The fake grave for Dodger was lost now, somewhere back in the trees. He sat outside for hours and listened as the wind whistled through his feathers. He spoke only to the priest, and the cat, and the air.

On the day of the funeral, he wore black and wondered if anyone would think it odd that he had a trench coat on in church. He'd mended his shirt early the night before, had stitched an even hem on either side of each slash in the fabric. If asked, he would say something about grief. *Inconsolable. Ravaged.* The tearing of clothes.

At the church, he kept to the walls and concentrated on keeping the wings folded low against his back, as inconspicuous as possible beneath the fabric of his coat. Most of the people there were friends of Doug and Carol. A few church parishioners, from what he could remember, and other faces he didn't recognize, couldn't place. But there was Julie, second row in. Bryan, in another pew, looking as out of place as ever. And then, surprisingly, the flash of Emma's hair at the back.

He stayed by the wall and left the family pew to Doug and Janet. Father Jim was so calm, so warm. Sam felt a rush of gratitude toward this man who had so easily dropped his life to come with him, this man so steady in the face of death. Yet even as the priest spoke, Sam felt his mother shrink down to nothing, a woman now dead like so many others. Weren't there more things to say? Or did this happen to everyone, an entire life summed up in a three-minute speech?

Father Jim motioned toward the back and called him forward. "Sam. Would you like to say a few words?"

No. And yet his feet brought him up to the altar, his pace slow, inexorable. For a moment he wondered what he looked like—the grieving son, bundled in a trench coat in a church that was too warm—and then he remembered Emma, and Father Mario, and wondered what they saw.

He opened his mouth, and nothing came. He wanted to tell them about Dodger, about what his mother would have said if she could see him now. About the turnips that she'd planted in the garden, turnips that always failed to grow. About how she'd loved Julie. How she'd wept, when they told her of the child.

He cleared his throat. "A lesson to all of us, I suppose. You can't stop death from coming." He paused. There had to be something else; there wasn't. He stepped down from the pulpit, then walked down the aisle and through the doors and there was the Jetta, waiting. He climbed in. Turned the key. Joni came on the stereo, and he drove back up to the house.

He was a dutiful son, and had everything ready when the guests came traipsing back to Carol's house. Juice. Booze. Egg salad sandwiches for Doug, tuna salad sandwiches for everyone else. He scooped the tuna from two sandwiches onto a plate and took it to Chickenhead, who had been banished to one of the guest suites upstairs. She had her claws in the couch when he walked in the door.

"Don't do that," he said, not meaning it. "What will Doug say?" He put the tuna on the floor and watched the cat pad over and sniff it. The recent episode with the tuna juice—perhaps, even, the episode with the truck, *that* episode—had reinvigorated her appetite. She ate the tuna and left the celery. When she finished, she jumped onto the couch and settled in his lap, her customary purr a dark rumble against his stomach. He ruffled her fur and pictured Father Jim, ushering everyone back to the house. Priestly platitudes ready at hand. Janet would be angry, perhaps even Doug. He did not care.

He closed his eyes and dreamed strange things of light and shadow, dreams that flickered on the edges of his mind and then disappeared, like old letters, fading away with age.

—

"Sam."

He opened his eyes. Julie, in the bedroom. She'd been crying. She wore the dress that Carol had given her three years ago as an engagement present. Red and white, a white lily in the dark twist of her hair.

He sat up. Chickenhead jumped off his lap and onto the floor. "I didn't hear you come in."

"You were sleeping." She sat at the opposite end of the couch. "You looked tired. Up there, I mean."

Up there, for the eulogy-that-wasn't. "I am tired." He rubbed a hand over his face. The wings stirred, ruffled, were still. "Is Derek here?"

She blinked. "Derek? He's at work."

"Not at Buddhism class."

Julie bit her lip. "Sam."

"I'm sorry, I'm sorry." He stood and rolled his shoulders, heard something pop in his back. "Thank you for coming."

"Don't thank me," she said, irritated. "As if I wouldn't come."

"I don't know," he said. "I didn't think so."

She opened her mouth, closed it. He'd hurt her, again. "Fine. I came for her, then. Look at it that way."

He sighed. Chickenhead wound around his feet and then, surprisingly, stepped over and rubbed her head against Julie's ankle. She stooped and scratched the cat's ears, casual, an afterthought. He noticed again the cut of the dress, the luster of her skin against the red.

The words came almost without thought. "Are you pregnant?"

"What? No. *No.*" She flushed, turned her head.

He pressed on, did not know why. "But you want to be."

"And?" Julie turned back to him, her face sharp. "So what if I want to be? We're engaged, Sam. I am allowed to want a baby." Her voice louder, dancing on that shrill edge he knew so well. Then, "I shouldn't have come. I thought it would be good, you know, to say goodbye. I loved her. And you were up there and you said those things, and I thought—someone needs to come back for him." Deep breath. "I guess I was wrong."

He laughed. He thought of two running steps, a break through the window glass, of soaring away from the house. Chickenhead, as if on cue, marched back to him and snaked a claw through his feathers. The sudden shock made him gasp, which he covered with more laughter. Then he raised the wings and passed them to and fro in front of his face, watched as Julie's eyes grew dark. Yes, that was fuzz, a slight lessening of focus. He closed his eyes, raised his hands to his head. "I'm sorry," he said. "Forgive me."

A long pause. "You should come downstairs," Julie said. She stepped forward and put a hand on his arm. "Everyone wants to know where you are."

He opened his eyes, and she was so close he could see the mole on the underside of her chin.

"Sam," she said. Now she looked worried. "Your hair. It's falling out."

He pulled his hands away from his head, and indeed, there was hair lying flat against his palms. He thought back to that day just over a week ago, when he had stood in front of the mirror and stared at the skin beneath his scalp.

"It's stress," he said. He ran his hand over his head again and more hair flaked through his fingers. "I think. I don't know. I don't know what's happening to me."

Someone knocked at the door. Julie shot him a puzzled look and then crossed the floor and opened it. Bryan, disheveled and timid and looking intensely uncomfortable.

"Julie," he said. He shuffled into the room and then looked at the floor. "Hi."

"Hi Bryan," she said softly. The door closed. It was quite possible, Sam thought suddenly, that the two of them hadn't seen each other in over two years. What was that his students would have said? *This is awkward. So awkward.*

"Dude," and Bryan looked up, over at Sam. "You okay? You beat it out of that church like a bat out of hell."

Sam laughed. The slight frown on Julie's brow made him laugh even harder. "Yeah, well," when he could speak. "You know what I'm like at a funeral."

"Are you gonna eat?" Bryan had a napkin in his hand. "Those sandwiches are disappearing fast. Not that they're all that great." Then he looked at Julie again, and blushed. So much for his bravado of before. *You're humping a fucking rock.*

"They're funeral sandwiches," Julie said, already annoyed. "Obviously they're no good for the chef, but I think the rest of us will muddle along okay."

"It's fine, Julie," Sam said.

"Of course it's fine," she snapped. Then she saw the plate with the leftover celery. "Don't tell me you fed a sandwich to the cat."

"It's his cat. Can't he feed her whatever the hell he wants?"

Julie stopped, closed her eyes. "I didn't *say* tha—"

"Easy, kids," Sam said softly. "And here I thought this was going to be such a joyful reunion."

"Times change," said Bryan, bolder now. He looked at Julie. "Don't they."

Now it was her turn to blush. "Look—we're not getting into a fight. Any of us."

"Who said anything about fighting? We're all as happy as can be. In fact, Sam and I were out just a little while ago, living it up with some nice young ladies from—"

"Bryan," he said. The room was suddenly so hot. "We don't need to go there."

"Why not? I say we kill two birds here," and even Bryan winced at the choice of words, "and hash it out. You need to move on, the two of you."

"We've moved on," Julie protested.

"Sure. *You* have, with the professor. What about him?" and he jerked a thumb at Sam.

"What about him?" Julie threw her hands out to her sides and narrowly missed hitting one of the wings. "It's his life, Bryan. He made that very clear."

Sam pressed his hands to his temples. Two years ago, Julie and Bryan had been his closest friends in the world. "We should go back downstairs."

Bryan rolled his eyes. "Fine." He reached back and pulled the doorknob and almost collided with Father Jim, who stood with his hand poised to knock on the door. "Oh."

Bryan shook his head, once more embarrassed. "Sorry, Father."

Chickenhead made a strange sound, then ran to Father Jim's feet and rumbled. He bent and picked her up. "That's all right." He nodded to Sam. "Are you all right, Sam? Everyone downstairs is worried."

"I'm fine," he said. No one would believe him, but only the priest knew exactly what he meant. "I just wanted to rest."

"There aren't that many people," said the priest. "Doug, Janet, and Kenneth. A few people from the church, and your friend, Emma. Father Mario. Everyone else went home."

"Emma?" said Julie. "I don't know an Emma."

"She's from school," Sam said. "A student. It's nothing."

Father Jim looked from Sam to Julie to Bryan, then back. "You don't have to come down," he said. "I can tell everyone that you'd prefer to be alone. If you like."

"No." Sam moved toward the door. "I'll come down." They followed Bryan down the stairs, Sam at the rear so no one could step on the wings. Then they were in the kitchen, and there was Emma, there was Doug. There was Father Mario, small in a corner of the room.

He ignored the glare from Janet and made his way to Emma first, because she was alone. Alone, awkward, uncomfortable. Pale. She hovered over the sandwiches and held a glass of juice in her hand.

"Mr. Connor," she said. "I'm so sorry."

"No one calls me Mr. Connor here," he said, trying to be funny. "To everyone here I'm just Sam. You might as well say it too."

"Okay." She took a gulp from her glass. "I know I shouldn't be here—I just wanted to say—"

"It's nice that you're here," he said. Somehow, surprisingly, it was true. "It was nice of you to come."

She shrugged. "I just wanted to say—I'm really sorry. It must have been such a shock."

"Yes." Shock was everywhere. In the air, in the floorboards beneath his feet.

"How are you . . . otherwise?" She was looking at everything except the wings.

"Fine." He could see Julie watching them, trying not to pay attention. "I'm fine."

"Have you told anybody else?" Why was she speaking so low? Couldn't she see everyone turning toward them, flagged by the drop in her tone? Julie's eyebrows were so high they looked fake, painted on.

"Father Jim," he said. "He can see them. Father Mario too."

"Really?" She glanced over at the priests. "What does that mean?"

"You tell me."

She looked troubled. Her hair shone against the blackness of her dress, and her eyes were very green. How had he not noticed her eyes before? "They . . . they look like they're taking all of your energy. Like leeches."

"Leeches." That was a good word. He hadn't thought of that word. "You could say that."

"What do they say?" She gestured to the priests.

He snorted into his fruit punch. *Everyone wants to know why—even me.* "Religious psychobabble. God works in mysterious ways. Etcetera."

"Maybe it's not psychobabble," she said. "Ever think of that?"

"Yes." He wasn't lying. "All the time."

Emma nodded jerkily. She drank the rest of her juice and

then placed the glass carefully on the table. "I'll pray for you," she said. "If it helps at all."

"Thank you." So many people, so many prayers. The wings twitched at his shoulders.

"You can... call me," she said, awkwardly. "If you need anything."

"I don't have your number." This was ridiculous. This was dangerous ground. He could see Julie inching closer, her own glass in hand.

"Here," Emma said. She handed him a scrap of paper. "My number. And my email. Use it whenever you want." She smiled. "See you later, Mr. Connor."

"Sam," he said, but she was already moving, making her way to the door. He watched until she left, and then he turned his head, and there was Julie.

"Are you *sleeping* with her?" she asked. Her voice shook.

"What?" More shock. Underneath it, yes, a hint of laughter. *So much hysteria, so little room.* "Of course not."

"Oh." Julie ducked her head. "It just—you just looked so intense, the two of you."

Intense. There was another word. "Are you sure you're not pregnant?" he asked mildly.

Her voice went even lower. "I don't know."

"Oh."

"You can't have sex with a student, Sam."

God, he was tired. "I'm not having sex with a student," he said. "Don't you think I have other things to worry about?" He drained his glass. "I think you should go."

Julie bit her lip. How many times had he seen her do that, over how many years? "I'm sorry."

"It's fine," he said. "I'm just—I'm tired, Julie. I need to lie down."

"Okay." She leaned in and hugged him. Her arms slid beneath the wings, effortlessly, unknowingly, as though she'd been hugging him like this forever. Then, surprisingly, she kissed his cheek. "Call me. Please? If you need anything?"

"Sure." He pulled away. When she left the room, he walked over to Bryan, who looked amused and antsy all at once. "Don't. Don't even think about it."

Bryan shrugged. "If you say so." He shot Sam a strange look. "Are you okay, Sam? I mean, apart from this. You seem . . . weird. I don't know. Since that day."

"Since the hangover to beat all hangovers?" He tried to laugh—it came out forced, too loud. Everyone looked over. "No. I'm okay. Really."

"All right." Bryan, of course, was not convinced. Disheveled or not, he wasn't stupid. "Well. You know I'm leaving this week, right?"

"Yes," Sam said, though in truth he'd just remembered. A tour of northern Italy for the haphazard chef. Who was not, in fact, all that haphazard when it came to his work.

"I'll be back just before Christmas," Bryan said. "But you can email, if you want. Or call. When I figure out the number, I'll send it to you." He paused. "I really am sorry, Sam."

"I know." Yet he wouldn't be all that surprised if Bryan went to Italy and disappeared. He wasn't even surprised to realize that this didn't bother him, though the fact that he didn't care made him uneasy. Who was he, now, that his life had become so small?

"We should go out again when I get back," said Bryan. "And do . . . something."

"Yes. Something," he echoed.

Bryan cleared his throat. "Okay. Well—I should go."

"Sure." He walked Bryan to the door and got his coat. His normal, stylish coat that did not have rips in the back. "Let me know how it goes."

"Will do." Bryan had one arm in the coat and was already halfway out the door. He clapped one hand against Sam's shoulder and began to amble down the front path. Then he stopped and came back. "Tell Julie I'm sorry," he said, sheepish. "I didn't mean to . . . everything feels so *strange*. You know," and he cast his hands in circles, "you and her and me and . . . everything's just so different now."

"I know," he said. "I'll tell her."

"Okay." Bryan nodded, then walked down the path. This time he did not turn back.

Sam watched him get into his car and drive away. He stepped into the house and closed the door. He avoided the kitchen and went back up the stairs, into the bedroom, and there was Chickenhead, once more twitching her tail on the bed. He fell on the duvet and spread the wings over the bed, until they were both cocooned in feathers.

Bryan would be back at the end of December.

He would not be here at the end of December. The knowledge was heavy in his stomach. His mother's life had ended without warning; his own days were counting down, now, to only God knew what.

When he came down hours later, Father Jim and Doug were in the dining room, drinking tea. Janet had bought more Chinese food. More chopsticks. The sweet and sour sauce, in its pristine Styrofoam container, had a radioactive sheen.

"The house, you know," said Doug. Without preamble, without looking at him. "The house belongs to you."

"What?"

"When I moved in, Carol asked me if I would stay, were anything to happen." He shook his head. "I told her I didn't want to stay if she wasn't going to be there. So she gave it to you. It's in the will."

Strange that this news, of all things, should shock him so. He slid into a chair, the wings hunched behind him. "She never said anything about that."

"Why say anything?" Doug's face twisted into a smile, a frown. "She thought she had years left. We *all* thought she had years left." He lifted the teacup to his mouth. His hands were shaking; tea slopped over the brim of his cup and splashed over the saucer onto the floor. "Fuck."

Doug was forty-two. Just past forty and a widower—but that's what one might get, you could argue, when one married a woman fifteen years older. *Chasing cougars. What a MILF.* The kids still made fun of that kind of thing at school. And yet here was his stepfather, newly old and alone in this great wide house. The unfunny end to the joke.

What might have happened, had he been there in time? A casual drop-in, just to say hello—a hand outstretched, another jolt of power from his abdomen, and Carol blinking up at him instead of his goddamned cat. But no—the *cat* was more important. The cat was the vehicle that would show him his power. His mother, the deer—these were expendable creatures, things that could disappear.

Janet came in from the kitchen. She slapped the top back on the container of sweet-and-sour sauce and slid into the chair across from Doug. "I think you should get some sleep." She reached across the table, grasped his hand in her own. "I've got everything here, Doug. It's fine."

"What am I going to do?" he said. He still hadn't looked

up at them. "I don't know what to do, Sam." He took a breath, deep and ragged. "Can you tell me what to do?"

He did not miss the glare from Janet, or the way that the words hung in the air, or the way that Doug's hands shook around his teacup like those of an old man. "I think Janet's right, Doug. I think you should get some sleep. We can worry about everything else later."

Doug nodded. He stood and padded out of the room without saying anything else.

Janet looked from the door to Sam and back. "I'd like to stay," she said. "For as long as he needs me."

He wanted to be back in his own house, or walking the streets of the city, or back in Tofino, throwing mud at trees. "It doesn't matter to me," he said. "Stay as long as you like."

"Are you going to go home, Father?" she asked Sam. "Today?"

He looked at Father Jim, who shrugged. "Sure. If that's what you want."

"I think it isn't good for Doug to be around anyone else right now," she said. "He needs to be around family."

"Sure." He did not point out that his own family was gone now, that his house held empty rooms and a cat. That it was his mother they'd just scattered over the ground. Instead he stood, took his coat from the peg by the dining room door, and whistled low between his teeth. A moment later Chickenhead trotted into the room.

"Make sure you call if you need anything," Sam said.

Janet nodded. "We'll be fine. But thank you."

They walked outside and got into the car. Sam settled the wings around the driver's seat and turned the key in the ignition—and then there came a whisper, a sudden shake of the world. His hands convulsed around the steering wheel and for a moment, he was and was not there. *The angel takes a breath, and struggles in the car.* He leaned against the horn and let it blare, let the sound pull him back.

"Are you all right?" Father Jim grabbed his shoulder. "Sam. *Sam.*"

"I think you should drive," he said, drawing the words up from who knows where.

"We don't have to go now," said the priest. "We have time. Why don't you go back in and rest?"

"I want to get home." He unbuckled the belt as he spoke, pushed the door open, and almost fell out of the car. He stood and rested his hands above the doorframe. He looked up to the house—Janet stood at the window, watching them both.

Father Jim got out, crossed to the other side of the car, and clasped Sam's arm. "Are you sure you're all right?"

"I'm sure," he mumbled. He stumbled over to the passenger side, keeping one hand on the car. When he was inside again, buckled and somewhat calmer, he turned to the priest and tried a grin. "How long has it been since you drove stick?"

"Years," said the priest. His hands were hard and nervous around the wheel. "But God will get us home. Eventually."

—

When they walked back into the house, Chickenhead murmured in joy and stretched herself onto the hardwood. Sam stepped across the threshold and let his jacket fall to the floor.

"So," he said. "That's that." He shot a glance at Father Jim, who had closed the door and was unlacing his hiking boots. "Why did you ask me up there, at the church?"

The priest looked up at him and then out the window.

"Sometimes people want a chance to say things."

"I didn't," he said. "Surely you knew that. Surely you knew how that would make me feel."

"Well." Father Jim moved his boots against the wall. "It's done now. There's nothing more to do."

"No." They had taken the ashes down to the ravine that morning and sprinkled them among the dirt and water. "I suppose there isn't."

They moved to the kitchen, and the priest went to the refrigerator, pulled out potatoes, carrots. "Stew?"

Sam wasn't hungry. Had he been hungry, at all, since the day the wings had arrived? "That's fine."

Father Jim took out a knife and began to chop the carrots. "I spoke with Julie for a while," he said. "Back at the house, while you were asleep."

"And?"

He shrugged. "There's a sadness there that I don't remember."

It was two years ago. It had only been two years. "It was a sad time."

"What happened, Sam?"

"She was pregnant, and the baby died." He coughed. "A few months before the wedding." And then what? A mistake, a fumble into another woman's apartment late one Saturday night. And then another mistake, and another. "She was too sad," he said, hating the words, hating himself. How to explain? How to make it believable, and understandable, that feeling of not knowing what to do, what came next? "I couldn't—I didn't know what to do. I wanted to be there for her, and I ended up being there for other people. Other women."

"I see," the priest said. Was that contempt? Was he

imagining it? "So she was the one who called off the wedding."

"Yes." Sam rested his forehead against his hands. The wings slid forward so that feathers tickled the back of his neck. "She moved out, and met Derek." Derek the professor. Derek the would-be Buddhist. "And now, here we are."

Father Jim shook his head as he diced an onion. His fingers were squat and strong around the knife. "There's something unfinished there. Between you two."

"It doesn't matter," Sam said. "Not now. Whatever I did to make this happen—it's done. She's done."

"And who else is there, then? In your life?"

He shrugged. "No one. I've been busy, with teaching. And now, with this."

"And other friends? Other people?"

"There's not much else." The job. The cat.

"Time was, Sam, that would have been different."

"I know." He shrugged. Time was, he'd been surrounded by people. "They were Julie's friends. They sided with Julie. Who could blame them?"

"There's no one else?"

He thought of Emma. "Not really."

"That's not good."

"This from the man who lives with trees for ten months of the year."

"You think I'm not involved?" said the priest. "You think I don't do things, see people?"

"I'm involved," Sam protested. But already he could feel the argument thinning, becoming tired. He was not close with his kids anymore. He skulked the halls—had done so, truth be told, even before the wings. There was Bryan, whom he'd seen more in the past two weeks than he had in months.

Janet, Doug—they would disappear now, eventually. There *was* no one else.

"It's not good for man to be alone," Father Jim said softly.

Sam snorted. How many classes had he taught, how many times had he argued and tried to make them see how words could structure things, make the world new from one syllable to the next? "Maybe I'm not a man anymore."

The priest sat unfazed. But then, he was someone whose path had not changed, whose life had not become something other. "I think," and Sam had the impression that the priest was choosing his words very carefully, "that I'm going to stay here for a while. With you."

"I'm not an invalid," Sam snapped. Then he was ashamed, and sorry, and he turned to hide it. "Everything's been taken care of. It's fine."

"It's not fine," Father Jim said. "But that's all right."

"Don't you have—" and he waved his hand "—duties? Classes, retreat issues, that kind of thing? What on earth will the brothers do without you?"

Father Jim ignored the jab. "I think you need me here. That's all."

"That's . . . that's . . ." *Pathetic*, he wanted to say. But the word would not come out.

The priest shrugged. "Call it whatever you like. But you'll need someone here, Sam, before all this is through."

He waited until Father Jim had finished with the onion. "What do you think you'll have to do?"

"We bear witness," said the priest. "It might be useful, Sam. Someone to believe."

He laughed. "In me? Or in God?"

Father Jim shrugged. "In you, or in God," he said, echoing those words that Sam's mother might have voiced, given the chance. "Or both. Does it matter?"

—

Later that night he woke in the dark, in his own room, Chickenhead a rumbling mass at his feet. For a moment he couldn't remember why he'd awoken, and then he moved his shoulder and felt it, that sharp spike of pain. Deep breath. He turned his head slowly and saw that the left wing had somehow become tangled in the sheets, in the space between the bed and the nightstand. He twisted around and a muscle in his back popped, then popped again. He reached his hand over and pulled the wing out of the gap, unwound the sheets. The material was damp, as though he'd been tossing in fear.

Freed, the wing bounced softly in the air just above his ear, the feathers crumpled and bent. He raised both hands and pulled the wing between them, smoothing down the feathers. Chickenhead, oblivious, slept on.

The wing slid through his fingers like water. It was soft, and yet not-soft—the wispy down of each single feather a mask for the ribbed cartilage that lay beneath. He lay still and listened to Chickenhead, snoring faintly at the end of the bed. Perhaps he could fly now, if he wanted. If he gathered the courage to try. The world both above and below, and people spread beneath him like children, so completely unaware of how their lives could change.

VII

On Wednesday, Lilah and Debbie have a dinner date, so instead of scouring the evening streets for Timothy, Lilah finds herself in a West End café, eating scrambled eggs out of an avocado. Debbie is in yellow and has flowers in her hair.

"Tell me everything," she says. She eats wholegrain pasta and orders a cup of herbal infusion, what the junior manager at the office, Colin, calls *lesbian tea*. "You've been too quiet this whole week. How did it go?"

Lilah pours hot sauce onto her spoon and licks it straight. "It was . . . interesting." Israel, above her. Israel, around her, inside of her, everywhere. She taps the spoon against her teacup. "We went to the Indian restaurant, the one on Eleventh."

"Yes," says Debbie. "The one that everyone talks about. Did he pay?"

For some strange reason, this makes her laugh. "Of course he paid. And he had his chauffeur drive me home."

"Lifestyles of the rich and famous." Unbelievably, there's a note of envy in Debbie's voice. "And?"

"And what?"

"And then what happened?"

"And—nothing." Lilah shrugs, suddenly thrumming with fear. How much of this is she going to tell? Once upon a time she'd have had a gaggle of girlfriends to regale. Now there is only Debbie, eager on the other side of the table. What would she say if she knew?

"Come *on*, Lilah. You went on a date with Israel Riviera! The entire office is talking."

"Sure they are."

"I'm serious." Debbie pours more tea. "You aren't in those meetings. You don't see the way that Penny looks at him. Like she wants to kiss him and squish him beneath her shoe all at once. *Everyone's* scared of him, and *everyone* adores him, in a weird, worshipping kind of way, and last Saturday he went out with you. And now you're going around the office and sitting in front of your computer like it's no big deal." Debbie picks up the spoon and stirs her cup of tea, her nonchalance so studied it's almost comical. "That mark there, on your lip—did you fall?"

"My brother," Lilah says, her hand going automatically to her face. Luckily the Timothy story makes sense. She told Debbie about Timothy some weeks ago. This is the other thing they share in their sterile, stupid office—stories of a boy, lost and wandering on grey city streets.

"Oh." Debbie relaxes. "Is he okay?"

"He's fine," she says, because Timothy is as fine as Timothy can be. Lying over a grate somewhere or shivering in some alleyway or stealing food from a restaurant garbage bin. She pulls concealer from her purse and dabs more of it over her lip.

"So?" Debbie asks. "Come on, Lilah. How was the date?"

"The date was fine."

"Does Joel know?"

"I don't think," Lilah snaps the concealer case shut, "that Joel will be around much anymore."

"Ah." Debbie, bless her, lets her keep this, lets Lilah turn back to her meal. "Are you going to go on another date?"

She thinks of Timothy, somewhere on the streets. The crack of Israel's hand. "There are—there's so much other stuff going on, Debbie. I don't know."

"Of course. I'm sorry." Debbie is an only child and has been in one relationship forever. "I just—it's exciting. He's quite striking, Israel. I've always thought that."

"He's very . . . intense."

"I'd expect so." Debbie says, her voice firm with the confidence of the young. "A man can't have hands like that and be wishy-washy. It just doesn't mix."

Lilah laughs in spite of herself. She wonders what Timothy's hands say about him. "He has these crocheted doilies all over his apartment. Apparently his mother made them, and she's been dead for years. Don't you find that creepy?"

"My mother made doilies," Debbie says. She plunges her tea bag in and out of the cup, clears her throat. *So you went to his apartment.* "She won't do it now because they've gone out of fashion, but when I was little we had them all over the house. Didn't your mother do things like that?"

"I suppose." Roberta was into macramé, when she wasn't raging against men or praying at the church. She made Lilah a hideous green wall hanging that had pockets for her books; whenever Lilah had friends over, she took it off the wall and crumpled it under the bed. Eventually, though, the macramé stopped. By the time Lilah moved out, Roberta was too occupied with Timothy to do anything other than pray. But perhaps she's begun again now, these years on. From what Lilah hears of her during their strained hours on the phone, there isn't much more for Roberta to do.

"Anyway," Debbie says, "that's kind of sweet. He must have loved his mother."

She moves her hand up to her jaw and traces the skin. "I guess."

Debbie's eyes narrow. "Lilah. Come on."

"It's nothing." Debbie has been living with her partner for most of her young adult life. They go to the cheap two-for-one movie showings every Sunday and are planning to buy a condo next year. It hurts, knowing that for some people there is this much happiness in the world. "It's just different from anything else I've ever done. I don't really know how I feel about it."

"You can't know how you feel about someone on your first date," Debbie says, her voice solid with authority. "Maybe you just need to give it time."

"Maybe." Lilah bites into her avocado and lets it slide around on her tongue.

Debbie crunches into her sandwich. "Or maybe it's just weird because it's a work thing. I'd sure feel weird if my boss started whisking me away to dinner. At least at first."

She winces. "Yeah. Sorry about that."

"Why be sorry?" Debbie shrugs. How funny, that she can be so romantic and yet so practical all at once. "He's interested in you. You're interested in him. He's the boss—why not take advantage? *I* would."

"I don't believe you."

Debbie laughs. "True. But then, this isn't happening to me. Although I'll admit that it's nice to sit at my desk and watch Penny go white and terrible with rage."

"I'm going to lose my job." Lilah covers her face with her hands. "This could be a disaster."

"Maybe," Debbie says cheerfully. "I mean, I can't imagine it would be comfortable if things were to go wrong. Think what it would be like at the office, even if you didn't lose the job!"

"Thanks."

"Just see it through, Lilah. Who knows what could happen? Maybe you'll fall madly in love." Debbie claps a hand over her heart. "With the *Hass Avocado*. How romantic."

Inexplicably, this thought fills her with terror. "I think it's a little early to be talking love."

"Love is best when it happens early," Debbie says, earnest. "You never know, Lilah. This could change your life."

"Maybe," Lilah says. She finishes the rest of her meal and thinks about Roberta, ensconced in her house on the other side of the Strait. Timothy, making his way down some street in the city. And Israel, who is also there now, who has his own little spot in her mind, his voice and his smile inside of her, pulsing with energy. How much potential heartbreak is it possible for one person to hold?

"Well," Debbie takes a sip of her lesbian tea, "*are* you going to go out with him again?"

Or perhaps it's not the heartbreak that scares her, but the possibility. The possibility of a heart more than whole, or a life that reaches so far beyond what's expected that you can't see where it ends and forever begins. "Friday," she says. "He's cooking."

"Good." Debbie claps her hands like a child. "Make sure you tell me everything."

—

Timothy went to the video store, those months ago, and did not come back—that's what happened. Twenty-four hours later Roberta issued a missing person's report; forty-eight hours after that someone found him across the water, crouched in a Vancouver alleyway, dirty and disheveled but very much alive. He wouldn't leave. He sat hunched on the ground, shivering, and when Lilah tried to touch him he shied away.

They went to the station, but the police were no help. "He's old enough," they said. They meant age of majority; Roberta heard it literally.

"How can someone be old enough to live on the streets?" she raged, back in Lilah's kitchen. "That's ridiculous. That's *inhuman*, Delilah."

"It's his choice," Lilah said. The words felt like dust in her mouth. She drank cheap Earl Grey and thought of her brother, the fever in his hands. "He'll come home if he wants to."

"I haven't been a bad mother," Robert said, looking at her. "Have I?"

"No." Mediocre. *Not enough*. "No, you haven't."

"He doesn't have his medication," Roberta said. "I don't know what he'll do."

"The police will keep an eye," Lilah said. She had her doubts. But you had to have faith. You had to put it somewhere.

"I don't know what happened, Delilah," Roberta said then. "I tried so hard."

Lilah ignored this and waved her cigarette in the air, so that the smoke swirled between them like a veil. *Trying*—and *there*. Such a gulf in between. "Mom—he's eighteen. You can't make decisions for him forever."

"I know that." Roberta's hands twitched at the table. "But he's sick. How is he going to survive? How—who is he going to talk to, who's going to pray for him? Should I talk to the diocese here? Maybe we should ask them to talk to him. To take him in."

"What, so he can suck some priest's dick just for a place to sleep at night? He's not going to get help from the diocese."

Roberta slapped her so quickly it stunned them both. "You," she said, breathing hard, "are a terrible human being."

"*I'm* terrible?" Lilah snapped. "I'm not the one out there destroying children's lives. I'm not the one building wars for God, or going into sub-Saharan Africa and telling women that birth control could send them to hell." Her own fury was brittle, yet familiar. "Why the fuck should Timothy listen to what a priest has to say when odds are they're just as fucked up as he is, if not more?"

"How is it possible," said her mother, "that you've travelled and experienced so much and still have eyes that see so little?"

"Timothy's never left the province and he feels the same way."

"How do you know?" Now Roberta was merciless, unforgiving. "You haven't been there."

"You think that just because I wasn't there while you indoctrinated him means I don't know these things? He's not stupid."

"He's a good boy," Roberta said dully. "He's just—I need to believe, Delilah, that he'll be okay."

"The world eats good people," and as her mother's face

crumpled Lilah pushed her own guilt away. "My *experience* taught me that. And no amount of praying will change it."

"What did I do wrong?" Roberta whispered. "With Timothy, with you?"

"Jesus Christ. Will you stop that? He left school at fifteen, Mom. He didn't have any friends, and he didn't play outside, and when I was home all we ever did was stay up late and drink hot chocolate. He read too much. He was too sensitive." Dyspraxia, Asperger's, or maybe even autism. *Schizophrenic tendencies.* Doctor speak and fancy labels that in the end all meant the same thing. Strange little boy who became a strange young man. She would do anything for him, and destroy anyone else who ventured to say such a thing, but still, it was true. "That's not your fault. That just happened."

"He hates crowds," Roberta said. "How is he going to survive in this city?"

"Vancouver has plenty of places for people to disappear," Lilah said. She stubbed out her cigarette, lit another. The urge to vomit was almost unbearable. She closed her eyes, and eventually it passed.

"You need to stop smoking."

"I have stopped. I'm stressed. You stress me out."

"Oh." Roberta sniffed. She reached for her bag. "Fine. I'll go."

"You know you can stay, if you want."

"And stress you out?" Roberta threw on her coat. "I wouldn't dare." She pulled out her wallet and tossed a few bills onto the table. "This is for Timothy. When you see him. Get him whatever he wants. Whatever he needs." She strode to the door, opened it, and slammed it behind her.

She called Lilah later that night, once she was home. "Will you call me if you see him? Will you let me know he's okay?"

"Of course I will." This family, her family, splintered like glass. She cradled the phone and did not say it, although they both knew it was true. Together they were broken; the three of them. So different, and so lost.

Israel is not in the office on Friday, but halfway through the day a message comes through to her desk. Emmanuel, wanting to know when he should pick her up.

"I'm fine," Lilah says. "I'll take the bus."

"Mr. Riviera specifically asked that I pick you up, madam." His own accent is not as rich, not as exciting. But Emmanuel sees Israel every day, and some of the other man's power seeps through the phone. "It is not, as I understand it, a request."

"Well," Lilah says brightly, "you can tell him to go to hell, then."

A pause. "Madam," Emmanuel says. "That is . . . hardly appropriate."

"Emmanuel. Tell Mr. Israel Riviera that I will be there, at seven, and that if I see your car downstairs before I leave I won't come out of my apartment. Is that clear?"

"Madam, I really would advise—"

"I don't care what you'd advise," she says, still in that cheerful tone. "You tell him that I'll be there, and that I won't be picked up like some hooker."

Another pause, this one heavy, disagreeable. "I will let him know," Emmanuel says finally. He hangs up without saying goodbye.

"'Like some hooker?'" Debbie's hands are poised over her keyboard, her eyebrows arched, amused. "I bet that's going to get you brownie points."

"I don't care." She does not want brownie points. She wants him angry, she wants the righteous slap of his upturned hand. "If he thinks I'm going to answer to his beck and call—fucking men."

Debbie laughs. "It's just a date, Lilah. You're so wound up."

"I'm not," she protests. But Debbie just smirks and turns back to her desk.

Lilah leaves the office at four, goes home and soaks in her tub for an hour. She climbs out with wrinkled fingers, towels off, then pads naked into her bedroom and picks her outfit for the night. Red dress, neckline low, no jewellery. She wears hardly any make-up, and twists her hair so you can't see the early bits of grey. Then she slides the black shawl out of her closet and hooks the black peep-toes onto her feet. Not quite glam but not quite office. Her bruises faint but there. Waiting.

She takes the bus downtown and walks the rest of the way to Israel's apartment, careful in her heels. She is exactly on time. She stands outside of the building for a moment, looking in. The lobby is sleek on the opposite side of the glass. She raises a hand and presses the buzzer. She will not run away.

"Delilah." His voice over the intercom is cracked, knotted with power. "Come up."

This time, she rides the elevator alone. There is no music—this feels strange until she remembers that there was no music before, either. Just a steel and glass box rising silently into the night. She focuses on the marbled floor and thinks of Emmanuel, Israel, breathes in deeply. Brownie points. The elevator slows and stops. She raises her head, and the elevator doors slide open.

"Hello," Israel says. He stands before the elevator, waiting for her. He's wearing an apron, black pants, one oven mitt. If this was any other man he'd look ridiculous. But this is not Joe-with-an-L. This is not any other man.

"Hello." She holds her breath and waits for more, but there's nothing, so she steps over the threshold. Israel smells of cedar and incense, like the apartment. Heavy, waiting. He slips Lilah's coat from her shoulders, slings it casually over his arm. "You must remove your shoes," he says. "Please make yourself at home."

Lilah slips off her heels and sinks her feet into the carpet. Plush. Even the floor here is expensive. The apartment is lush and calm, a soothing mix of beige walls and recessed lighting. She hardly notices the doilies now. The front foyer opens into a great room that looks out over the city. City lights twinkle at them through the glass.

"I've made tortellini," Israel says. "Stuffed with pork and rosemary—I trust you don't object?"

"No, it's fine," she says, and she follows him into the kitchen.

Israel pauses at the counter and passes her a glass of wine. Red, this time. "Good."

Lilah perches on a bar stool and watches him move through the stainless steel expanse of the room. This hulking, beautiful man in a kitchen apron and oven mitts. Saxophone music drifts from the stereo by the window.

"Emmanuel called me," she says suddenly. "I told him I didn't want to be picked up."

He smiles. "I know what you said."

"Are you . . . upset?"

Israel shrugs, then turns from her and fiddles with the oven knobs. "You are here. If you would like to be stubborn and walk instead of being driven, who am I to argue?"

"I didn't walk the *whole way*," as though it matters. "I took the bus."

"Oh." His voice is smooth. "Excuse me." Then he nods in the direction of the music. "John Coltrane. An American saxophonist."

"I know who he is."

"Do you," he says. "That is interesting. In my experience, most women do not."

"In your experience, do most women also crochet?"

He chuckles and slides a casserole dish out of the oven. "Every woman should know how to make beautiful things for her family."

She doesn't know what to make of this, so she says nothing. The wine is heavy, delicious.

"You should tell me more about your family, Delilah." He takes two plates out of the cupboard and slides them onto the counter. "I am very interested. You can tell me now, while we eat."

"You didn't tell me anything about *your* family," she counters. A childhood in Mexico, a struggle with math that mirrored her own. "Anything important. You first."

He laughs. "Very well. I am an only child, and my mother is dead." He spoons the tortellini out as he speaks, the movement of his wrist quick and sure. When he finishes, he reaches for the bundle of parsley sitting on the counter, then tears two sprigs and places one on each dish. "My father . . . became irrelevant years ago. I am alone in the world. Is that what you want to hear?"

"You don't have to be so blunt," she mutters. "Jesus. I thought you said you knew how to tell a story."

His expression flickers, unreadable. "I said I had many stories to tell. That is different." He slides a plate in front of her and sits on the opposite bar stool, then takes the cream napkin that sits next to his plate and unfolds it over his lap.

"You asked me a question, and I answered it. Would you prefer a fairy tale?"

A fairy tale, a happy ending. She unfolds her napkin and spreads it carefully across her knees. "So you haven't seen your father," she says. She picks up her fork and then puts it down again. "In years."

He shrugs. "It is not a problem. He is dead in every way that matters." He nods to her plate. "You can eat. I won't poison you."

Lilah frowns and scoops a forkful of pasta into her mouth too fast; she coughs and narrowly avoids spitting everything back out onto her plate. Israel smiles. She avoids his eyes. She pretends to concentrate on the food and says nothing.

"Your father is also gone," Israel says idly. "You haven't seen him in years, either."

She stops eating and stares at him. "Who the hell told you that?"

He laughs. "Surely you don't think you hide it all that well, Delilah. You have—how would you say it? Daddy issues."

"I do not fucking have daddy issues."

"But your father is gone, yes?"

Lilah puts her fork down. "Why the fuck is it important?"

"People show who they are when they are upset," he says. So calm. "I am trying to know who you are."

"Why can't we just talk about hobbies, or favourite books, like normal people?"

"Normal people are mediocre," he says. "Is that what you want? Is that truly who you want to be?"

The door is just on the other side of the foyer. All she has to do is take her shoes and go. "Don't tell me what I want. You have no idea."

"Hmm," he says. He winds a hand around the stem of his

wine glass and stares at her. "That could be true." Then he reaches forward with his other hand and strokes the skin on the back of her wrist. "But I think—I think I am not wholly wrong."

She looks away and mutters her words in the direction of the floor. "My father left fourteen years ago. I don't care if I ever see him again."

"I see."

"Why is it so important?" she says, her eyes still lowered. "Why do you want to know?"

"Ah," he says. "As to that—how can I know who you are if I don't also know what your family think of you? If I don't know where you come from? I do not have a family, Delilah, so families interest me. It is that simple."

Lilah shakes her head. "We're not that interesting."

"You think so? And yet your brother lies trembling on the streets, changing even as you watch. Disintegrating, disappearing, despite all your efforts to save him. And you love him? You'd forgive this sad, ungrateful wretch?"

She snatches her hand away. "Fuck you. You don't know anything about my brother."

"You'd be surprised what one can learn." He reaches for her hand again, and this time he does not let her go. "Suppose he disappears, Delilah. Suppose there is no more Timothy. What would you do?"

"Shut up. Just shut up. He's not going to disappear."

"But what if he does?" His voice pleasant, relentless. "You'd need something else to live for, no? Perhaps your mother, who is also dying? Tell me, Delilah—what happens if she goes too? If you have nothing? Would you not want something else?"

"They're not going anywhere," she says. She cannot move her hand. "Stop it. They're not gone."

"Haven't you wished, sometimes, on some level, that they *would* disappear?" He tightens his grip more. "Tell me, Delilah—in your heart of hearts, do you not secretly imagine what life would be if they were not here?"

Tears spill from her eyes. "Why can't you just leave it alone?"

Israel releases her hand. "You've left it alone for too long," he says. "All this guilt you carry—perhaps your brother just deserves to die."

She throws her fork at him without thinking. He ducks it easily—the fork hits the kitchen cabinet and clatters to the floor. "Goddamn you." Her voice cracks with tears and rage. "God*damn* you, you fucking son of a cunt."

"What did you say?" His voice is low.

How she hates him, suddenly, this man who loves his mother. "I said, *you fucking son of a no-good cunt*. I bet she was nothing more than a whore."

He hits her so fast it doesn't register. The force sends her reeling, knocks the wine glass off the counter so that it shatters on the floor. He hits her again, and her head crashes against the wall. She stumbles from the bar stool, no doily there to save her.

"Jesus fuck," she gasps. She should run to the door, call for help. Something.

"You have a filthy mouth," he says. He is already standing over her. He rolls the sleeves of his shirt slowly, deliberately, and extends a hand to her. Lilah takes it without thinking. He pulls her back from the wall and then smacks her again. Blue-white stars explode behind her eyes. And suddenly she is humming, glowing, alive with energy. She blinks, breathes hard.

"I have so much to teach you, Delilah," he says. "I have so

much to *give* you. But you're not listening. How long before you pay attention? How long before you learn?"

She lets him strip her, right there in the kitchen. He leads her into the bedroom and uses the black shawl to bind her hands to the bed. Then he pulls the sheets away—these beautiful sheets, the duvet that probably cost more than she makes in a month.

"I will teach you," Israel says. "I will set you free." He opens the bedside cabinet and brings out a delicate whip. Even the brush of the whip along her thigh makes Lilah shiver.

"Do it," and she clenches her teeth, arches her back, waits for the pain and that breath of infinity along her ribs. Small Timothy. Sweet Timothy. The brother, yes, she has wished away a hundred times.

Israel holds the whip above her, his hands ready. But he tosses it aside and kneels before her, and he traces her face in the dark, his thumbs warm against her wet cheeks, her salty eyes. Over and over, until his fingers are damp and her face feels as raw as if he'd taken the whip to it after all. Then he stretches a band of cloth across her eyes, and ties it gently behind her head.

She clenches her hands as he draws away, and readies herself. She hears him remove his clothes, feels him stretch out beside her. He places his arm across her breasts and says nothing. She is blind and bound, waiting. Maybe he'll whip her now. Maybe he'll make her scream.

Minutes pass, maybe hours, as they lie there in the dark.

Finally. "I don't want him to disappear." She aches under the weight of his arm and listens to him breathe. The fury has passed through her like a migraine and left her giddy, yet strangely calm. "I get frustrated. Sometimes I imagine what it would be like if he wasn't here. Yes. But I don't know what I would be without him."

"You would find out," he says. "Eventually."

"I don't *want* to know what I would be without him."

"No one wants to know," he says. "But who knows, Delilah, what gifts might lie in wait beyond that sadness?"

"Of course. I forgot. 'Perhaps God has other plans.'"

His shrug is soft beside her. "You are quick to blame God," he says. "I find it amusing."

"My mother always said that Timothy would lead us to God," she says. What is it about this man that draws the words from her? Her throat feels oddly raw. She swallows; the feeling does not go away. "She thought he was destined for . . . something. And she expected that that would change . . . everything."

"What do you think?"

"Some destiny," she says, bitterly. So much freedom in the darkness of that cloth across her eyes. "He might as well be locked away."

"But you follow him anyway," he says. "You follow, and you hope." Suddenly he reaches across and takes away the blindfold—the room is so dark that for a moment she can't tell the difference.

"Follow who? Timothy? Or God?"

"Does it matter?" He rests his hand against her cheek; with his other hand he reaches up and pulls her wrist free from the shawl.

She doesn't wait for the blood to rush back into her

hand— she slaps him, twists her wrist so that her nails catch at the corner of his mouth. Israel grunts. Her arm is a live wire, her own blood pulsing back into her fingers. The pain is brilliant, excruciating.

Israel swings a leg across her torso and frees her other arm. He places a hand on either side of her ribcage. As her eyes adjust to the light, she watches the energy flow through her arm and explode against his face—fireworks, a supernova that settles into the air around his head. Dark man with a halo of blue-white stars. She is pinned against the bed; she's never felt more powerful in her life.

Suddenly, the crack of his palm against her temple. "Let him submit absolutely," he whispers. "Let him offer his cheek to the one who strikes it, and receive his fill of insults."

She shuts her eyes and thinks of Timothy. Israel bends close, puts his mouth to her ear. He presses his hand against her stomach and the sudden pressure makes her arch up in pain. "Can you feel that?" he asks her, still whispering.

She nods and shakes her head, both. "No." She vaults up and scratches a line across his face with her free hand. "Hit me harder." Then she pulls his face toward her own.

SIX

He went back to school, because there was nothing else to do. He avoided Stacey. He was curt with Emma, almost abrupt. The wings had begun to pulse waves of pain across his shoulder blades. He took codeine, which did nothing. Every time he stood in front of the class it was a performance: Sam the magician, Sam the disappearing, winged freak. They watched the puzzle. They watched him.

He'd begun to get migraines. They were worst in the early morning and came with auras, a terrible sensitivity to light. The students in his morning Shakespeare class had halos. Some were golden. Others shone orange, a few of them a light pink that faded into white. Emma's halo was purple and sat nicely against the brightness of her hair. Stacey shone yellow and red, like the top two-thirds of a traffic light. *Caution. Caution.*

At home, Father Jim—whose own halo was blue, the calm colour that Sam imagined Hindu monks meant when they spoke of nirvana—cooked for him, like a housewife. He even walked the cat. "We'll call it a sabbatical," he said. "I can leave whenever you want me to go."

"No," Sam said. It was morning and the priest had made coffee; he stood now in front of the stove and fried sausages, stacked pancakes. Maple syrup drizzled between each layer like glue. "It's nice, the company." He'd forgotten how nice. How easy, to slip into the routine of being alone. "What will you do then, while you're here? Will you give Mass at the cathedral?"

"Maybe. Pancake?"

"Do you think they'll have pancakes in heaven?" Sam asked, only half joking.

The priest shrugged and slid a stack onto Sam's plate. "Why not? No sense in giving up on a good thing, I say."

"Seriously."

"Sam. How the hell am I supposed to know?"

The pancakes were fluffy, soaked in syrup, delicious. He would have fed a piece to the cat had Father Jim not swatted his hand away.

"Don't do that. That's not good for her."

"It's just a pancake!"

"All the same." The priest sat down across from him and began to cut into his own stack. "No wonder she follows you around all of the time. That's cupboard love, is what that is."

"It is not," Sam said, offended. "And anyway, she's fond enough of you."

The priest shrugged. "Maybe. Have you heard from Doug?"

"No." One week, and not a word. Sam had called Janet a few times, just to make sure things were okay. It seemed that she'd taken up permanent residence in the house. She'd also gone back to being the Janet that he'd always mildly disliked; her answers were monosyllabic and irritated, as though calls from him were a ridiculous waste of her time. "But I'm sure we'll hear if anything happens."

"Hmm," said the priest. He drizzled maple syrup over a piece of sausage and put the whole mess in his mouth.

"What does that mean, *hmm*?"

"Nothing, really," Father Jim said. "I just wonder how he's coping."

His mother had been gone now for over two weeks. Why did it feel so far away? "He'll be fine. It will take him a while, sure. But he'll be fine."

"And you?"

"Me." A week and a half ago, they'd hit a deer on a twisting Vancouver Island road. A week before that, he'd brought his own cat back from the dead. And a week before that, wings had sprouted from his back like flowers from the ground. He opened doors extra wide now as a matter of course, no longer thought it strange to wear his trench coat at the school. He could see auras. The wings were heavy against his back and yet, somehow, the most natural thing in the world.

"I'm fine."

The priest snorted into his coffee. "You look fine."

"What else am I supposed to say?" What did they say, the prophets, during that space of time before acceptance, when the world was still the same around them and they had not yet become lost?

"Have you spoken to Bryan? Julie?"

"No," Sam said. "But I don't talk to Julie. Not really. And Bryan's been away." Against all expectation, an email had come to Sam several days ago. It was characteristically blunt, awkward. *Sam. Hope you're feeling better, see you when I get back.*

"And Emma?" the priest said, watching him. "Looks like there's unfinished business between the two of you, as well."

He was avoiding Emma, considerable feat though that was. The curtness seemed almost to encourage her—she'd become a constant fixture at school. She was first in the room in the afternoons, her face always tense and then slack with relief. *You're still here*, she might as well have said.

He had forgotten about the infinity puzzle, but discovered it one day in class as he was rummaging through his desk during a test. He pulled it out and wound the string around the metal, through and through again. More knots. The room was hushed, save the sound of scratching pencils. He twisted the string again, and when he looked up, Emma was watching him. He tapped the puzzle against the desk and then hooked one finger in each end of the string and pulled. Nothing moved.

When he looked up, she was bent over her test. He put the puzzle in his pocket, and a few minutes later he forgot about it, again.

They were reading Graham Greene, and some of the students had issues with Scobie.

"Makes no sense," said one of the girls. Clara. He had to do this now, repeat their names to himself whenever they spoke. He was forgetting faces, blurring them all in their auras, in the light. Clara shone red. "If you truly believed as he did, you wouldn't do it. It's inconsistent."

"What's inconsistent?" he asked. "Greene was trying to express a different view of spirituality. His work is rife with this struggle. It's inconsistent against the dogma, not the faith."

"But they're the same thing." Jodi, the star hockey player with an eye for hard facts. Green. "Faith is all about rules. If you don't know the rules, or you don't follow them, then that's it for you."

"Not necessarily," he said. "You can't expect to think a world view that proclaims the ineffability of God could then be contained by a simple set of dos and don'ts."

Jodi laughed. "The Ten Commandments? Hello?"

"Spirituality is supposed to be about journeying," he said, and he waved the book in his hand. "Greene was fascinated by the struggle to find God—how easily man could discover and lose divinity all at once." How God could arrive in a rush of white wings and then go, just as quickly, leaving feathers behind Him to trail in the dirt.

"I still think it sounds strange," said Jodi. "You're telling me you don't find it all at least a little ridiculous?"

Sam shrugged. "Personally? I'm not sure. I wouldn't call myself an atheist. But I wouldn't say that I believe, either." Mildly surprised that he could still say it, that it still felt true. The wings swept over the floor.

"Then that makes no sense. If *you* don't believe it, why all the talk about journeys and whatever else? You can't stand up there and expect people to take you seriously if you're admitting right now that you're not sure?"

"Ah," he said. "But just because I don't believe it doesn't mean it isn't true, or that it couldn't be true for other people. I also happen to think," and here was a glimpse of Sam-before-the-wings, that long-ago teaching rock star, "that Paul McCartney died years ago and everything that's happened to 'him' since is an elaborate hoax. But just because I don't believe in the spectre of Paul McCartney doesn't mean that he couldn't still exist. How would I know?"

They were not convinced.

"There's nothing about the world as it is now that can't be explained by science." Clara again. "People want to talk about God because they think that science takes all of the mystery out of the world. That's all it is. People just want a good story."

Emma was tracing circles in her notebook. She hadn't said anything, which wasn't surprising. What could she say? What could either of them say, really?

"So science doesn't take the mystery out of the world, then?" What would Father Jim say, he wondered. What words were there at times like these?

Jodi shrugged. "I don't think so. There's too much about the world that we still don't know. It'll take years. It could take hundreds of years, and for all of that time people will still be thinking about this thing called God and worshipping the air like it's actually going to do something. I just think it's a waste of time."

Sam dropped his chalk, bent down to pick it up, and spread the wings out so that they touched either side of the floor. When he raised his head, Emma's face was pink, and no one else had noticed anything. "That may be," he said calmly. "It may be that there's no such thing as God, and it's all been one grand delusion. But you don't know. You might think that you know, that you have no doubts. But you don't know what you're going to see tomorrow." What might happen to you one morning, when you wake up with feathers in your sheets and down in your hair. "You just don't know."

"Who's supposed to build their life on something like that?"

"You're not supposed to," he said. "You just do. It just happens." He scratched his head and strands of hair came away in his hand—he heard a small gasp, a murmur from the girls, and ignored it. He shrugged and gave them the closest truth he could. "God or no God, guys, the world itself is shaky business. You never know what's going to happen next. And if you never meet God face to face, then that *not-knowing* is about as close as you're going to get."

He'd half expected her to walk out of class the moment the bell rang, but Emma hung back and stood by his desk. When the last student left, she slammed her bag against a chair. It was loud enough to startle him.

"You're a hypocrite," she said.

"I'm not a hypocrite. I told them the truth."

"'The truth,'" she mocked. "What truth, exactly? That you don't believe in God?"

"I didn't say that."

"You might as well have said it!" Her voice shook. "This thing—God, whatever—this is *happening* to you. How can you stand there and say otherwise?"

"But they can't see this," he said gently. "And even if they could—who knows? Maybe it has nothing to do with God at all. Maybe it's genetics. Maybe it's a disease." He thought of Father Jim's Portuguese story. "People grow extra limbs. Or they get tumours that have teeth. It happens."

"Don't talk to me like I'm one of your students!" she snapped. Sam looked up and saw a surprised face at the classroom door.

"We'll just be a moment." Then lower, to Emma's furious face, "You *are* one of my students. And you aren't the one waking up with feathers in your bed. Don't tell me you can explain this better than anyone else. I've been to the doctors, Emma." *Scars.* "I've been to a priest. And they either see them or they don't." Then, with more force than he meant, "What do you want me to *do*?"

"I want you to take responsibility," she said. The flash in her eyes was unnerving.

"For what?" A cat, maybe? A cat sitting in his house right now, possibly eating tuna and purring in the lap of his houseguest the priest? Or his mother, scattered in bits over the ground?

"You're being called to something," she said. "Called out of yourself."

"What do you expect me to do?" he asked. "Go doling miracles out to the blind?"

"You'll find out," she said. "God will tell you."

"And what if God doesn't? What if this is all that happens, and I'm just supposed to walk around like a freak for the rest of my life?" Why hadn't he noticed that zeal in her eyes before? The Emma whose hips he had liked—where had she gone? "This isn't happening to you," he said, sharply. "Don't presume to tell me what God may or may not say."

"But God will speak to you," she said. "You're a teacher. You understand. The lessons come, eventually. God is like that as well. It just takes time."

Had she gone insane? Did this happen to everyone hit by a sudden divine flash—did words go out the window, did logic rush out the door in the wake of holy power?

"You—don't—know," he said. He felt so old. He picked up his bag and lifted it over his head, then settled the strap carefully between the wings. "Emma—this could be something terrible. Or it could be wonderful." Or it could be both, and neither. Who was he to say?

"How are you supposed to decide anything if you don't know?" she snapped, echoing the others. "You need to build a life on *something*." She shook her head. "A lot of people would give anything to have this kind of opportunity."

The thought was so ridiculous it nearly stopped him where he stood—angel factories, the wings lined up and colour-coded like linen shirts. *Heavenly dispensation, right here, right now!* "Maybe," he said again. "If I find anyone willing, I'll be sure to let you know."

—

A few days later, she tried a different tactic. She began to follow him in between classes—he caught glimpses of her hair behind him in the hall, and she lingered in the doorway after class, an uncertain smile on her face that would then disappear as soon as it had come. That afternoon he caught her outside, standing by his car.

"You can't keep doing this," he said, again. "People will talk."

"People are already talking about you," she said.

"People always talk about me." He thought back to the student who had died. He shrugged and tried to make a joke of it. "I'm going bald faster than an eighty-year-old man. What's not to talk about?"

Emma looked at the ground. "It's not that."

"What?"

"You're sneaking around. You keep looking over your shoulder as if people are following you. And you're talking to yourself. You even do it in class."

"I do not." But he couldn't remember. Why couldn't he remember?

"Mr. Connor," she said. And then, "Sam." She was so pale. "They don't see what I see. They see you wearing a trench coat, or shirts with holes in them, and everybody knows that your mother died and you're losing your hair and you just—you look terrible, all the time." She stopped, took a breath. "Maybe it really is a disease," she said then, her voice small. "I think they're getting bigger. The wings."

She was right. He'd checked the mirror this morning. "I suppose that means more responsibility."

She winced. "I'm sorry. I just—I feel like I should be doing something. I can see the wings—that has to mean something. Doesn't it?"

"Maybe. Or maybe, again, it doesn't mean anything. There's nothing you can do, Emma." He ducked into the Jetta and settled his wings across the seat. "But you're right. I should leave. It's probably best."

"I don't mean go forever," she said hastily. "I just mean—you look terrible. Maybe you just need to take some time."

"And then what?" He shut the car door to mask his sudden rush of panic. "And then they'll disappear?" He watched her swallow, and for an instant he imagined he could see himself there, sucked into the throat of an unknown destiny.

He ignored her the next day, and the next. The day after that, he went to Stacey and handed in his resignation.

—

Three nights later, he went to bed and woke floating in water, the wings half-submerged. Salt water slopped against his mouth. He blinked, unsure, and then spun around, as wildly as the water would let him. Sky, the sun creeping up slow on the eastern edge.

He was in the ocean. The water off Jericho Beach, if memory served him right—the outline of the city just there, flickering on the horizon like the auras of his students. He kicked his legs and felt no bottom. A glance to the left and a buoy, there. He struggled through the water and climbed onto the buoy as best he could. He hung there, and tried to remember, and nothing came.

He'd fallen asleep in his own bed, Chickenhead beside him. And now here he was in the water. The ocean stank of salt and rotting fish. He turned his head and a wave washed up against the buoy, slapping seaweed against his mouth. The wings grew heavier with each second that passed. He clung to the buoy and shivered.

When he couldn't feel his fingers anymore, he slipped back into the water and struck out for shore. He swam slowly, the wings threatening to drag him down into the water with each laboured move toward land. Every pull of his arms made him warmer. He crawled onto the beach as the sun flickered at the eastern edge of the sky, and felt his own temperature rise as if to greet the sun. He staggered behind a rock and tried to wring the excess water out of his jeans as best he could. The wings were sodden and bedraggled, murky with seaweed and sand. He could feel them stretch toward the light like sunflowers.

He'd proposed to Julie on this beach, three long years ago—on a morning like this, the sun shining white, the air scented by the ocean and heavy with mist. He paused for a moment, water pooling in the sand around him, and rested his forehead against the rock. That life. Then.

He climbed up the beach and to the road, and walked until a bus stop came into view. No one else was there. He sat on the bench and spread the wings so that they covered the inside of the shelter in all of its grime, then rested his head back against the glass. He blinked, and colours swam before his eyes. The world seemed made of dew, the deep green of grass, the warm smell of dirt. He focused on the ground and saw each individual pebble, each crack in the concrete. A spider crawled out of a crack by his feet and scuttled over his toe.

The bus, when it came, was also empty. The driver took one look at him, shoeless and shirtless, and let him on, unmoved.

"Make sure you don't get those seats wet," he said.

"I'll stand," Sam said wearily. His jeans were damp, but drier than they would have been had he been anyone else. The air of the bus, after the cool calm of the shelter, was almost hotter than he could stand. He closed his eyes. The bus wheezed slowly into the city, and no one else got on.

They rolled into Kitsilano. He pulled the bell when they turned onto his street, and the bus lurched to a stop.

"You be careful now," the driver said as Sam approached. "This city isn't so nice in the morning."

"I know." It was all he could say. He left the bus—ducking quickly through the door so that the wings wouldn't catch as it closed—and made his way up to the housing complex, stood in front of his door. He could leave now, and no one would know. Walk through the city and up Grouse Mountain and disappear into the trees.

He opened the door with difficulty and walked into the house. No one stirred. Even Chickenhead was still on the bed, sleeping. He stripped off his jeans and climbed in beside her and lay there shivering, even though he was no longer cold.

—

Father Jim did not think that quitting was a good idea. "What will you do?" he said. "What about the condo? What about the house?"

"What about them?" Sam said. He felt like a petulant child. "My mother's house is paid for. And this one—I'll let it go."

"You can't 'let it go,'" said the priest. "What happens when the bank comes calling for their money?"

"I won't be here to see them. It's okay."

"You need something to fill up your time."

"Sure," Sam said. He hadn't said anything to Father Jim about the dreams. About that morning, waking up in the ocean, adrift. "Maybe I'll take up flying."

"I'm serious." The priest had cooked dinner again that night—rib eye steak, out on the tiny patio. They sat by the sliding doors and ate, drank wine. "You're not thinking straight. It just won't be good for you."

"Maybe we should swap places," Sam said. "You go teach Flannery O'Connor, and I'll move to Tofino."

"Rilke fought God," said the priest. "All his life. For him, God *was* loneliness, that drawing away into the self, rather than from. Is that what you want?"

"I didn't want to wake up in the morning with wings," Sam said. He felt as though he'd said it a million times. "I didn't want my mother to die. I don't want to be sitting here, drinking with you and wondering what comes next. I don't want any of it."

The priest looked at him, then away. He toyed with his fork and let it drop on his plate with a clatter. "You know," he said, idly, "they call it 'spiritual counselling' now. What we do. People are afraid to attach something larger than themselves to all of this. So we are no longer intermediaries, representatives. We counsel. We listen to stories and prescribe prayer and meditation, and that's it."

"If I wanted a therapist, I'd go to Julie."

"Those magicians," the priest said, ignoring him, "that lived during the time of Christ. They floated planks of wood beneath the water and knew how to distribute their weight so that they could walk on them and look like they were floating on the water. They were men who could, with sleight-of-hand and a few tricksy helpers, make five loaves of bread feed five thousand people. This is one theory."

"And you?" Sam asked, in spite of himself. "What do you think?"

"Isn't it obvious?" the priest said. "I think that we'll never know one way or the other. Theology, Sam, is nothing more than another story. You're the English teacher—you should know."

"Yeah," and he did not point out that he wasn't an English teacher anymore, "but I'm not in the business of telling people to base their lives around that story. There's a difference."

"Is there?" said the priest. "You dissect Flannery O'Connor and ask people what it means. Or you tell them to figure out for themselves what it means. And some people's lives will change forever because of that. A girl with a wooden leg, or a red wheelbarrow beside some white chickens. People build their lives around this too, Sam. And you think it's not the same?"

"It's not." He thought back to Jodi the hockey player. To his other life, where he had once been so sure. "Stories that you tell to make sense of the world around you are different from stories that people tell because they don't want to deal with what comes *after* the world around you. It's a crutch. It's people being sloppy."

"Right. And you're not being sloppy at all just now, despite the fact that a few weeks ago you woke up with wings."

"There could be a logical explanation," he said. "Even now."

"You don't believe that," the priest said, "so I'm going to pretend that you're not being an idiot. As for logic—who says that God isn't logical? God *is* a matter of logic for the theologian, Sam. A matter of thought. The most brilliant minds in the world will never be able to get past that. But for the mystic, God is a matter of experience. You either get that or you don't."

Experience. The pain, the possibility of flight. "So what happens"—again, so many repeated questions—"if this is in fact God? What am I supposed to do?"

"If it is," said Father Jim, "God will tell you what to do. Eventually."

"What if it's not that simple? No voice from on high, no vision? What if I misinterpret what it is I'm supposed to do?"

The priest laughed. "It wouldn't be the first time in all of history that's happened, Sam."

"That's really helpful. Thanks."

"You'll know." Father Jim reached across and took Sam's plate and stacked it on top of his own. "And as to what you'll do—well, that's different, according to each and every man. Some of us are called to action and others to observe."

"I wanted a small life," Sam said, his voice low. The chance to touch a few lives, to love them deeply and carefully and well. To make mistakes and claw back from them a broken, humbled man, fusing back together.

"Some men are born for greatness," said the priest. "And others have it thrust upon them. Isn't that how it goes?" His voice was deep and tired with knowledge. "Didn't you learn anything in those fucking catechism classes? *God does not ask, Sam.*" He sighed. "So you haven't spoken to Julie? Since the funeral?"

Had he talked to anyone, apart from the priest and Emma, those few moments in and around the school? "No."

"Shame," Father Jim said. He picked up his glass and tilted it so that the sunlight sparkled through the champagne. "I am telling you, Sam—withdrawal is not a good idea."

"Okay. So I seek out my ex-fiancée. And that's a *good* idea."

"As I said. Unfinished business there."

"Do they teach you this at seminary? How to grind in the obvious?"

"People always make the mistake of thinking that God is about the other. People forget that God is about people."

Sam poured another glass of wine and thought about plucking the feathers off his wings, one by one, as though he was about to roast a chicken. Pluck them out and burn the rest of them off, that's what he would do. "And that means what, exactly?"

"You don't know what might happen."

Chickenhead stepped out onto the patio and rubbed against his feet. He offered a piece of steak to her, let her lick his fingers. Her tongue was rough and strong.

"You feed her steak?" Father Jim asked, amused.

He shrugged. "Why not?"

"Hardly the cost-conscious choice for a man who's just walked away from his job."

"There is some money," he said, which was true. "In the house. In the bank. At least for a little while." Wealthy grandparents to thank for that. Carol had never liked to talk about the money, but there it was.

"You're going to have to do something," the priest said again. "You can't just withdraw from the world, Sam."

Watch me, he wanted to say. Instead he said nothing, and they finished eating in silence. When night came he left the house and walked down dark streets until it seemed the entire city was empty, the people as elusive as God.

Doug was having trouble with the house. He wasn't sleeping, and he wouldn't let Janet clean the bathroom or dust the shelves. He kept forgetting to water the plants.

"I don't think he should live there anymore," she told Sam over the phone.

"He probably just needs time."

"He's not eating."

Sam pictured chicken balls piling up in the fridge, unused cartons of sweet and sour sauce lying forgotten on the counter. "Of course he's not eating, Janet. His goddamned wife just died."

She ignored him. "I don't think it's good for him. And it's your house now, Sam. You should be living here."

"I have a house."

"Are you listening to me?" Suddenly she was shouting. "I don't care about you, Sam. But I will do anything—anything—for him. I will take him out of the house and leave it empty, and everything in there can rot. The rain can wash it all away, for all I care."

He spared a moment for the poetry of the image—a tsunami, perhaps, that would break in through the windows and carry away the plants, the old afghan rugs. "Janet," he said. Why couldn't he have had a sister? "I think you should take him away. You're right."

A long pause. When she spoke again, she was quiet, apologetic. "I think he needs to stay with Kenneth and me. At least for a while. That life is over for him now."

"I know," Sam said. So many lives were ending. "You do what needs to be done for Doug. I'll take care of the house."

"Thank you, Sam." She hung up.

Three days later the edges of the conversation had blurred, faded away. The next day he woke up and couldn't remember Janet's face, no longer found it strange that he hadn't heard from Doug at all. Instead, it felt inevitable and somehow proper. Appropriate. Who had room for family—almost-family, reluctant family, mildly disliked family—in the midst of metamorphosis?

On Sunday he gave in and took a razor to his scalp. He looked strange without hair—younger, more vulnerable. The hollows in his cheeks were dark, and his eyes seemed a more vivid blue. He stood in his bathroom and stared at himself in the mirror. Hair littered the sink. The wings stood firm on either side—his protectors, his companions. Carrying him who knew where.

Chickenhead, his other companion, jumped up on the counter and swatted at a stray piece of hair as it drifted down to the tile.

"You're not supposed to be on the sink," he said out of habit. But he put the razor down and picked up the cat, rested his forehead against her fur. The world was falling away. He could feel it: the ground becoming softer beneath his feet, the air beginning to whisper where before it had said nothing at all. He put Chickenhead down softly, and gripped the countertop as energy ran through his veins. God. The universe. Something.

Then it was gone, just like that, and he took the cat and went to bed.

—

The next day, he opened the door and there was Emma. For a moment he stood there, the door ajar. Then, "How did you find this address?"

"You're in the phone book." She looked nervous, unsure. Determined. "And I called yesterday. Father Jim said I should come."

It is not good for man to be alone. "Oh. Well—I'm fine. I just need some time."

"You left," she said. "Did you think you could just disappear? Do you—don't you think people might worry? That they might have a right to know?"

"Know what?" The wings perked up behind him, like ears. "People take bereavement leave all the time."

"You're not on leave," she said flatly. She shuffled on the step. "So—are you going to let me in, or what?"

"I can't let you in," he said. "It's . . . inappropriate."

"For fuck's sake," she spat. "*Inappropriate* is hardly what matters here. Besides," and she flung her hand out to stress the point, "it's not like you're my teacher now, is it?"

Sam laughed. He took a step back and held the door so that she brushed past him, against the wings. He closed his eyes. Then, because he couldn't help it, "You should be in class right now."

"*I'm* going to be valedictorian," she said, with a hauteur most un-Emma. "I don't have to do anything anymore. I already got into McGill."

"What's that they say about pride and falling?"

She shot him a glance and snorted. He shut the front door. In the hallway she looked smaller somehow, and once more unsure. She glanced from the wings to the door and back.

"You didn't think beyond getting through the door, did you?"

Emma lifted her shoulders and then let them drop. "Not really."

He sighed. "Of course not. Do you want coffee?"

Another shrug. "Why not?" She followed him into the kitchen.

He pulled the mugs from the cupboard, measured the espresso into the grinder and counted to himself—one steamboat, two—as the beans were whittled down to dust. He heard Emma slip into a chair behind him, the soft slide of her jeans against the seat, the thump of her bag on the floor. He tipped the coffee grounds into the espresso maker and turned on the burner, watched the flame lick the sides of the little pot.

"I like your house," she said, finally. "It's very you."

"That's funny. Most of this—pretty much all of it, actually—came from Julie."

"Julie," she echoed. "She was at the funeral. The one with the dark hair."

"Yes." When the milk had heated he let it froth extra long, the way he liked it.

"Still. It suits you, the house. It's very quiet and calm and . . . good."

"Good."

"Are you going to repeat everything I say?"

He waited until the coffee had finished bubbling, and poured the milk before he answered. He turned back to her, a mug in each hand. "Do you take sugar?"

"No."

"Just as well." He slid the mug across the counter. "I don't think we have any." He sat on the opposite stool and faced her across the granite counter. "So."

"So."

"Why are you here?"

"I wanted to see how you are," she said. "At school—they just said you left. They didn't say why."

"They can't say why. It's hardly professional."

"Well, whatever. I wouldn't have done anything—I wanted to, but I wouldn't have. And then Father Jim called. He said you might need some company, so. Here I am."

"Father Jim," Sam said. "He gets around."

"Is he here?" she asked. "He said he was staying with you."

"He's at Mass." He watched her study the wings. "He goes to the cathedral in the mornings now."

"Oh." She sipped her latte. "That's nice. That you have someone around, I mean." She put down her mug. "I brought you something. It made me think of you."

He wondered if she was changing her mind about the house. If she was regretting, now, those steps that had brought her to his door. "Another puzzle?"

She blushed. "No." She reached down into her bag and pulled out a book. A grey, scuffed book with torn edges.

"Fear and Trembling," he read aloud.

Emma put the book down and looked away. "I thought it might help somehow. To know—to know that other people have felt the same. That other people have struggled."

"I don't think that Kierkegaard felt quite the same." The wings were a dark mass behind his shoulders, radiating pain and quiet discontent. "Kierkegaard didn't have wings. Or maybe you didn't realize that?"

"I *know* that," and now there was a shake in her voice, and he hated himself. "I'm just—I'm just trying to understand. To help."

"You can't help," he said. "No one can."

"Fine," she snapped. She slapped the book on the counter and stood, pulled the bag over her shoulder. "Forget it. Thanks for the coffee."

He sighed. "Emma—wait."

She turned back to him. "What?"

"I'm sorry."

She fiddled with her bag. "Do you want me to go?"

Sam thought of Father Jim. "Yes. And no."

Another pause. When she spoke, she sounded completely unlike the Emma he knew. "I think you could be better, Sam. You taught all of us that we could be better."

"This is different," he said.

"It's not." She dropped her bag against the counter again and sat across from him. She opened her mouth—he braced himself for another lecture, but Emma just shrugged. "Can I see them? The wings?"

"You already see them."

"I mean, *really* see them."

"Oh." He watched her from across the countertop and wondered. He thought of Julie, somewhere in the city with Derek. Of Father Jim, at the cathedral, the benevolent puppetmaster of his new life. Then he slid off his chair and began to unbutton his shirt. His fingers were calm and steady, and the non-voice of God did not speak in his ear. There was only Emma, silent on the other side of the counter. And the cat, who knew everything anyway.

He let the shirt drop to the floor and stood before her, his palms raised upward, the wings stretching out behind him so that they obscured most of the kitchen, so spectacular now that they were almost ordinary. Emma swallowed and stepped off her chair. Chickenhead jumped to the ground, came to him, and wound herself between his feet.

Emma stopped inches from him, her eyes trained on the left wing, on a spot over his shoulder. "What do they feel like?" she said, her voice soft. "They look—they look wonderful."

"They hurt," he said bluntly. "All the time."

"That seems sad," she said. She held her hand in the air by his shoulder, not quite touching anything. "That doesn't—that doesn't make sense." Then she stepped to the side so that she was almost behind him, and this time her outstretched hand touched shoulder, then ribcage, then that first bit of cartilage that lengthened into web. She spread her fingers through the feathers as though combing it all into place.

"They're real," she said. "I can't believe they're real."

"Welcome to the club."

She ran a hand through the other wing. "I knew," she said. "But feeling it—this is different. I can't explain it."

"Try waking up and feeling it, just like that."

"Do they work? Can you fly?"

"I don't know. I haven't tried."

"Are you going to try?"

"No." He closed his eyes. "What's the point? If this is all part of some grand plan, flying will be the smallest thing I do."

Emma stopped and pulled away. He turned to look at her and was surprised to find her sad.

"I dreamed of miracles," she said. "When I was little. My sister died and I dreamed for weeks about bringing her back, about being strong enough to change the world."

He hadn't known that. "I'm sorry."

"It's fine," she said. Then she raised a hand and touched his cheek, softly, and he felt the warmth from his own skin reach out to the tips of her fingers. "You even smell different."

He would have laughed, except that it wasn't funny. "I hope that's not a bad thing."

"It's not," she said. "You smell like water. You smell like the sea."

The next morning, in the bathroom, he washed his hands and watched his fingernails flake into the sink, brittle and old, like skin that had dried in the night. He stood before the sink and shook. The veins in his hands grew darker, more pronounced. They travelled up his arms, across his torso, wove around his ribcage. Like spiderwebs, or calligraphy in a language he couldn't understand.

He stumbled to the shower, switched it on, and let the water pummel his face. Then he put a hand—a nail-less, blue-veined hand—up against the shower tile and leaned into it, and as he did so he imagined other veins stretching from his pelvis, outward, down across his legs. The wings fell forward against his neck. Calming. Cool. There.

He let the water run over him, and when he was finished he stepped out of the shower and drew the wings around himself, like a blanket. They were long and white and beautiful. They were the only part of him, now, that had not changed.

VI

Later, she'll discover that Catherine of Siena liked blood. That Saint Simeon the Stylite tortured himself to death for love of pain, that Teresa of Avila spent a life chasing that sharp, excessive sweetness. That the mystic Christina of Retters burned her own vagina with a glowing piece of wood, and called the pain her doorway to God. She will read about Hindu mystics who stand on their feet twenty-four hours a day, and sleep with their heads resting on vertical poles. Men who walk across fire, and say they do not feel it.

Pain is the alchemy that renovates—where is indifference when pain intervenes? Alone in her apartment, Timothy sharp in her heart and the taste of Israel Riviera soft on her tongue, she'll recognize the beat, the rhythm, the way that something in her heart opens just for this.

This is one theory: that Catherine of Siena, Teresa of

Avila, Joan of Arc—these powerful women, these figures whose lives Roberta has written on the back of her hand—were nothing more than children, beaten and abused. Beaten so badly that they couldn't help but see God, children who became the adults chasing that sweetness into heaven and beyond. Sexualized self-sacrifice, says the research she finds. Lashes. Haircloth. Burns. Finding God, creating God, out of childhood trauma.

Another time, she might have found this silly, ridiculous. But now she is here, touching something. God above her and below her, the lash steady in his hand. She is being beaten clean. She will become a child again, like her brother. She will save him—and this time she will know what to say.

—

"I have waited a long time for you," Israel says. He lies beside her and strokes her hair.

"For me?" The world seems hazy when they're not fighting, when there's no blue-white aura around them to illuminate the way. Lying here, in the dark, it is easy to believe that her world has shrunk to this fuzz of not-knowing. "Why?"

"You are fearless," he says, and his hand comes round to rest against her cheek. "So fearless, so angry. So perfect."

"I'm not perfect." As she says it, the realities of the world—Timothy, Roberta, the terror of her dead-end job—come rushing in. "Plenty of things frighten me."

His hands are so warm. "But you seek them out anyway. You spent years looking for those things that might terrify or change who you are. Your brother frightens you, and yet nothing could turn you away from him. I frighten you, and yet here you are. It is," he says again, "perfect. It is exactly what I need."

"What are you talking about?"

"What if you had no family?" he says again. "What if Timothy disappears, and your mother wastes away, Delilah? What will you live for then?"

"They're not gone," she says for what feels like the trillionth time. "I don't know why you—"

"Wouldn't you want your own family? Imagine," and his voice is soft, silky, low, "a child of your own. A child that would not run away or disappoint you. A child that could make you into the mother you always wanted."

She sits up so quickly her vision blurs—she pulls her hand away and looks at him in the dark. "I don't want a baby."

"No?" He does not seem surprised. "But you would be a wonderful mother. A woman who would protect and love her child to the end of the world, even as it broke her heart. Even then."

"I don't want a baby," she says again. The room comes sharp into focus. "I won't have children. I won't."

His eyebrows go up. "Really?"

"I'd be a bad mother. I'm sure of it." She clenches the sheet in her fist. "And the child could end up like Timothy, and taking care of him is hard enough. I wouldn't wish that on any human being. Even though I love him."

"Indeed," Israel says. Then he shrugs. "Well. We can discuss this again later."

"No." She shakes her head so vehemently that the world spins again. "No more discussions. I won't have a child—not with you, not with anybody else."

Now he sits up and faces her. "Perhaps," he says, still in that soft voice, "that is not entirely up to you." He runs his hand along her thigh. "Isn't this the kind of danger you've been chasing for years? All of these men, Delilah—all of these mediocre souls, and not one child from any of them. Haven't you been waiting, on some level, for the day when you stop all of the games?"

She swallows, then swings her legs around to the side of the bed. "If this is what we're talking about, I'm leaving."

He nods. "I will call Emmanuel." He reaches for the bedside table and picks up his phone. "I will give you time to think on it, and reconsider."

She pulls her dress from the floor, hands shaking, furious. "There's nothing to reconsider."

Israel taps out a text message and then shrugs. He stands up on the other side of the bed, naked, and flicks on the bedside lamp. He is lean and hard and beautiful, completely unconcerned. "You'll change your mind. Eventually."

"Actually, *no*, I will not." She yanks the dress over her head and glares at him.

He strides around to where she stands and pulls her close against him, hard enough to make it hurt. "I wish only," he says, his voice so lovely in her ear, "to make you see. To help you understand that there is nothing like the feel of a human life between your hands. That potential, that power. It is—Delilah, it is very great indeed."

"My brother's life is in my hands," she says. The words are muffled against his chest. "And mine in his. It's all the life I can hold."

"Yes, well." His hand is hard against the back of her neck, his heart a steady beat against her forehead. "Even that can change."

—

On Sunday, when Roberta calls, her voice is tighter than usual.

"Delilah," she says. "The doctors have found another lump."

"A lump." Lilah thinks back to Israel, her flippant words. *She's fine.*

"Delilah," Roberta says, "I don't have breasts anymore. So tell me, exactly—how is it that they've found a lump?"

"I don't know," Lilah says. She thinks of her own breasts, bruised and quiet. She thinks of Israel, who bit her nipple until it bled. And then she pulls out her calendar and counts the days. "When are you going for treatment? I can come over. Make you dinner."

"You can't cook," Roberta says.

"Look, I'm offering."

"Don't bother." Roberta is all business now. *Medicine. Treatment. Thought you should know.* "I was just keeping you informed." She'll get off the phone and rake her garden—Lilah can see it even miles away. "Have you heard from your brother?"

And for one insane moment she wants to lie, to tell her that Timothy is at home with her, in the shower, scrubbing the grime from his cheeks. To give her this one gift.

"No," she says.

"Oh. Well—maybe you can tell Timothy, if you see him."

"Of course I'll tell him." Three months ago he might have cared about news like this. She doubts he'll say anything about it now—he has no room for anything else, anything aside from these endless hours on the street. "Anyway," she lies, "I was going to go to Victoria this week, to visit a friend. I'll stop by."

Roberta sniffs. "Well, you do whatever you want, Delilah. I can check in to the hospital myself. I'll be fine."

"Of course." Lilah, Roberta, Timothy—they're all fine. They say good night and hang up at the same time, and miles away she imagines that Roberta folds her right hand in the crook of her left elbow, just as Lilah is doing right now.

—

"Listen to this," Timothy says. He presses down on the pages of a book and ignores the food Lilah spreads out on the grass. More apples, more sandwiches, more chocolate. Fruit Roll-Ups. Juice boxes, and plastic pointy straws. A careful picnic. "Rilke. 'Once the realization is accepted that even between the closest human beings infinite distances continue, a wonderful living side by side can grow up, if they succeed in loving the distance between them which makes it possible for each to see the other whole against the sky.'"

"Where did the book come from?"

He looks away from her, hurt. He is so thin. "The library. I got it at the library."

"You don't have a library card."

He won't meet her eyes. "I go there, sometimes, and sit. The librarian gave it to me because I look at it all the time."

She takes a juice box and struggles to manoeuver the straw out of its plastic. Her fingers are stiff and cold. "So. Infinite distances."

He nods. "It made me think of you."

"Why?"

"You," he says again. "You and me."

She stabs the juice box with her straw. "I'm right here."

"I know." He closes the book and puts it down. "But—you're not, at the same time. You never were." He breathes hard, and his hands shake like those of an old man. "You understand, Lilah, don't you?"

"No," she says, even though it isn't true. "No, I do not fucking understand."

"Don't swear," he says.

"Well?" She throws a hand out for emphasis and the juice from the box dribbles onto the ground. Her scarf slips. "I come to find you. And you tell me the same goddamn thing every time. I need *something*, Timmy. I'm not the one who's not trying."

He ignores her. "What's that?"

"What?" Her hand goes to the scarf automatically, hiding the bruises beneath. "Nothing. It's nothing."

"That's not nothing."

"We're not talking about me." She clears her throat. "Anyway, I have to tell you something. About Mom."

Timothy nods. "There's a lump."

She can't hide her shock. "You talked to her?"

He shakes his head. "I knew." His voice sounds strange. "I just knew."

Lilah pushes her unease away. "It's not good, Timmy."

He still won't look at her. "Cancer's never good."

"I mean, really not good. She's going into the hospital." Roberta, alone in the house on the other side of the water. "She wants to see you."

"I'm busy."

"You're fucking kidding me."

"Stop swearing!" and this time his voice goes up. "Anyway—I don't see you over there."

"I'm going over," she says, and she can tell by the way his shoulders slump that he believes her. "Tomorrow." Unbelievable but true—days off in the middle of the week for administrative sludge. Penny, who had initially said no to her request, backed down after Lilah played the cancer card.

She'd considered playing the Israel card as well—fucking the boss, yes, and what are you going to do about it—but Israel, as it turned out, was not in the office. So she'd muddled through alone, apologized profusely, given Debbie the rest of her workload. Thankful, in some unapologetic part of her soul, for the fact that he'd been silent for the rest of the weekend, for the fact that he was not at work, sleek and powerful and troubling. "I thought—I don't know. I thought you could come with. And then you could come back here, if you wanted."

"Why are you so concerned when you hate her so much?"

"I don't hate her."

Timothy laughs, an ugly sound. "You can't stand her. I knew that when I was five."

"That doesn't mean I hate her."

"Doesn't it, Lilah?" and now he swings around to face her, his eyes dark, his arms spread wide. He waves the book in his right hand—a preacher, a prophet of words and solitude. "You could have fooled me."

She pulls her coat close and checks that the scarf is still in place. "So it's my fault, then. Everything." No answer. "What do you want from me?" she says quietly. "What do you want me to say?"

"Never mind," Timothy says. He tosses the book into her lap. "Here. You have it." Then he grabs a chocolate bar and shoves it into the pocket of his ragged coat. "It's just more for me to carry, anyway." He stands and starts walking away.

"Tim," she calls. He doesn't turn around. "Timothy." But nothing. She watches until he disappears out of the park, down the street, and then she gathers the juice boxes and the leftover sandwiches into a little pile. She leaves them there, on the bench, and as she walks away she hopes that rain won't come, that someone else will find the food and take it. She fingers the spine of the book and then opens it to the last page, where the stamp is faded and grey but still there. *Discard*. Left behind, just like the food.

She calls Roberta on the ferry. "I'm late," she says. "But I'll be there before seven."

"I made dinner. I'll keep it in the oven for you."

"Thanks."

"Is Timothy—"

"He's not here," Lilah says, looking out over the water. "I couldn't find him."

"But last you saw him, he was okay."

"Yes." She remembers the book. "He's been going to the library."

"He was always reading," Roberta says. "Maybe our lives would have been easier if he'd been into sports."

"Maybe," Lilah echoes, but she can't laugh, as much as Roberta wants her to. Timothy is scrabbling on the streets of Vancouver as they speak, ducking into libraries and avoiding them both. "Do you want me to bring you anything?"

"I'm fine," says Roberta. "Be careful when you come in. They're calling for rain."

"I'm sure I'll manage." She tightens the scarf around her neck and checks, once again, that her sleeves cover everything. "I'll see you soon. Okay?"

"Okay." Roberta hangs up. She always does this—no drawn out goodbyes from this mother, no hesitant words of farewell. Lilah closes her phone and once more looks out of the window, to where the setting sun glints over the waves. It hurts to sit down, but she's not moving. She tosses her phone lightly from hand to hand and thinks of her brother, scuttling in the streets.

She has chocolate and cigarettes in her purse, and a change of clothes in the overnight bag Roberta gave her years ago. Another sweater, another scarf. In the bathroom, just before the ferry docks, she pats concealer over her neck and ignores the other woman, a mother with two girls who pretends not to look at her bruises. Outside, she pays for her rental car and glides out of the parking lot, her hands steady on the wheel. She turns on the radio—Emmanuel does not have music when he drives—and flicks through the stations until something fits. Mahler, *Symphony No. 5*. Chopin when that is over, Schumann, and then Debussy, the notes long and soft. She smokes out the window for the entire drive, and throws her last cigarette out into the bushes that lie by the side of Roberta's lawn.

Her mother does not open the front door, just as she never says goodbye. Lilah walks into the house and puts her shoes at the door. "Mom?"

"Here," comes Roberta's voice. The kitchen. Lilah flicks on the hallway light as she pads into the house. The first thing she notices is that all of the plants are dying.

Roberta sits at the kitchen table, leafing through photos. A cigarette dangles between her fingers. Her hair is the darkest red it's ever been. She has lost weight, and skin sags in folds around her neck.

"Since when did you start smoking?" Lilah asks.

"I don't know. A month ago?" Roberta does not get up. "It can't possibly make much difference now."

"Don't talk like that," Lilah says automatically. She wraps

a towel around her hand and opens the oven, pulls out a tray covered in foil.

"Chicken stuffed with feta," Roberta says. "And olives. Your favourite, if I remember."

"Yes," Lilah says. "Thank you."

Roberta waves her hand in the air and weaves trails through the smoke. "It's not like I had anything else to do." She taps ash into a tray and watches Lilah spoon the chicken onto a plate. "Do you want more? I have extra in the fridge. I didn't feel like eating."

"I'm fine," Lilah says. She takes a bite. The chicken is soft, juicy, delicious.

"I can turn the heat up," Roberta says, nodding to Lilah's scarf and long sleeves. "If you're cold."

"I'm fine," she says again. She pulls out her own cigarettes and dumps the chocolate on the table. "I brought you this. It's Timothy's favourite."

"Chocolate," Roberta says. She picks the bar up between thumb and forefinger, as though it's covered in mud. "Please tell me you're feeding him other things. Did you give him the toothbrush?"

"Yes, I gave him the toothbrush. And yes, I'm feeding him other things." Hope. Despair. Fear like gut rot in her stomach, always there, always moving.

"Good." Roberta breathes out smoke. "Maybe I can bribe him the next time I'm in Vancouver."

Lilah laughs. She finishes the chicken quickly, surprised at how hungry she is. Then she goes back to the fridge after all. "Maybe. He's not much into bribes right now."

"Isn't he," Roberta says. She rubs her free hand against her hip. "But he's all right. He's alive."

"Yes. He's alive." Lilah slides her second plate into the

microwave, presses the button, and taps her fingers against the counter. This is where Timothy made her hot chocolate, all those years ago. *He's such a strange little boy.*

"Well. That's something, I guess." Roberta nods to Lilah's scarf again. "Are you sure you're not cold?"

"Really. I'm okay." The microwave beeps. Lilah takes her plate out and sits back down at the table. The words come out of her mouth and hang in the air. "I'm seeing somebody."

"Joel." Roberta's voice dips. "You told me about Joel. The one who doesn't have a job."

"He has a job," Lilah says automatically. "But no, it's not Joel. I'm not seeing Joel anymore."

"Oh. So who is it, then?"

"Someone I work with. He's from Mexico."

"Does he speak English?"

"Of course he speaks English. What a stupid question."

Roberta shrugs and stubs out her cigarette. "So what does he do, then?"

"He's in HR. In management." She stops, suddenly aware that there's not much else she can say.

"Mmhm." Roberta fingers another cigarette but does not light it. "And you're happy? Things are okay?"

Happy. Happy? "Things are... okay," she echoes. "As much as they can be."

"Mmhm," Roberta says again. "My therapist says that Timmy has abandonment issues."

"Wow. Some therapist."

"He *says*," Roberta continues, frowning, "that everything goes back to your father. Do you think so?"

Lilah pushes her last piece of chicken around. Timothy, who was four when it happened, has never mentioned their father. Not once. "I don't know."

"Do you feel abandoned?" Roberta presses. The word sounds strange in her mother's mouth. "Does it bother you?"

Lilah shrugs. "Why bother feeling bad about an asshole?"

Roberta stares at the table. "I keep thinking," she says, "that maybe I was wrong. Maybe I should have followed him, or tried to keep him closer, so that he could see the two of you. If there had been a man in Timmy's life, maybe this wouldn't have happened."

"Carl thought Timothy was strange," Lilah points out. This is what she remembers most. "I don't see how keeping him around could have helped anything."

"He didn't," Roberta says faintly. "He didn't think he was *strange*—he just didn't understand."

"He called Timothy a fucking spastic. That's the kind of role model you want for your kid? Really?"

"Well, if you're so sure, Lilah, then what was it? What happened?"

So this is what she thinks about, their mother, alone in this house with her dying plants. "For God's sake—I don't know. Doesn't your therapist tell you not to dwell on shit like this?"

"Don't swear," Roberta says irritably. "My God—you always look so beautiful until you open your mouth."

"Thanks."

"You're welcome." This time Roberta stubs out her cigarette half-finished. "I'm tired," she announces. "I think I might go to bed. You know where to find everything, don't you?"

"Yes." Lilah stands up and carries her plate to the sink. She watches out of the corner of her eye as Roberta gets up, her hands clasped against the table. She moves like a woman twice her age. "Do you need help?"

"No," Roberta says. "I'm tired. That's all." She puts a hand against the doorframe. "Will you want breakfast? I don't have that much food—we might need to go shopping, depending on what you want."

"I'm fine," Lilah says for the hundredth time. "If I want something, I'll go and get it. No big deal."

Roberta nods. "All right. Well—I'll see you in the morning." She shuffles into the hall.

Lilah watches her go, then dumps her plate in the sink and walks through to the back room, where the glass doors look out over a dark, overgrown yard. She pads out onto the deck and sits on the step, listening to the wind. Victoria is quieter than Vancouver—quiet and polite, its secrets buried deep beneath the ground. The church Roberta goes to is only a few blocks away. Secrets are buried there too.

She sits for hours, trembling with cold, until even the faint sound of downtown revellers has faded away. Timothy will be shivering on some sidewalk, alone. Israel Riviera will be sleeping, or thinking about children, also alone. And Roberta, who sleeps behind her in the house, will perhaps be dreaming of those days before Carl left, when their paths were laid like flagstones, ordered and precise.

When she can't take it anymore Lilah goes back into the house, where memories drift slowly through the air, and she goes to bed in the room of her childhood, where the old macramé from Roberta sits on the wall like a guardian.

Roberta has to check in to the hospital late Wednesday afternoon. She was right; there's hardly any food left in the house, so they go for breakfast at the neighbourhood café. It's the same café Lilah worked in all those years ago, before she left for Toronto, and nothing has changed. The paint still peels in the corners, and the muffins are still delicious. Lilah almost sneaks one into her bag just because.

Roberta doesn't eat anything. Instead, she drinks tea and watches Lilah finish a giant helping of scrambled eggs and potatoes. "You have your father's metabolism," she says. "I always envied that." In the daylight she looks more gaunt than she did in the kitchen; gaunt and smaller and old. "Timothy had it too. God's gift to both of you, I suppose."

"Right. Because God's been big on the gifts in this family."

"You're so bitter," Roberta says. But her anger has no force, no conviction. "It's not God's fault, Lilah."

"How can you say that? Look at you. Look at—if you could see Timothy, you wouldn't say that."

"Maybe," says her mother. "But Delilah, I can't help it. You can't possibly understand."

She hears the echo of Timothy even as Roberta speaks the words. "I guess not." Potatoes done, Lilah drops her fork onto her plate and nods to the waitress. "We'd better go."

They don't speak during the drive to the hospital. They park in front of the cancer centre and Lilah, laden with bags, follows Roberta through to the admissions desk. The triage nurse checks them in faster than any hotel receptionist.

"Room 304," she says. "They'll have gowns there for you."

They trudge down the hall until they find it—a small room with a single bed, a thin couch against the wall and one TV bolted to the ceiling. The walls are light purple. Mauve. The air smells of disinfectant and bleach. But there is a window that looks out onto green. Victoria is still green, even into these middle days of November.

"Home sweet home," says Roberta. She drops her purse on the bed and looks away from Lilah, out the window.

Lilah's mouth tastes like dust. "I'm just—I'm just going to go to the bathroom," she says. She ducks into the ensuite, locks the door, and turns on the fan so that Roberta can't hear her throwing up. The scrambled eggs and potatoes go straight into the toilet. Her ribs hurt when she's finished.

She washes her hands slowly, the fan still on, and then flushes. She shoves a stick of peppermint gum into her mouth. She can hear laughter now, over the fan. Laughter, a faint male voice. Roberta, flirting with the nurses already.

But when she steps back into the room, it's not a nurse at all.

"Delilah!" Roberta says. She hasn't changed into her hospital gown. She is smiling now. "You didn't tell me he was *lovely.*"

There, sitting on the bed, is Israel Riviera. Looking completely at home against the purple of the walls, and talking to Roberta as though he's known her all his life.

"Well," he says. He winks—at Roberta, at both of them. "Delilah likes to keep secrets. But they are not hard to figure out, I think."

"No," Lilah says. She puts her hand up against the doorframe. The world shifts and rearranges itself right beneath her feet. "I suppose not."

FIVE

In his dreams, he crept down corridors of stone, stood on a windswept beach, and found himself fumbling for words in the dark. He walked, barefoot, and listened to the shuffle of his wings.

Awake, he walked the streets of Vancouver and made his way through a world filled with auras. He wore gloves to hide his hands. Colours were sharpened, everything around him crisp and saturated. He could smell the damp even when the sun was shining, and hear children laughing hundreds of feet away. He often found himself out of breath, as though he'd been running. Walking was the only thing that kept him calm.

Some mornings, he crept into the cathedral and watched, hunched in a pew at the back, as Father Jim said Mass. How well he remembered this—the uneven hush of the cathedral floor, the terrible quiet in the air. The priest at once commanding and unobtrusive, calm. *Amen*, he said. *Go in peace, to love and serve the Lord.*

Father Mario, who seemed happy to sit back for these sessions, often sat with him in the pew. This other priest, whose part in the story no one could quite figure out.

"It is good to see you here, Samuel," he said once. "Are you well?"

"No," Sam said, his voice low. In front of them, Father Jim read the Gospel. A story about a son who returned to his household after a long time away.

"You should not be afraid, Samuel. God would not want you to be afraid."

"Really?" he said. In these moments with his head above the water, why was it that the rage and the sarcasm came so easily? "But surely if I feel fear, it comes from God Himself. Surely He wants me to feel this way. Otherwise, why bother with the wings at all?"

"You mistake fear for cowardice," said the priest. "Fear that turns one immobile does no one any good. But fear that draws you out of yourself is a different thing entirely."

"I don't want to lose myself," he said. He thought of Julie, Emma, and Bryan. All these parts of his life, falling away. "I don't want to disappear."

"Every man is destined to disappear in the face of God," said the priest. "How could someone maintain their individual nature in the face of the Almighty? It is just not possible. But God will give you strength."

"God has not given me anything."

"Many people say this. But the truth is merely that God has not given them what they want."

It went like this often, which is why he walked instead. He traversed the streets of his neighbourhood so frequently people stopped registering his face—no more Sam, just another body in the grey. He walked, and he thought. About his mother, scattered in tiny pieces over the water. About the wings. About Emma, who had started, he could see, to be afraid. And he thought about Julie.

Julie had left three messages on the machine since he'd seen her last. *Sam. Sam, I need to talk to you. Please call me back.*

Two weeks after she'd left the first message, and he still hadn't picked up the phone.

"Are you going to leave those on the machine forever?" asked Father Jim. They sat in the kitchen and drank coffee, as they had begun to do in the mornings. "They take up space, you know. Someone else might be trying to get through."

"Stacey," he said. He watched Chickenhead bat dust balls in the corner of the room. "Or Emma. That's all, really." Bryan was still out of the country—there was another face he found himself forgetting.

"Sam," Father Jim said again. "I think you should call her."

"I'm going to call," he said. "I've been busy."

"Mmm," said the priest. He nodded, suddenly, to Sam's hands. "What's with the gloves? You can't possibly be cold."

Sam took the gloves off and spread his hands. They seemed strangely effeminate now, without nails. It had become difficult to pick things up if he dropped anything—he wore the gloves for this purpose now as much as any other.

"Ah." Father Jim didn't flinch. "I wondered."

"They just came off. In the sink. It just . . . happened."

Father Jim shrugged. "Maybe it's just stress, Sam. Maybe they'll grow back."

"Maybe," he echoed. Then he tried to make a joke of it. "Or maybe I'm just evolving. You know—onto the next stage. No more ass scratching or fumbling in the dirt for me."

The words were hollow, bereft of humour. Father Jim reached over and squeezed his hand. But he didn't say anything, and after a while Sam put the gloves back on.

He called Julie at work, finally, and she left her office to see him. They went to the coffee shop she loved—the one on Denman, so close to the shores of English Bay.

"How are you?" she said. "I've been so worried. You look *terrible*."

That made him laugh. "Well. I've had better days." Weeks. Months. Years.

"I heard that you left your job," she said.

"How?"

"Stacey told me."

"*Stacey*?"

"She's a client." Julie waved her hand. "It doesn't matter. But she said that she asked you to stay. That you're not returning her calls."

"I don't work there anymore," he said. A lifetime ago, that's what that was. "I don't have to call her."

"She's worried about you."

He stared at her. "Should you even be telling me these kinds of things?" The wings curled around the metal backing of the chair. "Besides—I'm hardly any of Stacey's business."

Her eyebrow went up. How well he remembered that, another lifetime away. "Just like you're hardly any of that student's business? Ella?"

"Emma," he said instantly.

She held his gaze for a moment and then flushed. "It's just—you always have these women. All the time."

"So you phoned me," he said, slowly, "again and again,

and left messages, just to meet with me and tell me about my 'women'?"

She tapped her fingernails against her mug. The sound echoed. "I just want to know how you are."

"I'm surviving." What a strange word. "I just—it's hard, Julie."

"I know." Unexpectedly, she reached across the table and took his hand. His new hand, hidden and safe within the glove. "You know I'm here for you, Sam."

"Sure," he said. "You look good, by the way."

"Oh. Thank you."

He coughed. "How's Buddhism class?"

"Sam."

"Seriously."

She shrugged. "It's all right. Derek's really into it."

"You know," because he couldn't help himself, "studies have shown that Tibetan Buddhism has a large part to play in the prostitution problem in Thailand."

"Really." She let go of his hand.

"Yes." He dragged his coffee cup in small circles around the table. "Tibetan Buddhists believe in reincarnation. You'll know this, obviously."

"Yes," she said, her voice going thin.

"So they teach that prostitutes are on the streets paying for the sins of a past life. I think it's a funny doctrine."

"It's not a class in Tibetan Buddhism."

"Oh. *Well* then. I guess that's fine."

"We were having a nice time," she said. "Just now."

"We had a lot of nice times," he said. "But in the end that didn't seem to matter, did it."

"What's with you?" she muttered. "You've got all of these people around you—Father Jim, me, Bryan, that student. All of these people, and you're just—this isn't you. This isn't the Sam I remember."

"That's astute. Did you not hear me, five minutes ago, when I said I was having a hard time?"

"I know you're having a hard time." Her own hands were rigid against her mug. "But people die, Sam. It's horrible, but it happens. You have to keep going."

"Bryan, by the way, says that he's sorry for being a dick. He's in Italy. He's not exactly around right now."

Her mouth hung open just the tiniest bit—that lip, that red lip that he loved. "What is wrong with you?"

He laughed. "Nothing. Never mind." He lifted the coffee cup to his mouth. It was empty, but he pretended to drink from it anyway. "What else did Stacey have to say?"

"I think you should see somebody," she said. "A doctor. A—"

"Priest?" He bit down on the sudden urge to laugh again. "I have a priest living with me now. He even cooks. He makes fantastic pancakes." He talked faster to hide the panic. Her lips were too red, her coat too green, the pulse of veins beneath her cheeks visible when he should have seen nothing at all.

"That's good," she said. "I'm glad you're not alone."

Two nights ago he *had* woken up on Grouse Mountain, halfway up a tree. Where would he be tomorrow? Would he wake up in the air this time, floating over that beach, then crash to the ground and pierce his wings on the rocks that sat below? "I have the cat," he said. It was all he could say. Even his own voice was too loud.

"Sam?" Her voice was worried now. "Sam—are you sick?"

"Yes," he gasped. He could not stop shaking. Just before his head hit the table he prayed that he would not disappear, that he wouldn't wake up in the ocean, soaking and afraid.

He woke up in his own room. Julie sat in a chair beside the bed, Chickenhead in her lap.

"Hi," she said softly, when he registered that she was there.

"She's in your lap," he said. The wings were bunched around his head and draped halfway over his face, and the gloves were still on his hands. He was so hot. The room swam in colour, floated in stale air.

"I know," and she ran a hand through the cat's fur, as though she couldn't quite believe it herself. "She's been here since I sat down."

"How long have you been here?" The migraine, or whatever it was, had receded. He felt wrung out, limp.

She shrugged. "A few hours? I'm not sure."

He tried to sit up, and shook the wings out so that they stretched over either side of the bed. "You didn't have to stay."

"I know," she said. She looked calm and regal, composed. "I wanted to make sure you were all right."

"How did I get home?"

"I called your house," she said. "Father Jim came right away. And I called an ambulance. They were ready to take you to the hospital, but Father Jim said you'd be all right. He said you were probably just tired. That you haven't been sleeping."

"That's true."

"He said you've been sleepwalking, Sam."

So he knew. "That's also true."

"You've never sleepwalked."

His mouth tasted of decay. "Not that I remember, no."

"What's wrong? It's not just your mother." Not so calm

now, not so composed. “That day, when you came to see me at work. You asked about Father Jim. Something was wrong then—I knew it. Are you in trouble? Do you need money?”

He laughed, it was so absurd. “No. I don’t need money. There’s the house, remember?”

“Then what?” She bit her lip. “I need to know, Sam. I think about you all of the time. I can’t sleep. Even Derek’s noticed.”

She wouldn’t believe him. He knew she wouldn’t believe him. Yet he was struck, all the same, by a rush to let her know, to have someone else believe. “I’m just...”

“Yes?” she said, impatient. “You—what?”

“I have wings,” he said. “I woke up a few weeks ago, and they were there. I’ve had to cut my shirts, Julie. And then Chickenhead got hit by a car, in front of me. And I brought her back. From—wherever.”

Her hand hadn’t stopped petting the cat. He stared at it and continued.

“And then Mom died, and I went to find Father Jim. He can see the wings, and so can Emma, and so can Father Mario. But you can’t. You can’t see them, and you think I’m crazy. Right now. And I’m dreaming strange things and waking up all over the city in the early hours of the morning, and I don’t know how I’m getting there. I really don’t.” She was still petting the cat. “Chickenhead can see them too, by the way.”

Julie nodded. “I see.”

He let his breath out in a rush. “That’s why. That’s why... everything.”

The line of her shoulders was set, firm. She stared at him until he began to fidget on the bed. “Sam, I think you need help.”

“You do think I’m crazy.”

"I don't think you're crazy," she said, hastily. "I just think—"

"Talk to Father Jim," he said. "Father Jim will tell you."

She frowned. "I think that Father Jim is enabling you. He wouldn't even let me take off those silly gloves. Maybe he's doing it because your mother died—I don't know. But I think you're in serious trouble, Sam. You need help. Professional help."

"Father Jim is a professional."

"You know what I mean," she said.

He pulled off his shirt and tossed it to the floor. "You can't see anything."

"See *what*?" She let the cat down, then pushed herself off the chair and stood beside the bed, her hands clenched. "There's nothing to see, Sam."

He closed his eyes against the nausea. "You should probably go."

She blinked. "I'm trying to help you."

"You can't help," he said. "No one can."

Julie cleared her throat. She was so close. "Well," she said stiffly. "You know where I am if you—if you need me."

"I know," he said. "Thank you."

"You're welcome." She stood up from the chair and went out of the room without speaking. The door closed very quietly.

"She didn't believe me," he said. To the air, to the cat. What kind of prophet could he be, when even those he loved could not see him, could not see what he was becoming?

Chickenhead climbed onto the bed, purred against him and slept.

Later, a different woman beside him. "Tell me about your sister," he said as they walked around the pond. Chickenhead bounced ahead of them in the grass.

"She was hit by a car," Emma said. "She was playing on the sidewalk, and this truck came up onto the curb and pinned her to a tree."

"I'm sorry."

"The driver was seventeen. She'd just gotten her full license, and she was driving her father's truck home from the mall. She said she couldn't see anything, that she lost control because of the sun through the window."

"What happened?"

Emma crossed her arms, tucked her hands into her armpits. "My parents called the ambulance, and they got her to the hospital while she was still conscious. But there were head injuries. She went into a coma later that night, and died in the morning."

"How old were you?"

"Eleven. Corrie was eight."

"And you wanted a miracle."

"Of course I wanted a miracle," she said. "Who wouldn't?" She uncrossed her arms and shoved her hands in her pockets. "Anyway, she died. And my parents almost divorced. It's been seven years, and sometimes I still come home from school ready to tell her things."

It hadn't been a month since his mother had died, and even her face was disappearing. "Emma, I'm sorry."

"There's no use in being sorry." She pointed to Chickenhead, crouched dangerously close to the edge of the pond. "Should she be that close?"

"She's pretty good on her feet," Sam said absently. "But she does like to show off, yes." He bent down and scooped her up. She grumbled, then nestled against his chest and started to purr.

"It's very nice here," Emma said. "It would be a good place to pray."

He laughed. "I don't think my neighbours would agree, but okay."

She looked at him. "Tell me," she said. "What would you pray for, now, if you had the chance?"

He thought of Father Jim. "Don't we always have the chance to pray? Isn't that the point?"

"But you don't pray. So. If you wanted to, what would you pray for?"

Yes, he'd want a miracle too. To wake up the next morning and be a normal man. To wake up and have a life that was once more ordinary and uninspired.

She saw it in his face; the disappointment in her eyes was almost tangible. "You'd still give it back. If you could."

"Yes." He hugged the cat and would not meet her eyes. He would give it back, and make his last conversation with Julie disappear. "I would choose a life that I knew over this. Is that so terrible?"

"It's not terrible." They reached the patio. Emma stepped into the house before him and then turned to face them both, poised over the threshold. "But I can pray and pray, Sam, and my sister won't come back. My life is different now. So what I ask for—that has to be different too."

"I want a sign," he said, and even saying it made him ashamed. "I want God to give me a sign."

Emma smiled. "What—wings aren't enough for you?"

"I want God to speak to me," he said, and he tightened his grip on the cat. "I want to know what to do."

"No one ever knows what to do," she said. "But eventually

we do something. Sooner or later, Sam, you have to stop fighting."

He couldn't sleep. He dressed and left the cat on the bed. The light from Father Jim's room shone as a thin golden line across the floor. He slid down the hall and went out the front door, then closed it quietly, like a thief stealing away.

He walked all the way into town and followed the water, the waves soft on his left-hand side. Into and through Stanley Park, the wings glowing white behind him. He remembered Cathedral Grove and imagined himself disappearing into the trees. He walked to the eastern side of town, the lights of the city flickering green and red and hesitantly blue. He padded past a bar fight, through the edges of a drunken wedding party, down countless streets that shimmered with rain. A dog followed him for six blocks, barking at the wings. He unfurled them in front of an all-night Chinese restaurant and glared at the dog. It fled, whimpering.

He saw the boy on Seymour, after he'd started his way home, curled up over a grate and shivering in the dark. A boy with a sharp nose and patches of dark, greasy hair, through which his scalp shone like ivory. A boy with wings spread out before him like blankets. The feathers were dirty, grey, slick with grime.

Sam stopped walking. He did not know what to say. His own wings shifted, stretched out into the air. He crept closer until he stood over the boy. The heat that rose from the grate was overpowering.

"Hello," said Sam. He could not breathe.

The boy stirred, opened one eye. He saw Sam's feet and

closed his eyes, did not move. Sam moved his own foot forward and poked the boy's knee. "Hello," he said again.

The boy sighed without opening his eyes. "Leave me alone," he said. "I just want to sleep."

"Look at me," Sam said. "I want you to tell me about—those."

Something in his voice made the boy open his eyes again and look up. He blinked and sat up slowly. His face showed smears of dirt. The holes in his jacket were ragged, the material billowing in the wind. His wings were crumpled from being so close to the ground—they unfurled sadly and sat there, bedraggled, the feathers closest to the sidewalk dingy and limp.

"Oh," he said.

"Yes," said Sam. "Oh." Even in the dark, he could tell that the boy's eyes were blue, like his own. He wanted to shout, to jump in the air and weep. "Tell me," he said. "Tell me everything."

He takes her for coffee in the hospital cafeteria, and pulls out her chair as though they're back in the Indian restaurant.

"Why are you here?" Lilah asks. She does not sit down.

Israel shrugs. "Emmanuel enjoys the ferry. And it is such a beautiful day—I thought it would be nice for a drive."

"You're a liar."

He leaves her standing and sits down in the opposite chair. "That is not a very nice thing to say."

"You didn't take the ferry because you liked the drive."

Israel shrugs again and spreads his napkin over his lap. "You may think whatever you want. But I am here now. You can come back with me tonight. Emmanuel, as you know, will not mind."

She sits down because there is nowhere else to go. "And if I don't want to go?"

He moves a spoon in circles through his drink. "But you do. You cannot wait to leave."

Her hands shake around her mug and coffee spills over the edge and onto her tray. Is it that obvious? Is this the kind of person she's become? "I can't stand seeing her like this," she says.

"Yes," Israel says. "That is why I am here."

She wants to weep, she's so tired. "I don't believe you."

He smiles. "How surprising."

She has no answer for that. They finish their coffees and walk back to Roberta's room without speaking. Israel makes her mother laugh in a way Lilah hasn't seen in years. They stay until visiting hours are over.

"I'll call," Lilah says, and she hugs Roberta for the first time since she's arrived. "And I'll be back on the weekend. I promise."

"Yes," says Israel. "We will be back. And perhaps we will bring Timothy, if we can find him."

"I'd like that," Roberta says. Her voice is thick with longing.

"Yes," Lilah echoes. She breathes deeply to hide her sudden fear, and looks away, out the window, to where the sky is dark and quiet. To where Timothy stands on some street somewhere, shivering and lost in the cold. She hugs Roberta again, and feels her mother's heartbeat slow against her chest.

"I'll be okay, Lilah," Roberta says. "Remember—we've been here before."

A human life between her hands, a human life beating next to her own. Lilah nods. She hoists her bag onto her shoulder and glances at Israel, waiting by the door. Then she follows him, and they walk out of the hospital and into the night.

They stop at Roberta's house to collect things—Lilah's bag, more clothes for Timothy. Lilah pulls the old raincoat from Roberta's closet and shoves it in with everything else. She works quickly, silently. She hasn't said a word to Israel since they got into the car.

"I like this," Israel says. His voice carries a hint of danger. He stands in front of the crucifix over Roberta's door and pats it as one might pat a lover. "Always watching."

"If you like it so much, why don't you have one in your own goddamned bedroom?"

He laughs. Then he backhands her, casually, but with enough force to send her reeling over the bed. "And here I thought we were making such progress. You shouldn't take the name of the Lord thy God in vain, Delilah. Surely, if you remember one thing, it can be that."

She holds her stinging face against the quilt and inhales the scent of Roberta. One breath, two. The flicker of electricity behind her eyes, a whiff of charcoal in the air. Is that the smell of her life burning? She turns onto her back and spreads her arms. "Surely God is man enough to handle it."

This time he hits her in the stomach, a fist down into her solar plexus. She moans and crumples into a ball on the bed. "You do not know anything about God, Delilah," he says, breathing hard. "You cannot possibly know whether God is man enough or not." He climbs on top of her. A dancer, swift and sure. He bends forward and tangles his hands in her hair so that her head tilts back, her neck is exposed. The world is soft and hushed and silent.

They fuck quickly, on Roberta's bed, with the breeze coming in from the window and Emmanuel waiting outside.

No antics this time. No pain. When they finish, Lilah strips the bed and leaves the sheets in a pile on the floor. She lets Israel go out before her, and as he ambles down the hall she slips back into the bedroom and touches the crucifix, reaching toward it in the night like a blind woman. Not praying, not exactly. Just holding the wood, and hoping as she does so that Timothy will go on disappearing, that he will fade into the night like smoke into the air so that Israel cannot find him. So that Israel cannot bring him back to Victoria, subdued and broken, like a slave.

—

They take the ferry back across the water, and they do not speak, and then they drive to Lilah's apartment and sit in the car without touching. Emmanuel, as ever, is a silent ghost behind the wheel.

"Why did you say that," Lilah blurts. "About Timothy. What do you want with him?"

Israel shrugs. "You and your mother—you're both avoiding the truth. Putting your faith in something false, something hollow. Like children, believing in Santa Claus."

"But I thought that made me special," she says bitterly. "Following him to the end of the world, even as he breaks my heart. Isn't that what you've waited for, all these years?"

"The quality is what makes you special," he says. "It's not about Timothy. You say that his life is all you can hold—I say he just holds you back. Even so, I find your devotion to him . . . curious. I would like to meet him, and see what it is about him that you think is so extraordinary. What it is about him that keeps you from me."

"Don't be stupid. He's not keeping me from you. I'm right here."

"But you aren't," he says. His hand so hard around her wrist. "Not yet. And I want nothing less than all of you."

"That's creepy." When he only smiles, she looks away out the window. In a few moments they'll be in her neighbourhood. She can climb the stairs to her apartment and crawl into her bed and forget, for a while, the murky, layered mess that is her life. "You didn't use a condom," she says. She pulls her hand away and grips the folds of her coat between her hands. "Back there, at the house. Did you think I wouldn't notice?"

"Are you afraid, Delilah?" Israel asks. "Are you afraid of what that could mean?"

"I won't allow it."

He looks out the window and speaks to her as though she isn't really there. "Perhaps it is time, Delilah, to recognize that there might be a higher purpose for your life."

"*Higher purpose*?" She almost spits the words. "God has nothing to do with it."

"God—in a way—has everything to do with it."

"I don't even know what this is. What we are. What kind of life is that?"

"For you? Or for a child?"

"Both." She swallows. "You won't wear a condom now," she says slowly, echoing what she already knows. "Will you. Even though you know how I feel."

"No."

"There are things I can do instead," she says.

"You won't."

For a moment, she imagines cracking his head against the window. A dark bruise, and the brightness of sun on shattered glass. "And how the fuck would you know?"

"Because," and suddenly his hand is around her throat,

squeezing tight, the darkness of his smile flickering before her like a grainy film, "I know." She gasps for air, and nothing comes. He pulls his hand away and the light comes back, slowly, filtering in. She rests her head against the back of the seat. Emmanuel, up front, says nothing.

"I don't want a baby," she whispers. Yet even as she speaks she feels the excitement well up inside of her—the excitement, the shock of remembered pain. She doesn't want a child, or she wants him to beat it into her.

She hates him. She wants him.

Pick one, Delilah.

They are parked in front of her house. They've been parked here for some time.

On Thursday, she wakes up with a fever. She drags herself into the office, then pleads sickness halfway through the day and scuttles out under Penny's disapproving eye. Once free, she buys as much fast food as she can carry and walks the downtown streets out of habit, despite the fever and the migraine climbing slow behind her eyes. There he is, suddenly—a thin boy sitting on a corner bench, twisting a knotted loop of yarn between his hands. She approaches him slowly, as though he is a wild animal, ready to get up and run.

Before she reaches him, he starts talking. "Remember when Mom took us to the hot springs?" He doesn't look at her.

"Yes." They'd gone to Banff a year ago, to celebrate Roberta's remission. Roberta spent most of her time in the water; when they weren't soaking with her, Lilah and Timothy spent hours outside, looking at the stars. Now she sits beside him gingerly, her muscles ready for sudden flight. She reaches into the bag and hands him food.

"I peed in the water," he says now. He eats a hamburger so fast that ketchup streaks down his mouth. "Every time."

"I was sitting right beside you!"

"I know."

"That's disgusting."

He laughs, high and childish. "I just thought you should know."

"Please tell me you peed when Mom was in the water too."

"Absolutely."

"That makes me feel better." She eats her own hamburger slowly. When she reaches for her napkin she finds it spread across her lap, even though she can't remember taking it out. Israel, whose influence is spreading faster than she can see. Israel, who ignored her at the office today as though she was an unrepentant child.

"That was after Montreal," Timothy says, oblivious. "When you came back from Montreal, and those years in Toronto."

"Yes," she says, puzzled.

He turns his head to look at her, mushed hamburger at the corner of his mouth. "You were sad. It hurt to be around you."

"What?"

"You left people behind you, in the city," he says. She doesn't remember talking to him about this, ever. "Sad people."

She shrugs this off and ignores the chill that settles into the tips of her fingers. "I made silly mistakes. I broke some hearts. Everyone does."

"Not like you, Lilah." He licks his lips like a frog.

"Well." Another shrug. "It doesn't matter now." She avoids the napkin and wipes the grease from her fingers onto her coat.

“I miss those days in Banff,” he says. “Those five days.”

“I miss them too.” She reaches for his hand and this time he lets her take it. There’s even a hint of a squeeze. “But we could have more days, Timothy. You know that.”

He takes a handful of fries and jams them into his mouth. He speaks through them, so that the words are slow and disfigured. “No. I can’t go back now. It’s impossible.”

The hospital, her unspoken words in front of Roberta’s door. “You don’t have to go back to Victoria. You can stay with me. For longer, this time.”

“It’s not Mom,” and he’s going, disappearing right in front of her. “It’s not you. It’s everything else. It’s just too hard, Delilah.”

“But we can help you.” She grips his arm. “Mom, me—we love you. We can help you see people, talk to people.”

He shakes his head, whimpers. “There’s nothing you can do.”

“But—”

“Nothing.” His voice is so broken and so final that she lets go. He stares at the ground between his feet. His hands lie open on his lap, bundled in a threadbare pair of gloves. “How is she?”

Now it’s her turn to stare at the ground. “They think she has a few months left, maybe.”

His eyes well up. “Tell her—tell her I’m sorry.”

Lilah takes his hand and winds her fingers in his own. “I know,” she says. Her words are hard and sure. “I’m sorry too.”

She gives him the rest of the food and leaves him on the bench. As she turns the nearest corner, she looks over her shoulder and back, but he’s already gone.

Another corner and suddenly Israel is there, in front of her, dark man in a trench coat and smooth leather shoes.

"Delilah," he says. "I thought you were ill."

"I was," she stammers. "I am." She keeps walking, quickly. "I just wanted some air."

"How interesting," he says. He falls into step slightly ahead of her, his coat flapping in the wind. "Surely there is air close to your home, as well?"

"I like being by the ocean."

"It is a pity you're ill," he says. "I thought we could go look for your brother this afternoon."

"Oh. Well—maybe tomorrow. Or the day after. Depending on how I feel."

"Yes," he says. "Depending on how you feel. Shall I have Emmanuel drive you home?"

"Emmanuel," she says, suddenly irritated. "Does he do anything else? Or do you keep him chained beside you like a dog?"

He chuckles and squeezes the top of her arm so hard it hurts. "Emmanuel is very loyal," he says. "We have been through so much together."

Lilah tries to shake her arm away, but Israel does not let go. "I can walk. I don't mind."

"Nonsense," he says. They round another corner and there's the car, waiting. "Emmanuel will take you home. He can also drive to the pharmacy and get you anything you need."

"I'm *fine*," she snaps. But it's like arguing with Roberta. He walks her to the car and opens the door, then pushes her inside, gently, and closes the door. He raps on Emmanuel's window. The driver nods and starts the car. They pull out onto the street and move away. Israel dwindles behind them until he is a dot in the middle of the window.

Emmanuel takes her home and parks in front of her building. He walks her through the foyer and up to her apartment, his hand steady on her elbow. "Goodnight, Delilah," he says at her door.

"Goodnight," she says wearily. Even though it is only afternoon. She lets herself in and shuts the door behind her, then stands listening in the front hall. Emmanuel shifts on the other side of the door, and waits, and a few minutes later he moves away.

She drops her clothes as she moves to the bedroom—first coat, and then shoes, and then she kicks off her pants and leaves them crumpled in the hall. Blouse. Bra. She crawls into bed in her underwear and shivers beneath the duvet. Her head is hot. Her hands are cold. She sleeps fitfully, and sweats into her sheets.

She dreams that she's standing in a stone corridor, her feet bare, the walls flickering from the light that shines at the far end of the stone. The man stands in front of her. Now he has wings, white and terrible. In his right hand he holds a spear, black and pointed to the ground. She opens her mouth to speak and he raises the spear and pierces her stomach. Pain bursts through her like pomegranate seeds on the tongue.

She drops to her knees. He withdraws the spear and pierces her again, this time through the shoulder. When she looks up, the man's eyes are large and dark and filled with tears.

"Let nothing trouble you, Delilah," he says. "Let nothing make you afraid."

Sometime in the night, she wakes up and staggers to the bathroom. She passes the window on the way back to bed and she sees the car in the lamplight, dark and quiet, nestled beneath the trees. Emmanuel has the light on, and from where she stands she can see him leafing through another book. Reading. Waiting.

She goes back to bed, and when she wakes some hours later, her fever is broken and the car is gone.

FOUR

The boy's name was Timothy. He was from Victoria, but had been living on the streets of Vancouver for almost two months.

"Since they arrived," he said. He flexed his hands around the mug. They sat in a coffee shop and drank coffee that was too strong, ate cinnamon buns that were stale. The girl at the counter had been puzzled when Sam asked for two of everything. *Two,* he'd said, and pointed at the boy. She blinked and nodded. *Of course.* The shadows of Timothy's face were smaller, darker than the shadows Sam had begun to carry. He rocked in his seat and darted glances around the room, looking at the waitress, the old man by the window, the couple who had staggered in laughing and drunk, looking for a coffee fix at four a.m. No one paid them any attention.

"What happened?" asked Sam.

Timothy shrugged. "I woke up and they were there." He picked at his bun. "What happened to you?"

"The same." Now that they were here and speaking he found thinking difficult. The air of the coffee shop felt oppressively warm. The boy was so thin Sam could see the veins beneath his skin. His dark blue, holy veins. "Can anyone else see them? Your wings?"

Timothy shook his head. "I don't think so. You're the first."

"The first."

"Yes. My mother, my sister—they don't see anything." He slurped the coffee and did not seem to notice when it dribbled down his chin. "You?"

"Three others," he said. "Three others can see."

"Oh." Timothy nodded. "What do you do?"

"About the wings?" he asked.

"No. What do you do. In your life."

"I used to be a teacher," he said.

"What do you do now?"

Sam shrugged. "I walk, mostly. I don't know what else to do."

"What does your family think?" said the boy.

"There is no family," Sam said, as though saying the words for the first time. "They're all dead."

"Your friends?"

"They worry," he said. "But I'm not sure that there's anything they can do." He leaned closer and noticed as he did so that the boy moved his head away, down, made it look natural. "What is this?"

"I'm damned if I know," Timothy said. "Damned." He finished his coffee and put the cup down with a loud clang.

No one looked over. “O foolish anxiety of wretched man,” he whispered.

“What?”

The boy looked at him. His mouth moved and sound came out slowly, like mist through the air. “*O foolish anxiety of wretched man, how inconclusive are the arguments which make thee beat thy wings below!*”

“Dante.”

“Yes.” Timothy nodded. “We are beating our wings together now, you and I.”

—

“You could come home with me,” Sam said. They had finished their coffees some time ago. “There’s room.” A priest, a cat, two men with wings.

“I shouldn’t,” said the boy. “There’s too much to do.”

“Too much to do?” Sam asked. “What do you do, then, on the street?”

“I sit,” Timothy said. “I walk.”

“Yes,” said Sam. “I know that too. But,” and here, unbelievably, was an echo of Father Jim, “you need to be around people, Timothy.”

“My sister finds me,” he said, the smallest note of pride in his voice. “Almost every day.”

“Then why aren’t you with her?”

“She doesn’t understand,” he whispered. “She doesn’t see me anymore.”

Yes, he knew that too.

“What’s going to happen?” said the boy. That’s all he was, a boy. A boy with a hooked nose and ratty hat and hair that was falling out, even as they sat hunched at the table. “Sam. What’s going to happen to us?”

"I don't know." He stood and picked up both mugs, carried them to the counter. "But tonight you're coming home with me." Timothy looked about to protest, and then nodded. "All right."

They walked home to Kitsilano in the dark, single file along the sidewalks. It was now almost six o' clock in the morning. The flowerbeds that dotted the path to his house were spiky with frost-frozen leaves, stark black shapes in the darkness. Sam led the way up the path, stepped up the stairs, and unlocked the front door. He turned the knob and opened the door into the house. All was dark and silent, save for the faint glow of a light at the end of the hall.

"You live with people," said the boy. "I thought you said you lived alone."

"I do." Sam closed the door behind them. "I have guests."

Chickenhead appeared at the end of the hall, and then ran down to them, a soft blurry shape. She went straight to Timothy and butted her head against his feet, purring.

"This is the cat," Timothy said. He watched Chickenhead, wary, and did not move to pick her up.

"Yes." Sam moved to take Timothy's coat but the boy shied away, wound his hands around his elbows. "Come to the kitchen. Father Jim is up."

"Father Jim?" said the boy, but he followed Sam down the hall. "You live with a priest?"

"Guest. I said I had guests." He pushed open the kitchen door and Father Jim looked up, saw them both.

"Hello," said the priest.

"This is Timothy," Sam said. "I met him earlier this morning."

"Yes." The priest watched Timothy for one long moment. Then he stood up from the table and moved to the cupboard.

"Can I get either of you anything to drink? You look cold, both of you."

They said it, both of them, at exactly the same time. "I'm never cold." Sam looked at Timothy and then away. His hands shook.

"Can I have some water?" Timothy asked.

"You certainly may." Father Jim cracked three ice cubes into a glass, poured water from the tap. The other men, silent, took seats. Sam let his head fall forward and rest against his hands.

"So," said the priest, placing Timothy's water on the counter, "Timothy. How did Sam find you?"

"I sleep on the streets now," said the boy. "I was trying to sleep, and Sam . . . saw me."

"We went to a coffee shop," Sam said. "We sat and talked. He had nowhere to stay, so I brought him home."

"Of course." Father Jim nodded. And then, as though it was the most logical question in the world, "Timothy. Do you believe in God?"

Sam laughed out loud. "That hardly matters."

"I have to, don't I?" Timothy said. He flexed his hands around the glass. "But this is no God I've ever known."

Father Jim nodded again. He poured tea for himself. The steam ran up his neck, got lost in the thick of his beard. "Do you have family, Timothy? What do they think, about you being on the street?"

"I am trying to protect my family," Timothy said, still in that low voice. "They won't understand."

Sam thought of Julie standing in front of him. *I don't know where you've gone.*

"Your parents?" pressed the priest. "Surely they have something to say?"

Timothy shook his head, looked at the ground. "My mother is dying," he said. He glanced at Sam. "They'll all be dead, soon enough. That's what has to happen."

For a moment silence overwhelmed the house. Chicken-head crept back over to Timothy and poked at his wing—a feather broke free, fell into the ground. As they sat, watching, the feather crumpled and turned into black dust.

"What's that?" Sam asked. He leaned forward and touched a finger to the dust.

"It looks like ash," said the priest.

"I leave a trail wherever I go," said the boy. "I couldn't hide now, even if I wanted to."

Sam thought back to the day when his own feathers had fallen on the floor of the x-ray room. They'd gone in his pocket, the feathers. He stood and reached for the jacket, crumpled in the closet by the kitchen door. When he opened the pocket, he saw nothing but fine black dust at the bottom, as though it had been there all his life.

"I'm tired," the boy said suddenly. "I'd like to go to bed."

"Of course." Sam stood. He waited until Timothy got off the chair, and then took him into the hall. "The one on the right-hand side—that's the one you can use. I'm at the end, and Father Jim sleeps," arm out, "in the room across from you. Sorry about the mess—I've been meaning to clean."

"Mess." Timothy laughed. He looked surprised, as though amazed he could still find small things funny. "You should see my mother's house." He walked into the room and shut the door.

Sam stood in the hall for a moment, thinking of the fear on Timothy's face. That sudden panic in his eyes, underneath the laughter, and the way his hands gripped everything—the table, the railing, the doorknob—as though to anchor, hold him to the ground. That flash of something other in the boy's face just before the door shut. And the sound that came from the other side of the door? The hard thump against the ground, the little moan, the whoosh of expelled breath—someone else might have thought the boy was crying. Or having a seizure, perhaps.

He knew, though. He felt the rivers of God carolling through his own veins, hard and unrepentant. He knew. He understood.

—

He walked back into the kitchen. The cat made a running leap as soon as he appeared in the doorway—Sam caught and held her, firm against his chest. "Timothy," he said. "You can see him too."

"Yes." In the lamplight the priest looked exhausted. How many people weren't sleeping now, in this house?

"He's . . . further along than I am. With this thing."

"Yes."

"He doesn't know who he is half the time."

"I noticed that too." There was something odd in the priest's face. Recognition?

"Have I done this to you?" Is that what he was doing, during those long stretches of hours that he couldn't recall? Sleepwalking during the day now—wandering the streets of Vancouver and mumbling nonsense, mumbling prophecy?

"Yes."

The sudden drop in his heart, the sudden rush of fear. "So this is going to happen to me. This is already happening to me."

"Maybe." What he meant—what they both knew—was that the answer was *yes*.

—

Later in the morning, after a few stolen hours of sleep, Sam shuffled into the kitchen to find the boy already awake, staring out the patio doors. Timothy had showered; his hair was slicked close to his scalp, white patches evident. Like Sam, he wore no shirt, and his feet were bare on the kitchen tile. His jeans were filthy, full of holes.

"Good morning," Sam said.

"Hello," said the boy, without turning. "Hell-o."

He felt it, that pull of the infinite. The push of something other in the air. It whispered to him, called his name. He had to force words out of his mouth. "Do you want something. To drink. To eat."

Timothy turned to him slowly. "No." He was so thin.

Father Jim came into the kitchen then, and nodded to them both. "Breakfast?" he said, and he went for the cupboard.

"No." Both of them, again, at the same time.

"I want to go back outside," said Timothy. "I have to wait. For my sister."

Sam glanced at the priest, and then looked back at Timothy. "Sure."

"Are you sure you don't want something to eat?" Father Jim said, sliding into his own coat. "Just something for the road?"

"I don't want you to come." Timothy flushed. He looked restless now, antsy. Even more a bird, ready to jump into the sky. "I'm sorry. I just want—I just want Sam." He clutched at Sam's arm, panic sudden in his eyes. "But you can't stay with me when my sister comes. You have to leave."

Sam exchanged another look with the priest, and then nodded. "Okay. Just let me get my shoes."

They walked out the door single file, Timothy in front. "Where to?" Sam asked.

Timothy raised his arm and pointed in the direction of downtown. "That way." He set off. His feet made no sound as they moved onto the street.

"Does God speak to you?" he asked, after they'd been walking a few minutes. His voice, his stature—everything about him seemed to be shrinking, or fading away into the air. "Does God tell you anything?"

"No." Sam kept going. "And even if He did, Timothy—I don't know what He'd say."

"God is not talking to me," said the boy. "At the beginning, when it happened, I thought I heard it. I thought God said, *Give away everything you own, and come and follow me.* So I did. I came here, to be close to my sister. But now I don't hear anything, except for the noise."

"The noise?" Sam asked. It was another beautiful day. The air was still and calm.

"You'll know," Timothy said. "Soon enough. You won't be able to think in all of the noise. Everything will be—trying. To get inside your head."

You'll know. The priest had said that as well. Did they truly expect fireworks, or a voice that split clouds in the sky?

"I've been having dreams," the boy said suddenly. "I wake up and I don't know where I am."

"Yes," said Sam. "I know. I do it too."

"I walk—I walk because there's nothing else to do."

"Yes."

Timothy moved like a man asleep, oblivious to the cars that drove by, the horns that blared. As he continued in step behind him, Sam felt everything mesh together in light and fuzz and colour.

"I'm disappearing," the boy continued. "I look at my own hand and I don't know what it is." He stopped, shot a glance back at Sam. "Sometimes, when I wake up—I don't know what this is. Anything. The ground under my feet, the trees. I don't know what any of it means."

"I know," Sam said softly. "I don't think I would have understood you before," he said. Julie. Bryan. Emma. "But now—I do." His pilgrimage. Joni Mitchell singing to him on the open road. Camping trips with Julie and the one lost life that had broken them, had turned him away. His mother, whose face was fading. All of these memories and people who were gone, or in the act of disappearing. Is this what it meant, serving something larger, something different? That eventually all of the small things would fade completely?

"I'm glad you found me," Timothy said. He did not look back, and the words disappeared so quickly into the howl of the wind that for a moment Sam wasn't sure he'd spoken at all. Then, "It makes me feel better."

"I'm glad too," Sam said.

"What happens now?" the boy asked. "What do we do?"

"I think we just watch," he said. He remembered Father Jim. "We watch, and we wait."

"For what?"

"For God," he said. Finally. "I think that's what we're waiting for."

More research will tell her that pain causes changes to the brain, to one's physical chemistry. That the dopamine receptors in the brain are equally responsible for the increase in and relief of pain, that prolonged exposure to hurt will, literally, make someone into a different person. People who are in pain think differently, act differently. They build a world that operates around hurt and solace; they create nightmares, and lift themselves above in any way they can because when you hurt, freedom from it brings a release better than that of any drug. The highs of lacerated skin, the throb of a bruised and bloody mouth. The dark moments of stillness in between. Teresa of Avila beat herself and saw God; so too might Lilah's own penance bring with it visions of something else. A better world? A life where she is stronger, more than equal to her sins?

Or perhaps Israel is making her into a different person altogether now, with every slap of his hand. Remoulding her flesh. Rewiring her brain. Perhaps she will emerge from his hands like a newborn, her guilt burned away, ready to conquer that space between her brother and her story and that name across the stars. She doesn't have to travel far to cross it—all she has to do is lie still, and let him bring it to her.

"Do you ever have the same dream more than once?" This to Debbie, over pasta and baguettes. Lilah moves noodles around on her plate and watches Debbie eat—linguine, more lesbian tea.

"Like, nightmares?"

She shrugs. "Sure. Or just dreams, whatever."

"Sometimes. I dream about high school. But everyone has those. Why?"

Lilah pokes at her food. On the way to dinner, she kept her head down and ducked into the alley every time a black car passed down the street. And now she can't eat. Every time a plate's put in front of her she thinks of Roberta, chained to an IV in her starchy hospital bed. Every time someone passes by the window she expects to see her brother, cowering and helpless under Israel's hand. "I've been having some strange dreams lately."

"What are they about?"

"My brother." Debbie doesn't look satisfied with this, so Lilah continues. "Sometimes it's my brother, and sometimes it's another man. I think. He's thin. And we're in a stone hallway." A spear. "Or sometimes on a cliff, looking out over the sea." Maybe this wasn't such a good idea. "And I think—I'm not sure, but sometimes he has wings."

"Wings? You mean, like, an angel?"

"Um . . . yes." Is it, though? This man that shines, that makes entire oceans rise and fall under his hand—is this an angel? Are those really wings that flicker behind him, or just more tricks of the light?

Debbie dips a finger into her tea and then sucks it. This would drive Roberta wild. "You know you can get dream books from the library, right?"

"I know what the dreams mean," Lilah says. Her brother is lost, and she is looking for anything to save him, even God. Even a terrible, unfathomable God with a spear. It's not rocket science. "I just want to know why I'm having them all the time."

Debbie shakes her head. "I don't know. I can ask Jo, if you want." Jo, Debbie's partner, is a psychologist-in-training. Apparently she is all about dreams. No doubt she would shit her pants if she sat down with Lilah for an hour.

"It's not really important. I'm just curious."

"Hmm," Debbie says. "My dreams are so boring. I mean, showing up naked in science class is about as stressful as they get. Obviously, I need more excitement in my life."

Lilah laughs. "Maybe. But weird dreams and lost brothers are hardly excitement."

"You haven't heard from him, then?" Debbie asks.

"I hear from him," Lilah says. "But it's not the same. He can be right in front of me and miles away all at the same time."

Debbie nods. But she doesn't understand, either. "Maybe it's a phase, Lilah. I know it sounds ridiculous, but maybe he's just . . . I don't know . . . working through something."

"Maybe," she echoes. She pushes more noodles around. The waiter comes by a few minutes later and takes her half-finished meal away.

"It will get better," Debbie says softly. "You're a good person, Lilah. Good things will come to you. I'm sure of it."

A good person. A *nice* person. Is it true? Or is this just what people say? Three weeks ago she might have believed this—now, her life has splintered into so many pieces she finds it hard to call herself a person at all. Perhaps she is just energy, a blue-white pulse of power waiting for a moment to ignite. The days of her life losing focus, becoming one headlong rush to salvation, or damnation, or both. Timothy. Israel. Roberta. So much can change, Delilah, in a minute, an hour, a day. "I don't know, Debbie. I don't know anything, anymore."

—

In the morning she finds Timothy in front of the bakery, eating cupcakes. He licks icing from his fingers and grins up at her. His smile is so dazzling that she wonders, for a moment, if he's high.

"I love cupcakes," he says. "Don't you just love cupcakes, Lilah?"

"Yes." She sits beside him, on the ground, and sticks a finger in one of the cupcakes on his lap. The icing is chocolate buttercream. She licks her finger clean, and then runs it over the cupcake again. "You're in a good mood."

"You're going back to the hospital today," he says. He puts the cupcake on her knee. "That's what you've come to tell me."

"I am going to the hospital. Yes." She bites into the cupcake. How absurdly nice, to sit here with him in the cold December air and eat chocolate frosting. "You don't have to come. I won't force you. I just wanted to see you before I go."

"Now you see me. And then you won't. It's just that simple."

She stops mid-bite and looks at him, at how calmly he picks the crumbs from his jeans. "Timmy. Are you okay?"

"I'm fine," he says. Then he looks at her, at the scarf around her neck. "You're the one covered in scarves."

Suddenly the cupcake tastes like Styrofoam. "I don't know what you're talking about."

"I'm not dumb," he says, hurt. "You keep talking to me like you think I'm some kind of idiot."

Lilah swallows with difficulty. How many times have people said things like this? "It's not what you think."

"Let me guess. You fell down the stairs."

She pulls a tissue out of her purse and wipes her fingers. Slowly, carefully. "I've met someone."

"Someone who makes you fall down the stairs? That's nice."

"Tim. It's not like that."

"I don't believe you," he says. "You have bruises on your *neck*."

"I had hickeys on my neck all the time when we lived at home. You never said anything."

"I was a kid!"

"Anyway," she says, "it's fine. Don't worry about it."

"But I always worry about you."

She laughs. "Right. Because—clearly—I'm in worse shape than you."

"You wouldn't understand," he says. "That's why I don't tell you. Mom doesn't understand, either."

Lilah pulls her scarf tighter and shivers. "Is this going to go on forever, Timmy? I'm right here, and you won't talk to me. What do you want me to do?"

"It's a bruise," he says. "It's not a hickey. And you won't tell me anything else. So we're even, then."

"Even," she echoes. A woman steps out of the bakery and casts a quick glance over the two of them, huddled on the ground. She walks away quickly, without looking back.

"Mom took her rosary into the hospital," Lilah says. "I bet she's driving the nurses crazy."

Timothy snorts and looks at the ground. "Maybe. Or maybe they like it. Maybe it's comforting." He seems so far removed from tears today.

"If I was a nurse," she says, "it would drive me nuts."

"I think," says Timothy, "that when you're around death all the time, you can't help but believe. You'd go nuts otherwise."

Lilah remembers the crucifix in Roberta's bedroom, and her silent, hurried words. Not a prayer, though. Not quite. "People always want to pray when they're down. It's the easiest thing in the world."

"I don't think so. I think it's the hardest thing anyone can do. Because there's a part of you that always knows nothing might happen, that you might just be speaking words into air. And people do it anyway."

"Do you?"

"All the time," he says. He sounds so old. "Whether I want to or not."

She watches him, sprawled out on the concrete. Her little brother, fading bit by bit into the street. "And what happens?"

"Nothing," he says. "And at the same time, everything."

Roberta is thinner, weaker, confined to the bed. She's been puking so much that they've taken her off food altogether, and now there's an IV in each hand. One for the drugs, one for the food. It hurts her to use the TV remote.

"He didn't come," she says, as soon as Lilah walks through the door. "Did he."

"No." Someone has sent Roberta flowers, orange chrysanthemums that clash against the wall. Lilah drapes her coat over the couch and looks at the flowers, at the card. Church friends. *Get well soon, Roberta!* as though she's in bed with a cold. "But he sends his love."

Roberta laughs, or sobs—Lilah's not quite sure. "Yes. Yes, I thought he would."

"He's okay." Lilah sits in the chair beside the bed. "I saw him earlier today, and he's fine."

"I've been here," Roberta says, "all this time. Lying here, in bed, all day. And I think about Timothy, and I think about you, and I can't do anything. Do you know what that feels like?"

Lilah reaches over and takes Roberta's shrunken, withered hand. Her skin is crinkled, like tissue paper. "It's okay," she says. "Mom—it will be okay."

"You really think so?" Roberta doesn't look at her. "I can't see anything else, Delilah. I can't see a way out."

Lilah doesn't answer. She sits and she holds her mother's hand. Eventually Roberta falls asleep. Lilah sits there still, silent, until the nurses come in and ask her to leave.

—

She walks down to the harbour and sits by the water. She lights a cigarette and draws her feet up so that she is cross-legged on the bench. When the cigarette is finished, she lights another, and another.

After a while, she shifts so that she's lying on her back, exhaling smoke straight up into the air. The bench is cold beneath her head. The stars shine above her, seeming larger here than they are in Vancouver. She lies still and at some point she falls asleep. She dreams fitfully, anxiously—of her brother, Israel—and wakes shivering on the stone. But instead of getting up to walk home she turns over, brings her legs in, and stays curled on the bench.

Eventually she falls asleep again. The dreams are much the same. She wakes just before dawn, just as the sun is beginning to lighten the sky. She can't tell the difference between the bench and her own frozen skin. She stands, painfully, and walks back to Roberta's house, where she showers, eats oatmeal, and then makes her way back to the hospital.

—

She buys Roberta magazines and flicks the remote for her, all through that long afternoon. They do not talk about Timothy. When she is hungry, Lilah eats alone in the cafeteria. Otherwise, she sits in the room and reads *Cosmo* and *Vogue* while Roberta watches daytime TV.

"I can't believe people do this." Roberta waves her hand at the screen. *It's not his baby.* The talk show host is a young woman barely able to contain her glee. "Can you believe people do this?"

"People sink to all kinds of lows."

Roberta picks at her bedsheet. "I always thought you'd end up on one of those."

"A talk show?"

She shrugs. "Maybe. I also thought you'd end up in court."

"Thanks."

Roberta doesn't laugh. "You surprised me."

Lilah flips the pages of her magazine. "Oh."

"I thought your boyfriend was going to come," Roberta says then. "Didn't he say he'd come back this weekend?"

"Something came up. He had somewhere else to be."

"Oh." Roberta nods. "Well—it was nice to meet him, last week. He's very—"

"Striking." They say it together. Roberta laughs.

"Yes. Well. He looks like he's good in bed. Is he?"

"Mother."

Roberta shrugs. "What? Don't tell me I can't say these things *now*."

"I'm sure your church friends would love to hear it."

"Church friends, my darling, know a good fuck just like everyone else."

Is this the drugs talking? Lilah puts her magazine down slowly and stares at her mother. Roberta stares back.

"He wants to have a baby," she finds herself saying.

Roberta nods, as though this is the least unexpected thing in the world. "And you don't."

"What if the baby ends up like Timothy?" she whispers. "What if—what if I'm not good enough?"

"No one thinks they're good enough." Now it's Roberta's turn to grasp Lilah's hand. Her fingers are hot and dry. She stares at the bed, at the tubes poking into her arms. "But you'll have time to figure it out. He's a nice man. I'm sure he'll understand."

A nice man. Is that what other people see? Lilah nods and stares at their fingers, woven together. Roberta's knuckles are ivory beneath her skin, the IV bruise on the back of her hand an ugly greenish-brown. "There's so much sadness in the world," Lilah says. For some reason she thinks of Sabsatian, and his stories from that other part of her life. The unnamed woman who drowned in the river. "That's not—I don't think it would be fair to a child."

Roberta holds her hand and says nothing. Eventually she

falls asleep and Lilah leaves again. She goes back to Roberta's house to find the sheets still crumpled on the bedroom floor. She dumps them in the washing machine and throws in detergent and bleach, and then she takes a spare sheet from the closet and spreads it on the mattress. She falls asleep on this bed, in this room, away from the green macramé. She dreams of nothing.

It is dark outside when she wakes. She has enough time to catch the last ferry, so she waters the plants, locks the front door. She smokes out the window of the car. She thinks about Roberta as she boards the ferry—Roberta, and Timothy, and this mess they call a life. Could she sedate Timothy long enough to bring him back across the water? Would he forgive her, eventually? Ever?

Seated, she prays as she did in the bedroom—quickly and without thought. Except that it's not praying so much as asking, or begging. An imaginary conversation with someone who isn't there. The ferry moves through the water and people move around her and still she sits, and her thoughts bounce from her mother to her brother and back again, and nothing happens.

THREE

Within hours of that first meeting, he found himself mirroring Timothy—or maybe it wasn't the boy he was mirroring but just this shade of his new self, this final slide into strangeness. Things that had once been ordinary were now odd and new. The whisper of cloth against his skin, the tap of a toothbrush against the inside of his mouth. The click of Father Jim's pipe against his teeth. All these memories suddenly so hazy, so out-of-focus. What was it, that bush by the side of the road? That bright spot of colour in the air, following the child and parents who skipped over the bridge? Balloon. Yellow balloon.

He forgot words, forgot things. The veins in his arms and across his torso grew darker. Migraines came, went away, came back again. The world shimmered green and blue and gold.

The next day, they left Father Jim to his lunchtime whiskey and once more walked into the city. The day was cold and clear and the air carried a faint hint of snow. Timothy scuffed his shoes as they walked, and mumbled softly to the ground.

"Who are you talking to?" Sam asked when he couldn't take it anymore.

Timothy started, stopped. Flushed pink. "My sister," he said, his voice small. "I'm sorry. I know it's crazy."

"It's not crazy." He moved in step with Timothy so that the two of them spanned the sidewalk. A quick glance over his shoulder showed a small line of black dust trailing behind them, so fine that it was almost invisible against the cement. Dust. Blur. Nothing. "I'm sure she talks to you too."

"Maybe," the boy said. Then he shrugged. "I don't think so. We're—we're too far apart, now."

"Because of the wings?"

Timothy shook his head. "We were apart before. It's been that way for years."

Julie, standing before him at the funeral. White lily in the dark twist of her hair. The memory flickered, faded.

"My sister always wanted something else," Timothy continued. "Another city. Another life. It drove our mother crazy. *Drives*," and Sam remembered his words from the night before. *My mother is dying.*

"And now?" Sam asked. "What does she do?"

The boy shrugged. "She works in the city. She comes to find me on the street. She still isn't happy." He picked at a thread hanging off the cuff of his sweater. "Looks like *I* ended up with *something else*, instead."

"What's her name?"

"Delilah."

"That's pretty."

Timothy laughed. “She hates it. She always said our mother named her after the most famous whore in history.” He scuffed a shoe and started walking again. “She went to the hospital, yesterday. In Victoria. She wanted me to come, but I couldn’t go. I couldn’t.” Then he said something, too low for Sam to hear.

“What?”

“Lilah,” he said. “That’s what I call her. When I speak to her in person, and even when she isn’t there.”

“Oh,” Sam said. They kept walking. Men with wings, melting into the landscape. They walked along the edges of Granville Island, through the markets, through the colour. Even in these last days of November the island was busy, though for all the attention paid to the two of them, it could have been a ghost town.

“I still can’t believe,” Sam said, neatly sidestepping a young boy intent on walking and playing his videogame at the same time, “that hardly anyone can see us.”

“It doesn’t surprise me,” said the boy. “No one sees God anymore.”

“But we’re not God. Not even close.”

Timothy shrugged again. “Maybe not. Probably not.”

“What does that mean?”

“It means whatever it means,” said the boy. “Not God—but we’re not us anymore, either. We exist in between now.”

—

It came on him suddenly, inexplicably—that bone-jarring need for caffeine. Surprised that he could still want something, that the tastes of Sam Connor had not completely disappeared, he waited until they reached a coffee shop and then tugged on Timothy’s shirt.

"What do you want?" he asked, nodding to the café window. "I'll buy."

Timothy laughed, mischief sudden on his face. "I'm a penniless beggar. Of course you'll buy."

"Yeah, well. Espresso? Latte?"

"Hot chocolate. With whipped cream."

"No problem." Sam pressed against the café door, then paused. "Do you want to come in?"

"No." The boy shook his head. "Too many people. I'll wait. Here."

"Okay." Sam walked into the café and took his place in line. He held the wings close around his shoulders and shuffled with the others as everyone moved forward. When his turn came, he watched the barista blink, just as that girl had blinked at Timothy a few days ago. As though he was almost, not-quite there. Then she shook her head and smiled.

"Latte, you said? And a hot chocolate?"

"With whipped cream." He watched her fiddle with the knobs on the espresso machine. Someone knocked into him from behind, pushed into the left wing. A jostle, a nudge. Unintentional. He felt the pain slice into and down through his arm.

"Sorry," said a voice. A woman's voice. She sounded frazzled, embarrassed. He heard a child's giggle.

"It's fine." He didn't look back. The barista slid his drinks across the counter.

Then it came. *Sam. Sam, help me.* A voice out of nowhere, filled with terror. He looked up and saw Timothy, on the other side of the glass, speaking to a man in a long dark coat. A tall, balding man with a high forehead and dark eyes. That was all. He frowned, passed money across the counter, and glanced around—no one else had stirred. The child behind him smiled with white, shiny teeth. The call came again. *Sam*. He turned to the window and saw the sky darken, ever so slightly, saw the air shimmer and swirl around the man, whose elegant hands reached for Timothy. Everything went still.

Panic slammed into him like nausea, hard enough to make his fingers shake. He grabbed the drinks and sprinted for the exit. There were suddenly too many people in the coffee shop—his turn to jostle the crowd now and push his way ahead. When he finally got to the door and heaved it open with his shoulder, the answering rush of cold wind was sharp enough to make him dizzy.

Timothy stood on the sidewalk, alone.

"Are you okay?" Sam asked. He put their cups on the garbage can and balled his fists.

"That man," Timothy said, staring down the street. "He—knew." He blinked and turned his head slowly to Sam. "He *saw* me."

"What?" Sam turned sharply around, but the street was empty. "He saw the wings?"

Timothy nodded. "He just... walked up to me. Out of nowhere. He touched my forehead—" and the boy's hand went up, mimicking "—and he said, *Timothy. Ah, I see. I see you now.*" Even as Timothy spoke his voice grew darker, richer, more hypnotic. "*You have no place here. You have no power.*" He blinked. "Then he reached his hand out and he held the wing. Like this," and the boy reached over and pulled Sam's right wing tight into his fist.

Sam drew a breath, but Timothy didn't seem to notice. That darkness in the air, the weird shimmer of the glass. "What happened. When he touched your forehead."

Timothy blinked. "I—I don't remember."

"What?"

"I don't remember," he said, again. "It's . . . fuzzy."

"Fuzzy?" Sam said. "What do you mean?"

Timothy frowned. "I don't know." He let the wing go. "I'm cold," he whispered. "I'm never cold."

"Timothy." He gripped the boy's shoulder and shook him gently. "This is important. What happened when he touched your forehead?"

"I don't know!" Timothy cried, and he knocked the drinks to the ground. "*I don't remember. He made me not remember.*"

"Timothy," Sam said again. Just a hint of pressure, there, in the fingers. It's okay. It will be okay. "Calm down." He remembered. "You called me. In there, in the coffee shop."

"What?"

"You called me for help," he said slowly. He raised his hand and touched the boy's forehead. Touched skin and felt the blood rush beneath his fingers. The ground dissolved beneath his feet. He saw a flash of white light, and—a face? A woman? A boy? Then the light again—light at once soft and heavy, like snow.

He opened his eyes. Heard nothing. Timothy's mouth moved, but there was no sound. Sam blinked, and the world came rushing in.

"What did you see?" said the boy.

"I saw," and he put a hand to his temple, thinking back, "I saw—a woman? I think. I don't know. Is that what he saw?"

"I don't know," said Timothy. His ears were red with cold, or shame, or both. "I've never seen him before. I don't know anything."

Perhaps this was God—this insistent whisper, this uneasy rumble in the stomach. He fought the urge to take the boy's arm again. "What did he look like, the man?" His own memory was hazy now. A dark figure, a long black coat. "Maybe Father Jim will know who he is."

"Father Jim can't know everything," Timothy snapped. Then he flushed and looked away. "It feels like a dream," he said, his voice trailing off. "Or a nightmare." He lifted his shoulders so that his wings trembled in the air—still bedraggled, still limp. But lighter, now, since the day they'd taken him in. "*You have no power here*—what did he mean?"

"I don't know." Sam bent and picked the soggy cups off the ground. Adrenaline and confusion fought for space in his head. Power? Did Timothy—did either of them—have any power at all? "We should go home," he said finally.

"I haven't seen my sister," said the boy.

"We should go home," Sam repeated. The drinks made a sticky mess beneath their shoes. He threw the cups into the trash can. Not waiting for Timothy to answer, he started walking.

The boy followed a few moments later. They walked back to the house in silence, watching the road, the cars, each other. As they neared the house, Sam remembered the shimmer of the air around the man, the unfamiliar, accented tones of Timothy's altered voice. The uneasiness in his stomach intensified.

"Should I tell my sister?" asked Timothy. "Maybe she should—I don't know. Maybe she should know."

"What could you tell her?" Sam said. "She doesn't see you. And anyway," quickly, to guard against the sadness in Timothy's eyes, "we don't *know* that it's bad." Nothing but a feeling, a memory growing more unreal as they walked. "We don't know what any of it means."

"Maybe." They reached the house. Sam unlocked the door and held it open, let the boy pad down the hall, into the kitchen. He locked the door, rested his forehead against the wood and turned the deadbolt, just in case.

But nothing changed, and the feeling in his abdomen didn't go away.

—

Timothy stood by the counter in the kitchen, scissors in his hand.

"My hair," he said. "Take it."

"All right," said Sam. "Timothy—it's going to be all right."

"Please," he said. He shook, barefoot on the tile.

"All right," Sam said again. He went into the bathroom and got the razor instead. When he came back to the kitchen Timothy was sitting, Chickenhead purring loudly in his lap.

"All of it," he said. "All of it. Gone. Like yours."

The hair fell away in seconds. He ran the razor lightly over Timothy's scalp until everything was gone, until his scalp shone ivory and his ears revealed tips that were slightly pointed, like Sam's own.

"There," Sam said. "It's done now."

"Thank you." Timothy stood and brushed off errant bits of hair, then kept brushing, even as the hair disappeared. He rocked his head slowly from side to side.

"I think you're . . . okay," Sam said. Why were words suddenly so hard? He reached out to the boy.

Timothy shook his head and moved farther away. "No. No. Don't touch me."

"All right." Sam put the razor down and held up his hands. "I'm sorry. It's okay, Timothy. It will be okay."

"No."

"Timothy. You're home now." The deadbolt. "It's safe."

"No," the boy said again. He shook his head one more time and walked out of the kitchen, dark blue veins spreading out across the back of his head even as Sam stood and watched him go.

—

Father Jim came home an hour or so later, bottle of whiskey tucked under his arm. Sam, huddled by the back door, watched as Chickenhead jumped down from his lap and ran down the hall to the priest. She seemed lighter when the priest was around.

"Hey," he called. "Get your own cat."

The priest chuckled, then frowned as he came into the kitchen and saw Sam on the floor. "Are you all right?"

"Something happened," said Timothy. He came from behind Father Jim and stood between them, hands twitching, eyes looking from the priest to Sam and back. "We saw someone—"

"Someone who saw Timothy." Sam spoke the words to the floor. "Someone who saw the wings."

"And?" Father Jim's voice was crisp, focused. "What happened?"

"He touched my forehead," the boy recited, moving his hand. His voice had an odd, singsong quality to it. "He touched my forehead, and he said, *You have no power here*." He paused with his own hand in the air. "Then he went away."

"Did you see him?" Father Jim turned to Sam. "Did he speak to you?"

"I was getting coffee," Sam said. It sounded strange now. "I saw them through the window, and I panicked." He told them about the darkness of the air, that shimmer of the world through the glass. "But by the time I got outside, he'd left."

"So he didn't see you," Father Jim said.

"No." Sam shook his head. "He didn't see me. Just because I went to get coffee."

The priest turned his hands palm up in the light. "The world has turned on smaller things."

Sam held his hand out for the cat; she ambled over and then rolled on her back in front of him. He brought his wing around and brushed the feathers across her stomach. "I don't know what happened but it meant... something."

"Do you know what it means, Father?" Timothy shifted from one foot to the other.

"I don't know," the priest said, his voice quiet. "But I'm not surprised."

"What?" Timothy and Sam spoke at once.

"God is beyond mysterious." Father Jim sat at the counter and ran a hand across his face. How old he looked, Sam thought suddenly. "But you—you, me, all of us—we'd be foolish to think that God is the only unknown in the universe."

Sam grew cold, shivering as he hadn't in weeks. "Are you talking about—"

"I don't know what I'm talking about," the priest said sharply. "Isn't it obvious? I'm guessing, just like the two of you."

Sam pressed his hand into the cat's stomach. Fur, smooth skin, and beneath the flesh, organs that propelled her forward. An inner solar system, an inner rhythm. Did she see the world differently, now that her life had been dipped in a miracle? If she had been there beside Timothy on the sidewalk, would she have seen something else besides a man in a long dark coat?

"You can't talk about God," Father Jim said slowly, "or live through a miracle, without eventually seeing something else. Something other than God."

Sam took a breath and stared at his hands. A demon, a different kind of angel altogether. He thought of Rilke. *Almost deadly birds of the soul.* "What happens now?"

"Damned if I know," said the priest. "This isn't *The Exorcist*."

"So—we just sit here?" Timothy's voice went even higher. "We do nothing? What if I want to see my sister?"

"No one said 'do nothing.'" Father Jim poured whiskey into a glass. He passed it to the boy, who held it between one forefinger and thumb as though he didn't quite know what to do. "Liquid courage, my boy. If I had to come face to face with the Devil, I'd sure as hell not want to do it sober."

Sam snorted. He rested his elbows on his knees and let his hands hang above the floor. "We keep going," he said. "I don't see that we have any other choice."

"You *don't* have a choice," Father Jim said flatly. "Look—maybe you came close to something today. Maybe not. Maybe there's a thread in all of this that none of us can see. God is being revealed to both of you—but on God's time, not yours. You do not get to decide what makes sense, and whether something has meaning or not. You get to pay attention. You get to feel God in your blood. That's all."

"God does not feel all that great," said Sam. "He feels like . . . the flu."

Now it was the priest's turn to snort. "God is more terrible than anything you could imagine, Sam."

"That's your wisdom?" Timothy's voice was almost hysterical. His eyes were stark, haunted—the eyes of a fugitive. "That's your uplifting speech?"

"*Yet in my flesh I shall see God,*" said the priest. He paused and let the words hang in the air. "Only a fool would find that uplifting. If God is truly in your veins, gentlemen—changing your skin, changing your bones—there won't be anything left of you when it's over. Anything else is a toy, by comparison." Now he was quiet, sad. His words settled among them like the ash that had begun to drift, steady and slow, from Sam's own wings. "As to the rest—if I were God, the world would make me ill too."

The week goes by and she avoids them both, Timothy and Israel, as much as she can. It's too much. She runs errands. She calls Roberta. She pleads another headache, and another. She leaves work early every day and goes straight home, where she crawls into bed and goes to sleep. No dreams. No answers. Nothing.

On Thursday, she stops at a McDonald's, and from there takes the long way home. She finds Timothy by the water, perched on beach driftwood, staring out. He wears a hat she hasn't seen before, and as she steps closer he straightens, becomes more alert.

"Lilah." He turns around and takes off the hat. "Where have you been?"

"What happened to your hair?" she says. He has showered. He is wearing different clothes. He is bald. "Where did you get that shirt?"

"I'm just borrowing it," he mutters. He does not look at her. "I'll give it back."

"Who gave it to you? Why in bloody fuck did you shave your head? Are you in some kind of cult?"

"I was safe," he says. "Don't worry."

Worry. Worry is all she ever does. "You could shower at my house. You can borrow clothes from me."

"I can't borrow clothes from you."

"So I have tits. Big fucking deal. You can borrow a god-damned sweatshirt, at least."

"Don't swear."

"Well? For fuck's sake, Tim. What am I supposed to think?"

"This isn't about you," he says. "Isn't it enough to know that I'm safe?"

Yes. And no. "You're not . . . you're not . . . you know—"

He smirks. "No. Thanks a lot."

"Oh. Well, that's good, then." She stands above him, awkward, unsure. Someone else had Timothy in their apartment last night, when she was hiding under her duvet. Someone else had him safe.

"You always find me," he says then. "How?"

"I don't know." Other people get pulled around this city for food, for sex. Lilah follows her brother around like a shipman, lost at sea and following the sky.

"How's Mom?" he asks.

"She's dying. She wants to see you."

His breath comes out funny—a wheeze and a whimper all at once. He blinks and he runs a hand around his head. "Do you like my hair? It was falling out. I couldn't hide it anymore."

She shuts her eyes and imagines the story she'll tell Roberta. "Please tell me it's not a cult."

"A cult?" He is genuinely perplexed. "Why would I join a cult, Lilah? *God lives inside of me.*"

"It's falling out because you're not eating enough." She sits beside him, on the log, and pulls out the bag of fast food. All of this travel between Victoria and back has meant little time for groceries—Roberta would cringe to see the shit Lilah is feeding him now. But Timothy is oblivious. He eats his food without comment, and this time he wipes his face with the single napkin that was placed inside the bag.

"Thank you."

"You always liked Happy Meals," she says. She thinks of The Actor, who brought Timothy food all those weeks ago. The Actor, Joe-with-an-L, all these parts of her life that are falling away, disappearing. The guilt is sharp and sudden, but eventually it subsides.

"I'm not seven, in case you haven't noticed."

"I know." She reaches for his hand; as always, he pushes her away. "You're a grown man. Completely capable of making your own decisions. I'm aware."

"You laugh," he says. He begins, once again, to rock in his seat. "You laugh, but Delilah, if only you knew."

"Then tell me!" Suddenly she is furious. A woman walking past them jumps mid-stride.

"I won't hurt you," is what he says. "Just know that."

"Tim—you can't do this forever."

"Who said anything about forever?"

The sound that comes out of her throat is wild, uncontrolled. She throws the rest of her hamburger at him. Then she stands and shouts so loud that people fifty feet away stop to look at them. "I hate you!"

His face opens for her like a flower, dying even as it blooms. "I know," he whispers.

Lilah stalks away before she can do anything else. She doesn't look back. She doesn't cry. She walks through the city, blind with rage. She walks straight to Israel's apartment, gleaming tower of metal and glass. She presses the buzzer.

"Delilah." She whirls around to find him there, in front of the door, holding Chinese takeout in his sleek gloved hands. "How . . . unexpected. I thought you were in hiding."

"What—I can't come to see you? We do everything on your clock, is that it?"

He smiles. For an instant, he looks like every other man she's ever slept with. Then he takes her arm, and she remembers. "Hardly."

Inside, he splits the takeout onto two plates and pours wine for them both. Lilah sits at the counter and does not eat; the fast food turns her stomach. She runs her fingers over the granite. Timothy's face, opening and crumpling for her all at once.

"You have seen Timothy," Israel says.

She sniffs, and immediately hates herself. "No."

He laughs. "You are a terrible liar."

"Fine. Yes."

"Yes. And he is—not well?"

"He's fine," she mutters. "He spent the night at someone's house. He fucking shaved his head. Like he's in some goddamned cult!"

She doesn't see his arm move at all. Another backhand, so quick. "How many times must we do this, Delilah? You are more than your body. You are certainly more than your mouth."

"He's going to die," she says bitterly. She speaks around the pain, around her stinging cheek. Then she dips her finger into the sweet-and-sour sauce. "He's going to freeze to death on the streets, and there's nothing I can do."

"But everyone dies," he says. "Your brother. Your mother. Even you, eventually."

She stares. "Is that supposed to make me feel better?"

"The truth does not make you feel better or worse. It is merely the truth." He puts his cutlery down. "You build what you can from that."

Lilah licks her finger, catches the sauce at the corner of her mouth. Sweet. A hint of chilies. "I hate him."

"You don't hate him." Israel pats his mouth with his napkin. She watches the skin over his collarbone, dark and brown. The pulse in his neck has quickened, like her own. "You love him so much that it feels like hatred."

"Or I hate him so much that it feels like love?"

Israel smiles his crooked smile. "Yes," he says. "Yes, Delilah. You see—you are beginning to understand."

This time he ties her completely to the bed, her hands and feet stretched to the bedposts, her knees bent so that she's exposed, all of her, to the air. To him. She shakes with terror, with anticipation. The pillow beneath her cheek is damp with tears.

"You fear me," Israel says behind her, "because you think I have power over you. Because you are used to having power over men." A caress, then the crack of his whip against her thigh. "But what you don't realize, Delilah, is that this is where the power comes from. This recognition—it is *pain*, only that. It will disappear. You are infinitely more than your body." He stops the whip and then draws it back over her reddened skin. Agony; like nothing else she's ever felt. Lilah sobs into the pillow, into the bed. She pulls against the scarves until her wrists and ankles chafe—these will be harder to disguise, these marks, and tomorrow at the office Debbie will be overwhelmed with concern. But right now, here, she says nothing. She couldn't say anything even if she tried—in these moments of calm before the whip descends she's holding infinity right in her mouth, teetering on the edge of a climax so radiant it's a wonder her organs don't implode. Is this what they meant, the saints?

"'For the Lord disciplines the ones He loves,'" Israel intones, "'and chastises every son whom He receives.'" At *chastises*, he snakes an arm around her front and jams his fist into her mouth, so that her teeth clink against the gold of his ring.

She bites him because it is the only thing she can do, bites until his flesh breaks and the warm tang of blood spills over her tongue. Israel grunts behind her and then pulls his hand away. He rams his fist into her cheek—she hears the bone crack, or shift, and then her head hits the pillow again and for a moment she feels nothing. More blood in her mouth. She spits it out onto the pillow.

"I'm sorry," she says.

"Never mind." He pulls his hand through her snarled hair, rests his fingers against her cheek. "It will all come out."

Lilah rests her head against the pillow and smears her forehead with the blood. Her breath comes in short, ragged bursts. Her skin aches. Her ass shivers. And yet she is calm, focused. She feels Israel ready himself behind her. He presses close, so that her shivers become his shivers, his heat becomes her own. For a moment, just before he pushes inside her, the space between them is filled with something endless, something other. His arms come round and cover her, like wings.

TWO

Nearly a week after the encounter on the streets, someone came to the house. It was morning. They were on the patio. Timothy had come back from a solitary walk on the streets last night looking like a beaten dog. He'd gone into his room, and he hadn't spoken to anyone, and all three of them had slept around the noise of muffled sobs. Now he sprawled on the patio stones, his limbs loose and awkward, the joints pronounced, like some kind of wooden puppet.

"What if," said the boy, "what if this is what we *all* become?"

"What if," Sam repeated. Today everything felt like a struggle. "I don't know."

"This could be death. This could be why no one talks about it."

"But no one sees us to talk about it," Sam said. "And—

surely—if it happened to everyone, we'd know something. *You*," and he pointed to the priest, "would know something."

"What do you think?" said Timothy. His voice cracked with longing. "Father." Fa-ther.

"I think," said the priest, "that God is full of mystery. And perhaps he is already using you for something wonderful. There is always that."

"You didn't make it sound so wonderful before," Sam said.

"Things can be wonderful and terrible at the same time." Father Jim took a sip of coffee and continued. He'd slipped the whiskey straight into his cup this morning—a quick sleight-of-hand, but Sam had noticed. "You both have family you fought with, whom you love. You've both had your hearts broken, in some form or another. We human beings—we love and despise at the same time. Once you acknowledge this, and recognize the limitless possibilities of your own heart, you'll realize that God isn't that different."

"Still," Sam said. "'Everything else is a toy, by comparison'? That's what you said." A shimmer in the air, the weight of feathers on his soul. "Or something to run from. It's either/or—it can't be both."

"What you're fighting, that other thing—it has to be . . . charming."

Timothy laughed. "That's not what I would say."

"But it has to be." The priest was calm yet insistent. "Think about it, gentlemen. What would you do if the Devil came to you in a roar of smoke and fire, threatening pain and eternal damnation? I don't know about you, but I'd sure as shit be running for the church."

"I thought you already ran for the church," Sam said, his voice wry.

"The point, Timothy," and the priest faced the boy, "is that if there is a Devil, and there is a God, and the point of the Devil is to draw you away from that God, then the Devil—or this other force, thing, whatever—needs to be as attractive as possible. The Devil needs to make you an offer you can't refuse, to seduce you so deeply you can't see any other way forward. Gentlemen—fire and brimstone is not a selling point. It's that simple."

The doorbell rang and Sam went to get it, sliding back into himself as he walked through the house and up through the front hall.

It was Emma. He held the door open for her and she stepped inside.

"Hello," he said. Hell-o.

"I've been calling," she said. She was pale, shaken. "I left messages."

"I'm sorry." He wasn't checking the messages anymore. He slept, and he walked, and he waited. That was all.

"I thought—I thought it had happened."

"Thought what had happened?"

"I don't know." Her laughter was shaky, forced. "Whatever it is that's happening to you."

Whatever it is. "No. Not yet." Whatever that was. He swept his arm out and pointed to the back of the house. "Everyone's through there."

"Everyone?"

He stopped. Remembered. Then he took her hand and pulled her through to the back of the house. She saw Timothy, and her hand squeezed his hard.

"Oh," she said. It could have been a prayer.

Timothy sat upright, quivering and terrified. "Who are you? Who is she?"

"It's okay," Sam said. He released her hand. "This is Emma."

"Hello," she said. She sat next to Father Jim.

"Emma used to be my student," Sam said. "And now—"

"We're friends," she finished.

"Friends," the boy echoed. He looked at them both. "I never had friends."

"You have a sister," the priest said gently.

"She *hates* me." Timothy rocked on the ground. The sounds out of his mouth reminded Sam of the deer he'd killed, all those weeks ago.

"I'm sure she doesn't hate you," Emma said instantly, leaning forward. "Why would she hate you? Maybe she's just... upset."

"She doesn't understand," Timothy said. "She doesn't understand, so I have to keep everything from her." He looked at Emma and sobbed. "But you. You can see them. Why you and not her?" He stumbled to his feet, breathing hard. "*I want it to stop.*"

"Timothy," Sam said. This he could do, he could understand. Hadn't he helped children such as these in his other, long-ago life? He stood up, counting the seconds as he rose. He locked eyes with the boy. "I know. I want it to stop too."

"I want to go home," the boy said, weeping. His wings shone white and terrible. "Make it go away, Sam."

"Timothy," Sam said again, and he reached forward, took the boy's hands in his own. They were both so warm. And yet the hands of God, come down to touch them both, were sterile, strange, and cold. "I would," he said. "I would take it for you. I would take it all away from you, if I could."

The boy shook and cried. His own hands were nail-less, and crisscrossed with veins, like Sam's. "You can't. You can't do anything." He wrenched his hands away and ran into the house. They heard the front door open and slam.

Sam stood there, staring at the open patio door until he couldn't hear the slap of Timothy's feet anymore. The boy, stumbling down to the city, his heart pulsing with fear and grief and rage. He turned back to look at the others, who were both stunned and quiet. Emma wept silently, her eyes shimmering and dark as the grass.

"He's gone to find his sister," Sam said. "He has nowhere else to go."

"He'll come back," said the priest. "He will, Sam."

"I'm sorry," Emma whispered. They turned to look at her. "I'm sorry. I thought—I thought it was a miracle. You. Him. I didn't understand."

"It is a miracle," Sam said softly. "And we don't understand it, either."

"Will he find her?" Emma asked. "Does he know where she is?"

Sam and Father Jim looked at each other, then at Emma. "Yes," they said.

"Should we go after him?" she said then, even though it was already too late. "Does he need help?"

"He'll find her," Sam said. He rested his hands against the back of his head and saw Emma start. Yes—no gloves. "Or she'll find him. One way or the other. There's something between them. I don't think we can see it." He thought again of Timothy. Weeping. Running. Alone.

"I need a drink," the priest said suddenly. "Does anybody else need a drink?"

Sam laughed. "No."

"Emma?"

She shook her head. "No, thank you."

"Very polite." Father Jim nodded and stood. "I'll take myself to the bar, then."

"There's whiskey in the cupboard," Sam said.

The priest shook his head and offered them the tiniest bit of a smile. "No," he said. "There isn't."

They sat in the kitchen, on opposite sides of the counter, just as everything had started on opposite sides of the desk.

"It's going to happen soon," Sam said. "Whatever it is."

"I know." Emma ran her fingers over the countertop, then raised a hand to her mouth and bit a nail. "I can feel it."

"I'm sorry. That you had to see that, I mean."

"I'm sorry for Timothy," Emma said, her voice low. "And you."

He shrugged. The cat came and jumped into his lap. Still purring. For Chickenhead, there was still so much to love about the world. "Emma—talk to Father Jim. If I'm not here. He'll know. He'll be able to tell you . . . what happened."

She nodded. "I still don't understand why I get to see everything. Timothy. I don't even know him."

Sam remembered Father Jim again. "Maybe you're just supposed to watch. To bear witness. To tell me that I needed to grow up, and stop screaming." He paused. "I didn't thank you before," he said. "But you were—you were so right."

She laughed, sniffled. "Who knew." She took a deep breath. He could hear the sadness whistle through her lungs. "I'll miss you."

"I'll miss you too," he said. This unexpected soul beside him, this unforeseen friend.

Emma reached over and took his hand, traced her fingers around the veins across his palm. "It's terrible, what's happening to you. But. . . I want it to be beautiful too. Somehow."

He laughed. "Forever the poet, you. Always ready to find the thing that shines."

Emma curled his hand into a fist and held it between her hands. "Maybe," she said softly. "I'm going to hope for something beautiful, all the same."

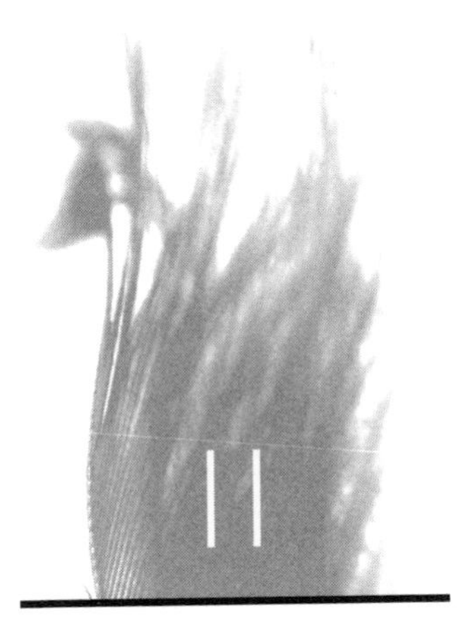

11

The next morning, there's no bruise.

"I don't understand," Lilah says, looking into the bathroom mirror. She runs her fingertips lightly over her cheek. The skin is white and smooth. "I thought you broke it. I *felt* you break it."

Israel leans against the doorway. "Everything feels different when you and I are together."

"But there's nothing. It's not even red."

He shrugs. "I did not hit you that hard. Perhaps it only felt that way at the time."

She thinks back to that moment, to the crack of his fist against her cheek. "Maybe." The rest of her body is mottled and purple, so much so that the sight of her white face is disturbing. Then she remembers something else. "I bit you. Are you all right?"

He laughs. "I am—Delilah, I am more than fine."

She peeks back into the bedroom. Even from the doorway she can see it—a stain on the pillow, murky reddish-brown. "I'm sorry," she says again. "I can buy you new sheets, if it doesn't come out."

"I do not want new sheets." He smiles and runs his hand through her hair. "I will keep it. It is a good reminder." Then he nods to her clothes, still crumpled on the floor by the bed. "Get dressed. It is still early—I thought that perhaps we could look for your brother before we both go into work."

She blinks. "What?"

"Your brother. Timothy. It is a beautiful morning. Perhaps he is out."

"I—I can't. I have plans."

"Oh?" His eyebrows go up. "What plans, so early in the morning?"

"I have . . . work to do. I'm so far behind. And anyway, I don't know if we could find him. I never know where he is."

"We would find him," he says with a certainty that unnerves her. "I think it would be . . . interesting."

"Why?" She walks back to the bed, pulls her shirt from the floor. "Because he's homeless? Because you think he has some weird power over me?" She yanks the shirt over her head. "Look, don't talk about him like that. He's not some—he's not a travelling sideshow, for fuck's sake. And I don't—" a sudden, painful truth, "—I don't *want* to see him. Not today."

"What a terrible sister you are," Israel says softly. He comes up behind her and bites her ear, so sharp that she stops for a second and closes her eyes. "Never mind—we won't go today. We will go later. Next week."

"Maybe." Lilah bends and steps into her pants. "Maybe not."

"You can't keep me from your family forever," he says. "It is *impolite*." A sudden smile widens his face. "But then, perhaps I was wrong. Did he not drive you to me last night? Maybe he does not hold the power over you that I thought. Maybe Timothy's purpose for you is. . . over."

"He's just a boy," she says. Sweet Timothy. She smoothes the wrinkles in her shirt and tries to calm her trembling hands. "He's just—lost."

Israel moves away from her, and tosses the duvet back over the bed with one twist of his arm. "Perhaps," he says. "But you forget, Delilah—even lost boys have a way of being found."

—

At the office, it's spreadsheets and telephone calls as though nothing has happened, as though nothing has changed. Halfway through the day, Penny leaves a note on Lilah's desk telling her to go and get coffee.

"You know," Debbie says, "I don't remember him asking for it once when you were off visiting your mom. Isn't that weird? I mean, normally the man drinks enough to kill a horse."

"Yes," Lilah says. She flips the note through her fingers and stares at Debbie, then pulls her coat from the chair. "Do you want anything, while I'm out?"

"That's sweet of you. But I'm okay."

Lilah nods. "All right. I'll be back, eventually."

Outside, she walks as slowly as she can, kicking at leaves on the sidewalk as she goes. She crumples the note, and then unfolds it. Penny's writing is black and perfect, the cursive of a schoolteacher. *Kopi Luwak. One pound.* One pound, and another look from the coffee merchant, who must go home and wonder exactly what it is that Lilah does to afford one pound's worth, every week, of the most expensive coffee in the world. Maybe she's an unobtrusive CEO, or a film actress just about to break into the world. Or perhaps she's old money.

Maybe she does other things entirely.

She pays for the coffee and walks out of the store, the coffee tucked deep into her purse. She dawdles on the way back to the office—sits on this bench, and then that one, and smiles at every person who passes her on the street. Penny would fire her for this, but Penny can't touch her now. Penny, who deals in ordered, civilized disciplinary hearings, and underhanded bitchiness. A woman who oversees office politics, and knows nothing of the currency of souls.

She turns the corner, close to the office, and there's a figure up ahead. Israel. He doesn't see her. He walks with purpose, with that even stride she knows so well. Israel, walking down toward the water.

She ducks into a side street and runs to the beach. Her purse slaps against her side and her goddamned heels are loud on the sidewalk. She runs, and she wonders at the same time why she's running, why it matters. How she could possibly know that Timothy will be down there, waiting.

But he is. Sitting on a wooden bench and staring out to sea, his shoulders bony beneath another sweatshirt that isn't his own. She sobs mid-step and keeps running. Then she reaches the bench, and her hand on his shoulder is firm. Insistent.

"Timmy," she says, breathing hard. "You have to go."

He blinks. His eyes are red and puffy. "Lilah. I didn't think you'd come back."

Israel will be here in minutes. Seconds. "I know, sweetie." I know. I know. "You have to get up. You have to go."

"I'm sorry," he whispers.

"Tim." She holds his face between her hands and kisses his nose, his cheek, his eyes. How could she have been angry? "Tim. Listen to me. Someone's coming. You need to get away from here. Now."

He stands. He moves so slowly. "I don't hate you," he says.

She shakes her head so hard that tears fly off her cheeks. "I don't hate you. I'll never hate you." It is so hard to breathe. Any minute now and he'll be around the corner, her lover, with power in his hands and darkness in his heart. "Run, Timmy. *Please*."

And he goes, down along the water and then back up the alleyway from which she's just emerged. Gone.

She whirls around to watch the other street. Seconds later, there he is, emerging from the intersection like a magician. He crosses the street at the end and walks up to her, his hands in his pockets.

"Delilah."

She nods, and tries to make it look as though she hasn't just been running. Her legs shake with the effort of it all. "Hello."

"Shouldn't you be at work?"

"Shouldn't *you* be at work?"

His eyebrows go up. "Perhaps I am. And you are . . . doing what, exactly?"

"Here," and she digs for the packet of coffee and tosses it at him so that, surprised, he must bring his hands up to catch it. "Running errands."

"You sound displeased."

She's so angry, or terrified, or both. "Why would I be displeased? Isn't this what every girl dreams of—fetching things for a man, like a dog?"

He laughs. He doesn't touch her. "I forget," he says softly, "how delightful you are. All of you."

"What?"

"Timothy was here," he says. "Yes?"

"I haven't seen him. I told you—I like being by the water."

"You are hiding him from me," he says and smiles. "How sweet. But—surely you must know this, Delilah, by now—unnecessary. Haven't I said this before? If I want Timothy, I will find him. Perhaps I already have. I found you, didn't I?"

"I don't know what you're talking about." She balls her fists to stem the sudden flush of terror. Then she nods to the coffee in his hand. "Anyway—you have it now. I'm going back to work." She starts back in the direction of the office. Israel doesn't say anything. He doesn't follow. She risks one glance back when she reaches the corner of the street. He stands in the same spot, staring at her, and as she watches he tosses the coffee in one hand, up and down, his fingers fast and sure and catching it, every time.

The next day, the last day, she finds Timothy on Beach Avenue. He's playing chess with a man in a pinstriped suit. The man's name is Bob.

"Just Bob," he says. "Nothing else." His hair is dark, flecked with grey, and gold-rimmed glasses swing from his breast pocket, an unsteady pendulum.

He is a good chess player, but not as good as Timothy. In fifteen minutes—ten moves, fifteen, Lilah's not sure—Timothy has the black king cornered. He shoots furtive glances at her when he thinks she isn't looking.

Bob surrenders with a smile, then nods to her. "He's good, your brother."

"I know," she says. She doesn't ask how he knows who she is. She reaches over to move Timothy's hat and ruffle his hair, and then remembers. *Bald.* He flinches at the approach of her hand and so she pulls away slowly, tries to make it look natural.

"Well," says Bob. He fumbles the chess set into a box as he speaks. "Time for me to get back to work. You have a good day now, Timothy. Miss," and he nods to her, then gets up and walks down the street.

"He seems nice," she says, watching Bob's dwindling pin-striped back.

Timothy nods, stares at the ground. "I've discovered a lot of nice people," he says. "Here. On the street." His fingers, clumsy and awkward in gloves, thread around and around the hat that sits in his lap. A red woollen toque, a ridiculous pompom.

Deep breath. "About before."

He rocks on the ground and says nothing.

"I'm okay," she says. Even though he won't believe her.

Still nothing. He rocks, and she notices two rips in the back of his jacket. Between them, flashes of skin. He's so pale. "Tim." She takes a deep breath. "You need to go away for a while."

Now he looks up, confused. "What?"

"I want you to be safe. There are—there are bad people out here too." Someone looking for you, a dark man in a trench coat and smooth leather shoes. "If you've found someone who can help you, you need to go there, to be with them. Please, Timmy. Is there somewhere you can go?"

"Yes," he says. His voice is very small. "But I won't see you."

"Even if it means I can't see you anymore." Especially then. "I can't keep doing this, Timmy. Wondering if you're safe." Another deep breath. "And you can't keep waiting here for me, because I'm not good for you."

"What? No." Timothy shakes his head. His lips are white and cracked—he runs his tongue across them, then across his chin, like some chalky lizard. "You are. You're what keeps me *here*."

"Exactly. You deserve so much more than this, Timmy."

"Why are you hurting so much?" he whispers. "It's not your fault."

"Isn't it?" She's led the Devil right to him. The shards of her life will kill him now, if he gets close enough.

"Sometimes things are bigger than you," Timothy says. "Maybe what's happening to me—maybe you're not supposed to understand, Lilah. Maybe there's nothing you can do." He takes her hand. A miracle. "I think even God would tell you that it's too much. Whatever you're doing, whatever it is that's making you feel so guilty. It's too much."

"I don't suppose God would listen to me," she says. "Not now."

"God always listens," he says. "He just doesn't answer all the time."

"Does God listen to you?" she asks, her voice low. "Does He speak to you, Timmy?"

"I don't understand what He says," he tells her. An answer, and not. "I don't understand what God wants me to do."

She pulls his hand close to her heart. "Me neither," she whispers.

"No one's safe," he says. "None of us."

"*Please*, Timmy. Is there somewhere you can go?"

"Yes," he says. He sits up. "I know the address. I can give it to you."

Lilah shakes her head. Could he find it, Israel Riviera,

locked somewhere in her mind? Could he bring it out of her, just as he brought out the story of her brother? "Don't tell me. I'll come and find you, when it's safe." She does not say when *safe* might be.

"Are you sure?" he says.

"I'm sure." She squeezes his hand.

Timothy looks at the ground. "I love you."

She pulls his head close and kisses his cheek. "I love *you*," she whispers.

Timothy stands, shakes off her hand, and walks down the street. Lilah sits rigid on the bench and watches him go. At any moment now, Israel will swoop down on Timothy and crush him into dust with one wave of his hand. Any moment.

But nothing happens. A thin boy walks to the edge of the street, then disappears around a corner. She hears no scuffle, no cry for help, nothing. There is no sound. There is no wind. There is no sign to show her that Timothy will keep walking, that he will go to his new home, that he will be safe—nothing but the knowledge now that he is passing into the hands of someone else. Even the birds are silent.

"You don't have to keep coming all this way." Roberta is ashamed. "I don't like it."

"It's fine, Mom," Lilah says. "Really." She smoothes the sheets by her mother's hand. "And anyway, I was thinking. I might come to Victoria for a while."

Roberta shakes her head vehemently. "You can't leave. What about Timothy?"

"He's safe," Lilah says. Strange benefactor, of extra clothes and unseen home. "He found someone who—who can help him, I think."

"He needs you," Roberta says. "You need to be there for him. *I* need you to be there for him." She points to Lilah's neck. "That spot, there. Is that a bruise?"

"I fell." Her hand comes up automatically. "I fell out of bed and banged it on the nightstand."

"Are you in trouble?" Roberta says sharply.

"No. I'm fine."

"Is your brother in trouble?"

"He's all right. He's surviving."

"He's in *your city*," Roberta spits. Suddenly she is incandescent, livid with rage. "You're supposed to take care of him." She shakes Lilah's hand away. "You're just like your father," she says. "You just don't care."

How easy, truly, to hurt the people you love. "I do care," Lilah says. "But I can't do everything."

"I'm not asking you to do everything," Roberta snaps. "But he's just a boy."

"What do you want me to do? Lock him up? Beat him senseless and drag him to the psych ward?"

"Don't be dramatic. You're always so *dramatic*." Her eyes well up. "You were always so good to him—surely you can convince him to stay with you. Surely you, Delilah, if no one else."

"I'm trying," Lilah whispers. "I'm doing everything I can."

"It's not enough," says Roberta. She looks like a spider, emaciated and picking at the sheets. "You, me—everything we do. It's like we're being punished just for wanting him to be safe, to be happy. I don't understand it." Her voice cracks. "Don't we deserve a miracle?"

Doesn't everybody? Lilah clenches her hands in her lap, stares down at her fists. What would Israel tell her, if she asked him? That miracles are for children, just like Santa

Claus or the Tooth Fairy? "I don't know, Mom. I think Timothy deserves a better miracle than me." Or maybe there are no such things as miracles—only good decisions and bad. Like the decision that brought her here, or the words that sent her brother away. Or the decision that will take her back to Vancouver, where a beautiful man waits to beat her.

—

"The pain is very bad now," says the doctor. He is young, nervous. "These things she says—it's just the pain."

"It's not just the pain," Lilah says. "She's angry." She presses a hand to her temple. "Can you give her anything? Anything more?"

"We can up her meds," the doctor says. "She'll probably sleep, a lot." He puts a hand on her shoulder and she starts. But he is only concerned. "Is that what you want?"

"Will the pain go away?"

"Most of it," the doctor says. His nametag says *Dr. Sand.* "She won't be able to talk very much. And if she does, you might not understand her."

Lilah shakes her head. "Do it," she says. "Just make her feel better." She goes back into the room and sits. The nurse comes in and adjusts the medication. Roberta continues to sleep. Just before night comes she starts to shiver, so Lilah asks for more blankets and when those do not help she climbs into the bed and places her arm beneath her mother's head. Roberta wakes up.

"Delilah." Her breath smells of stale air and fear. "Where have you been?"

"Right here," Lilah says. "I've been right here."

"You were gone," Roberta breathes. "I asked for you, and you weren't here. You were lost."

"Timothy was gone, Mom. But he's okay." Please let him be okay.

"Timothy?"

"He's okay. He's in Vancouver. He's safe."

Roberta frowns. "I don't. Understand. Who is Timothy?"

"Timothy, Mom. *Timothy.* He went to Vancouver, months ago. I've been watching over him. Like you wanted."

"I don't know who you're talking about."

Is this what the doctor meant? "Mom. He's your own fucking son."

"Don't swear," Roberta whispers, and for an instant, Lilah relaxes. "And don't... make up stories. That's not. Very nice."

"Mom." She pulls away. "*Timothy.* Of course you remember Timothy."

"I remember you," says her mother. She is puzzled, once more falling asleep. Yet her eyes are calm and clear now. Medication? Release? "I remember *you*, Delilah." She turns her head away, and sleeps.

Lilah stays on the bed until it's dark and listens to Roberta breathe. The nurses come and ago. God dances around the room, around them both. Capricious and clever, dark and wanting. God, whom she has begged to save her brother. Who has given her instead a man with a beautiful voice, a man with a soul so deep she can't tell where it ends. God in a trench coat and smooth leather shoes.

In the morning, the doctors tell her that it's likely Roberta won't wake up. That she could sleep like this for days or weeks. No one knows.

"What should I do," she says. She speaks to the young doctor and stares at the floor.

"Did she leave an advanced directive?"

Lilah blinks. "What?"

"I'm sorry," the doctor says, blushing. "Did she say anything, or write anything. About what to do if something like this happened."

"Nothing," she says. "It happened fast this time." Cancer in the breast. Cancer in the heart, the lungs, the liver.

"Is there someone else who might be able to help?"

She laughs. "There's no one."

"You should talk to someone," he says. "We have a therapist here at the hospital—"

"Not a therapist," she says. She breathes deeply and tries not to lose it, not in front of Dr. Sand with the hesitant smile. Then she says it again. "There's no one."

"Isn't there a son?" The doctor checks his chart. "She's listed here as having two dependants. Your brother?"

"He's gone," Lilah says dully. She has sent him away. And now Roberta will die and he won't know. "I'll just—I'll need to think about everything."

"Of course." Dr. Sand nods. "Let me know if there's anything I can do."

"Thank you."

"You're welcome," says the doctor. He blushes again and moves down the hall.

She stares after him, then stumbles to a chair and puts her forehead in her hands. People walk past her—feet slap hurriedly against the tile, others shuffle along, the slide of paper slippers quiet, unmistakable. At the other end of the hall lies the entrance to the hospital cafeteria; if she listens very carefully she can hear the faint clink of utensils, the clatter of plates. Laughter.

She gets up, eventually, and makes her way back to Vancouver.

It is raining in her city. The bus shelter is narrow and cramped. The man in front of her coughs something into his hand, then shivers with the damp. Everything around them is grey, dark, cold. The bus is little better. Lilah crawls into a window seat and watches the world rush by. She could get off the bus now and find another one that might take her somewhere entirely different. Seattle. The Interior. Or she could stay here, by this grimy window, until the bus reaches its end, and then start walking. Fade into the landscape, dissolve into the air like water.

But she disembarks at her old stop, and she's in front of her apartment, then in the foyer, then climbing up the stairs. She unlocks her apartment door and opens it.

He's there, in the hall, in front of her.

"Delilah."

Lilah drops her bag. "Jesus fuck."

Israel takes two steps and pushes the door shut. "I told you," and he's so close, his voice hot in her ear, "not to take the Lord's name in vain."

She closes her eyes. "How the fuck did you get in?"

"You left the door open." He stands over her, quiet. His arm is taut against the door.

"I never leave the door open." She tries for bravado but the words are a whisper. "Did you break in? I wouldn't put it past you. You followed me before."

Israel chuckles and traces a finger down her cheekbone. "Ah, but I am not going to follow you everywhere, Delilah. That would hardly befit a gentleman, no? Get your things," he says, his voice crisp. "Emmanuel is waiting for us."

"I was going to tell you something," she says. Forcing the words out before she loses her nerve.

"Oh?" Israel flexes his wrist.

"Take me," she says.

His eyebrows go up. "Delilah, how very kind of you. But surely you realize that that happened long ago?"

"I mean—you don't need to worry about Timothy. He's gone. He doesn't have a . . . hold . . . on me anymore." The anguish is so sharp she can't breathe. She turns her palms up and says it again. "You can take me. All of me."

"An offering!" He smiles. "How quaint."

"There's nothing *quaint* about it," she snaps. She holds tight to the fury and doesn't look away. "Do you want me or not?"

"But of course." He steps forward so that he's directly in front of her. His body blocks the light from the window. "I have wanted you for a long time."

"Yeah," she says. She tries to shrug but can't quite pull it off. "I know."

Israel laughs. "And haven't you waited for me?" he says softly. He steps even closer, traces a finger down her cheek. "Haven't you hungered for something else all these years? You were a child who saw holes in the nighttime sky, Delilah. Don't think I didn't notice, even then."

How is it that these words can still excite her, even as the kernel of fear in her stomach threatens to explode? She wants him. She wants him more than any man she's ever known. How terrifying, that she can be one thing and another all at once. And as Israel takes her hand and pulls her back into the hall, down the stairs and out into the nighttime air, she wonders if perhaps she was wrong about everything. Maybe salvation and damnation do not lie in Israel's hands after all, but her own.

ONE

He woke, and the light came off him in waves. Bright light, white light, light that wasn't warm. He looked up at the ceiling and spread his fingers, and rays leapt out from his fingers like sunshine. In his ears, a constant hum.

Chickenhead sat on top of the dresser, across from the bed. She twitched her tail and stared at him—wary, unsure. He stood and held out his hand. She did not jump down, did not come to him.

"Chickenhead," he said softly. "Chickenhead." It's me. It's still me. She didn't move.

Sam flexed his fingers, as he had flexed the wings so many times before, and watched the shadows leap and dance along the floor. Then he was walking, through the doorway, down the hall, down into the kitchen. Father Jim stood by the stove and took something out of the oven. Garlic, chicken, lemon juice. Sam stood at the entrance and watched the scene, the light pooling before him.

"Sam," said the priest, without looking. "Are you all right?"

The light. He was the light. "Timothy?"

"He just came back," said the priest. He turned, slid the oven mitts off his hands.

"She was afraid," Timothy said, coming into the room. The same light shone around his head, his hands. "She told me to go." Then his face relaxed, and the light dimmed. "She doesn't hate me."

"Why was she afraid?" Sam asked. He stepped closer, so that his light meshed with that of the boy.

"She's in trouble," Timothy whispered. "I don't know what to do." Up close, Sam could see fever in his eyes, hysteria only just kept in check. He lifted a hand and touched Timothy's forehead out of habit. Touched skin, touched stone, a void, a great gaping black maw. He pulled his hand away.

"Did you sleep well?" asked the priest, oblivious. "I came in and you were dead to the world. The cat wouldn't leave your side."

"Yes," he said. He glanced again at Timothy and then away. "I'm sorry. All I seem to do now is sleep."

"If you need to sleep, you need to sleep." Father Jim shrugged. "Who am I to argue?"

"The noise." Timothy nodded to Sam. "You hear the noise now, don't you."

A hum. A light that shone beyond and above him, through it all.

"This is the voice of God," said the boy. "This is what it has to say."

Father Jim, who had paused in the act of bringing lettuce freshly washed from the sink, put his hands down on the counter and took up a knife. "That may well be," he said, calm as ever, "but before God says anything, I suggest we eat. Sit down, both of you."

"I can't," said Timothy.

"Please," Sam said. They both sat. Sam watched the priest spoon out food and thought of Bryan, who was across an ocean now. He tasted nothing. He saw Timothy spoon a mouthful, close his eyes.

"I can't taste it," said the boy. "Every time I saw my sister I had to pretend that I could do it, that I was hungry—but everything I see is full of colour, and everything I touch is grey dust." He turned to the priest and let his fork fall to the plate. "I can't see beyond them. Everything is about the wings. Everything is about the light."

"It'll be all right, Timothy," Sam said. He reached across and squeezed the boy's hand, spoke with a certainty he didn't feel. "You'll see."

"You don't know." Timothy wrenched his hand away. "You don't know what happens next. And neither does he." He laughed. He pulled himself off the chair, still laughing, then stumbled out of the kitchen, down the hall. The guest bedroom door opened, slammed.

"He'll be all right," said the priest. "He just needs to sleep."

"Sleep won't help him," Sam said. "I sleep, and every time I wake up now, things are different." Light, spilling from his hands. He sighed. Chickenhead meandered over and jumped up into his lap. She went about making a nest, her paws on his legs slow and methodical until she found her spot and nestled in, a soft weight against his thighs. He ran a hand through her fur and felt it, that dark, constant rumble. "Is it better," he said then, "to believe wholly, or not at all?"

"You can't believe wholly," said the priest. "Or not at all.

One makes you an idiot, and the other brings you nothing but despair."

"Which one?"

Father Jim waved his hand. "It changes. All the time."

Sam thought about this, and ate as much of the chicken as he could. "So which one do you choose, then?" he asked. "How do you *know*?"

"You don't know." Father Jim said, his voice sad and sure. "God changes. *And* God is always the same. You and me—we're in God's shadow, Sam. We're always one step behind."

Timothy staggered into the kitchen late the next morning, his wings ragged, streaked with ash. They stank. Sam pushed him into the shower and left new clothes on the guest bed. There were feathers between the sheets. Feathers on the bed and a trail of ash leading back to the door.

He stared at it all for a moment and then went back to his room. Yes, there were feathers between his sheets too, and even as he watched, the feathers crumpled into ash. He heard the guest room door open and close, and the scuffle of Timothy pulling on the pants, the shirt. Then footsteps, and the boy knocked on his door.

"Hello," he said. The door opened.

"Hello." Timothy held his hand against the door. His other hand, loose against his hip, held Sam's old, red woollen hat. "My sister," he said.

"Yes."

"What do I tell her, Sam? What do I say?"

"Your sister," he said, remembering. "She's in trouble."

"Yes," Timothy whispered. "How do I tell her that God will save her, so that she knows? How do I make her listen?"

"Maybe God isn't going to save her," Sam said gently. "Maybe God's just waiting. Like us."

Timothy shook his head. "God will save her," he said. "I can feel it."

Sam looked at him and marvelled at how he could know. "It doesn't matter what you say," he said. "What you do, when you're with her—that's what matters. That's what she'll remember."

Timothy nodded. "Thank you," he said. "I'm going to find her."

Sam turned back to his room and listened. The front door opened and closed.

The standing mirror showed him a thin man with hollowed cheeks and long, pale hands. He touched a finger to the glass and it was cool, seamless. The mirror over the bed caught this reflection so that there was another Sam, another finger to the glass. Behind that another, and another. An endless line of men, of wings. Infinity. Forever, right there in front of him, his finger marking the spot where it began.

—

Sometime in the night, the boy came home. Sam, lying awake on his bed, heard the front door open and close, and then the shuffle of the boy's feet as he moved down the hall. The footsteps slowed as they approached Sam's door, then stopped.

"Sam?"

He sat up. "Timothy. Come in."

Timothy pushed the door open a crack and peeked into the room, then opened it further. Light from the hallway, and the boy, slid across the floor and over the bed. His wings cast a quivering shadow into the room.

"Did you find her?" Sam said when Timothy didn't speak.

The boy paused for a moment and nodded. "I did." He frowned. "She told me to go away."

He sat up. "What?"

"She's in trouble, and I don't think I can save her." Timothy stepped closer to the bed, whispering now. "It's all wrong, Sam."

Sam moved off the bed so that his own light mingled with Timothy's. The light that shone from both of them was so cold as to be almost blue, while the light from the hallway was golden, inviting, warm. He put a hand on the boy's shoulder. "You don't know that."

"I'm *supposed* to save her," the boy said. "Isn't that what God wants me to do?"

"I thought we didn't know what God wants either of us to do," Sam said. He took Timothy's hands and held them fast between his own.

"I hoped." Timothy's voice broke. "I prayed so hard. There's nothing for me if I can't help her. There's no reason to stay."

"Don't say that," Sam said. "Chickenhead would be so hurt." Even as he joked he felt the words become heavy, useless. Terror throbbed in his abdomen, sudden and dark.

Timothy managed half a smile. "Chickenhead has you," he said. He pulled his hands away. "And I have nobody. Why would God make me so lonely, Sam?"

"You're not alone." Sam reached forward and hugged him, careful of the wings, knowing it was not the same thing, being lonely and being alone. He wished for wisdom, for the words of Father Jim. But even words were beginning to desert him now. So instead he held the boy and said nothing.

—

"Sam. *Sam.*" It wasn't a shout, and yet the word carried through the house. He threw off the covers, stumbled out of the bed. He would have fallen but the wings pushed out and knocked against the bedside table, the bookcase, and calmed him where he stood. The call came again.

"*Sam.*"

He ran down the hall and into Timothy's room. The boy was on the floor, convulsing, his wings crumpled against the wood. Father Jim held his head. He looked up as Sam entered.

"I heard him fall out of bed," he said. The boy thrashed again, and moaned. "*Sam.*"

He knelt and spread the wings. "I'm here, Timothy." He moved in front of Father Jim, sat down, took the boy's head into his lap. "It's all right."

"Is this. What it feels like?" the boy whispered. He shook. "Death?"

"I don't know. Is this death?" Sam looked up at the priest and remembered a miracle by the side of the road, the deep green stillness of the trees. Chickenhead. The deer. Life and death. And something else.

He touched the boy's forehead and this time saw a woman with dark hair, a young boy. He could feel their sadness in his bones.

Timothy looked up at him. "I dreamed about them," he whispered. "The boy—he's lost. And the mother—she wants to believe in God. But I didn't know what the dreams meant. I didn't want to believe them, Sam. I wanted the dreams to be about my sister." His hand, blue-veined and strong, clutched Sam's arm. "I think—I think I need to go to them, to where they are."

"You're not going anywhere." He cradled Timothy's head

in his lap. Remembered, as if from a distant war, the face of the student who had died. "Timothy, we'll call an ambulance. You'll be all right. You will."

"But this is not death," said the boy, suddenly convinced. "You only think that it's death—you forget who you are. Sam." He stretched out a hand and the cat licked it calmly. Sam spared a moment to wonder: what else had she seen, did she know? Nine lives. The wings, the light, this boy, strewn across his path. Did she understand any of it? Or did she build her life around it, and make sense of what she could? She was wary, yet she hadn't stopped purring.

Then Timothy put his own hand against Sam's forehead. The calm wavered, and for a moment—one scintilla of time—he looked like a boy again. "*Oh,*" he said. "*Oh.*"

"Timothy?" said Father Jim, his voice sharp. "Tim—what do you see?"

"I was wrong," the boy whispered. And he smiled—a smile so dazzling it broke the heart. Then he disappeared.

There was no other word for it—he disappeared. He was there and then not there, just as Chickenhead had been dead and then not-dead those weeks ago. The clothes he'd been wearing crumpled to the ground. Sam held his hands around empty space for one more moment, and then dropped his arms to the floor.

"He's gone," he said.

"He's *gone.*" Father Jim was shaken, pale. "He just *disappeared.*"

"Yes." Sam felt calm. He heard the humming, saw the light stretch out from his fingertips, dance around the face of the priest. Could he see it? "It will be all right, Father."

"I—I need a drink," the other man said. He stood, and shook a little on his feet. "Can I get you a drink, Sam?"

"I'll come with you," Sam said. He followed the priest out into the hall, down to the kitchen. The room was dark—Sam spread his hands and watched the light from his skin touch the ceiling.

Father Jim had a new bottle of Scotch on the counter. He poured two liberal glasses and handed one to Sam.

Sam twisted his hands around the glass. "I wonder what's happening to him." A boy with dark hair and a broken heart. A mother who wanted to believe in God. And an angel, gone to them both. They drank in unison without meaning to, clinked their glasses against the counter at the same time. Chickenhead jumped on the counter and wound between them. He didn't shoo her off—he didn't have the energy.

"What should I be feeling right now?" asked the priest. "They don't teach you about this in seminary."

"Maybe they don't know," said Sam. Timothy, convulsing on the ground. Lying prone on the street, rocking on the other side of the guest room door. Sam reached for the whiskey and topped up his glass, then the priest's. Light filtered through the glass and the liquid. Eternal, bright. "Maybe this is what we all become."

"The glory of God," said the priest suddenly, *"is a human being fully alive.* St. Irenaeus."

"This doesn't feel like being alive." Yet where else could he see colours like this, be brought to his knees by the sound of the wind? This felt—it felt like much more than being alive. *"All, everything that I understand, I understand only because I love."*

"That's nice," said the priest. "It sounds biblical."

Sam shook his head. "It's Tolstoy. From *War and Peace*."

Father Jim shrugged. "No matter," he said. "I think God would approve." He took the bottle and upended it over his glass. He poured Sam another glass, and another. They sat like this, silent, and drank the whiskey until it was gone.

He lay in bed and thought of what he'd seen. A mother, a child. And that other face that had come to him, just for an instant—deep grey eyes, another sharp nose, a mouth twisted in sorrow.

Then the face dissolved, and in its place came nausea so violent, so overwhelming that he wondered for an instant if he'd also disappeared, become nothing more than roiling dark. When he opened his eyes, his fingers were clenched so hard around his sheets they looked like translucent, blue-streaked bone. Something else here that he was missing—God, elusive, teasing, so far beyond him as to be laughable. Uneasy rumble in the stomach.

Time was ticking forward now, so fast and yet so slow. The cat stood wary guard by the door. Against him, for him, who knew. Only God, and God wasn't telling.

At some point in the early hours of that last Saturday morning, his dick disappeared. He woke up and shuffled into the bathroom, dropped his pants and there it *wasn't*. A network of blue veins that arced upwards across his pelvis, spreading out from his groin like some kind of cobalt snowflake. That was it.

He shouted into the bathroom air. Just as he had those few weeks ago—months, years, ages ago—when the wings had first appeared. This time, after Chickenhead ambled into the bathroom, there was a sudden thump on the door.

"Sam? Are you all right?"

He leaned against the bathroom counter and tried to breathe. Couldn't. Dots swam in front of his eyes. Orange dots, red dots. Purple. The world spun. The snowflake did not go away.

"I'm—I'm all right," he said weakly. "Sorry. I'm okay."

He could feel the priest's hesitation on the other side of the door. "Are you sure?"

"I'm sure. I had a—bad dream."

Pause. "All right. If you need anything, I'm—"

"Across the hall," he said, sharper than he meant. "I know."

Another pause, then footsteps moving away.

He didn't have to turn on the light but did it anyway, and slumped against the counter, pants pooled at his ankles. He reached down and touched the snowflake. Touched soft skin stretched tight over veins, a shimmer of blue stretching up to his abdomen.

When he looked into the mirror, everything else looked the same. That was his nose. Those were his ears, his eyes. His teeth. Or were they chipped, the teeth, slightly pointed, slightly not quite the same? Were those really his irises—had his eyes always been that dark? He sucked in a breath and grasped the counter. Pressure locked in his knuckles.

His knuckles. The angel's knuckles. Him. It.

He opened the bathroom door and slipped across the hall, back to his room. He shut the door and spread his palms, so that the light arced above his head and shone out through the window like a flare from the sun. The bedroom was a gallery of dark, muffled shapes, the lattice on the window stark and clear and confining. He closed his eyes and searched for it—the noise, that feeling he'd had when speaking to the boy in the kitchen. The light was infinite and cold. Timothy was gone now. He was alone.

It. Could he be a man now? Why was it that he couldn't see Julie's face at all, couldn't see his mother but in shadow, felt his thoughts flicker out to the other man in the house with mild curiosity, as though he didn't actually know who he was? Of course he knew. Father Jim.

"Fa-ther Jim," he said. He left the room. He walked to the back, and into the garden, and held the door open out of habit, even though Chickenhead wasn't there. He let the door slide shut and stepped barefoot onto the grass. The sun was a faint grey line on the horizon. Frost touched everything—the footprints he left were deep and green. He flexed his toes and felt the soil cold beneath his feet, and then an answering hum from the ground travelled up his legs and connected with the hum in his centre. It was all he could hear. A hum, a pulse of life.

He walked out from the garden to the street. The angel walks the street and all is blue and green and red. The angel leaves bright footprints on the sidewalk. Even the air shimmers. Light flows like water from doorways.

The angel is a doorway—this much it knows, this much it remembers. But to what?

—

"Sam. *Sam.*" The priest held him, one hand around his head.

He was falling. Sliding away from all he knew, all he remembered. *Is this what it feels like, death?*

"Take care of Chickenhead," he said. "If. . . just if."

"Sam." Father Jim's voice was sharp. "You're not *dying.*"

He looked away, across the asphalt. The sun shone a pale ivory over the trees. "I'm not dying," he agreed. But the boy was gone now, and with him, an anchor that Sam hadn't even realized was there. What was that he'd said? *There's no reason to stay*. He pushed his hands into the dirt and focused. The hum from the ground became the hum in his head.

"I saw you," said the priest. With his voice, another anchor, a hand to pull him from the dark. "You walked out onto the lawn and collapsed." He held Sam's shoulder hard. "Would you like me to stay here with you?"

"I'll be fine," he said. "It was just a spell."

"You shouldn't be alone right now."

Is the angel alone? Or is everyone else alone, and lost? "I have—the cat. Chickenhead."

"I don't know." Father Jim frowned. He was doing a visit today, down at a neighbouring church. "I think I should cancel."

"Go," Sam said, forcing the words out. "You shouldn't stay because of me." Then a joke, a weak one, just to show that he could still do it, that he was still *Sam*. "Think of all the souls that will be lost without you."

The priest snorted, and helped him up. "Or the souls that will lose their way when I arrive."

"That's cynical," Sam said, and gasped. He closed his eyes and let the world reverberate in colour beyond him. "Even for you."

"God loves a cynic," the priest said, but his tone was unconvincing. "There's just no greater challenge."

Sam laughed. He wanted to say thank you. To weep. "He's met his match in me, then, I suppose."

"Yes." Father Jim smiled. "But then, you've made great work of the Almighty, Sam. God will be thankful, I am sure."

After the priest had gone, Sam walked through the house, touching everything. The photos, the pillows, the clothes that had belonged to Timothy, the clothes they still hadn't moved from the floor. The connection to Father Jim grew fainter. He went outside so that he wouldn't be there when the priest came back. So that he wouldn't disappear and leave the priest alone.

He walked as far from his old life as he could, and found that his footsteps had taken him to the front of the old cathedral, where he had said goodbye to his mother only weeks ago. This cathedral. Yes. He spread his wings and stepped inside. The air smelled of stone and earth and sorrow.

He saw the priest at the far end of the building—the small priest, the one with the dark hair—and walked toward him. The priest, hearing his footsteps on the stone, turned to Sam and spread his hands.

"Welcome," he called.

"Fa-ther," he said. Moving his mouth slow around the words. "Fa-ther Mar-io."

"Yes." But the priest frowned. "I am sorry. I forget your name."

Name. He blinked, and remembered. "Sam. It's Sam."

"Sam..." The priest frowned again. "No. I don't remember a Sam. Perhaps we haven't been introduced?"

He held out his hand, and unfurled the wings so that they spanned the centre aisle. White wings, the tips of the feathers becoming darker now as he watched. He was himself, just for a moment. "Are you sure, Father? I remember you."

"No," and the priest took his hand. He smiled. "I always remember a face."

"Do you remember Carol?" he asked. "Carol Connor?"

"Ah, yes." The smile disappeared. "So tragic, that. I see her husband almost every day."

"And her son?"

The priest frowned. "Son? They had no children. They were alone."

Alone. He nodded, took one step back. "I see."

"Were you a friend of Carol's?" the priest asked. His own eyes were blurred now, unaware. A miracle come down to touch him, there and then gone. "I do not remember seeing you at the funeral."

"Yes," he said softly. "Yes, I was." He took another step backward, shook his head. "Forgive me, Father." Fa-ther. "I didn't mean to bother you." Then he turned on his heel and began to walk back to the entrance.

"Sam?" But he didn't look back, didn't answer. Stepped beyond the door and into the grey light of the day and it was there now, *the noise*, everywhere. He thought of Father Jim, who might forget him now. Timothy. Julie. Bryan. His mother. An ordinary life, an extraordinary life. He thought of Emma and was sad. Then he turned into the alleyway behind the church and let the light spill onto the ground, up into the trees.

"*Mraiou.*" The cat. His cat. She stepped out from behind the tree and came to him, stood by his feet. He looked and could not quite believe. His cat. Chickenhead.

"This is just the beginning," he said. The word rumbled in his mouth, rumbled the ground beneath his feet.

He let everything go.

The cat stood watching him, and did not say a word.

—

The cat walks up to the angel, mewling. The cat winds itself around the angel's feet. *Mraiou. Mraiou.*

"Go," says the angel. The cat stares. It is upset, anxious. The angel hooks its foot under the cat and pushes it away. It hisses, howls, stops. It is only a cat.

"Go," the angel says again. The angel has a message to deliver. It opens a hand and lets light stream out from its fingertips. Then it turns and begins to walk away. The cat runs beside the angel for a moment, mewing. The angel stops one last time. And one thing flickers at the edge of the angel's mind. A memory.

"Chickenhead," it says softly. "*Go.*" This time the cat sits, and when the angel walks away it does not follow. The cat. The animal. The thing with fur.

When the angel reaches the corner, it looks back and sees the animal sitting there, waiting. Fear dribbles from the animal onto the ground. Fear and something else—something darker, deeper, more alone. The angel keeps walking and does not understand. The street becomes a tunnel, the tunnel becomes a corridor, and the corridor moulds beneath the angel's feet until it bears the groove and the dull shimmer of stone.

The angel walks. There is no memory. There is only God.

Finally, at the end of the corridor, a doorway wreathed in shadow. On the other side of the door, a woman. A woman with blonde hair, and despair deep within her soul. The angel walks through the doorway and dissolves into the air.

There is a message to deliver. There is no time for sadness.

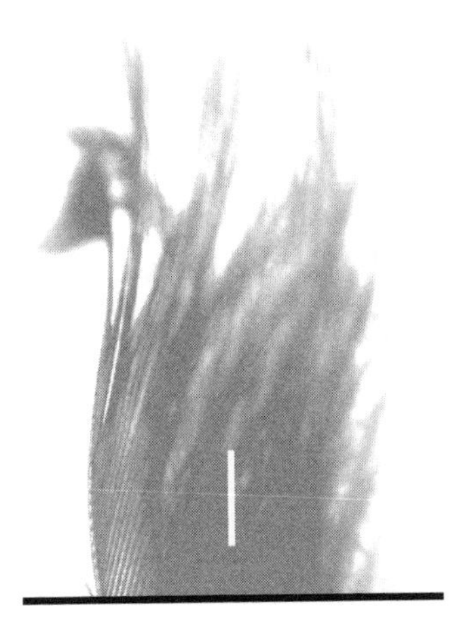

SUNDAY

She dreams of wings of her own that burst from her back like light, like a migraine given form. They split her skin and push from her shoulder blades like children. She feels it all—the stretch of cartilage and sinew, the growth of each tiny feather. She stumbles out of her bed and watches in the mirror as they grow, lengthen out into the room. White wings, so bright they reflect light back into her eyes.

Suddenly her bones feel lighter than air. She stands at the edge of her bed and leaps out of the window, and the wings stretch into the air as though she's done this all her life. The currents carry her like a lover. People scurry far beneath her like the tiny ants they are—this way, then that. Meetings and family and money and fights. She looks for her brother and does not find him. She is flying above, beyond the world.

She wakes in Israel's bed, sore and alone. He leaves no note. She dresses quickly and runs away from the house, into the rain.

MONDAY

The day passes slowly. Israel comes in late and then leaves the office at lunch hour—without speaking to her, without speaking to anyone. Lilah counts her times tables as her hands move over the keyboard. Minutes. Typing. Penny's watchful eye. One times one is one, one times two is two.

He comes back an hour later, frowning, and stops by her desk before continuing to his office.

"Delilah." He smells of the cold and the ocean.

"Did you have a nice walk?" She keeps typing and doesn't look up. "A nice beachside stroll?"

Israel chuckles. "I did." Then he frowns. "You left, yesterday. You did not say goodbye."

Two times two is four. Two times five is ten. "I might say the same for you."

"I do not need to explain myself to you," he says.

She still doesn't look up. "And I do?"

For a moment he is silent, the power of his gaze unmistakable even from where she sits, her eyes cast low. She hears him shrug. "No matter. I merely wanted to remind you—we're having dinner again, on Thursday. The Indian restaurant."

Lilah nods. Her fingers keep moving. "Fine. I'll be there."

"Of course you will." He turns to go to his office.

"Israel." Now she looks up. Across the desk, Debbie is staring at the both of them, transfixed.

"Yes?"

"Did you find what you were looking for?"

"Ah," he says. "No, Delilah, I did not." He smiles faintly. "But this does not surprise you, no?"

She shrugs—the relief is so immediate and strong, she can't say anything. The phone rings, and Debbie picks it up.

"Hello?" Pause. "Yes it is. . . Yes, she's right here." She puts the phone on hold and nods to Lilah. "It's for you."

Lilah picks up the receiver and switches the call to her line. "Hello?"

"Delilah?" says a voice. "Delilah Greene?"

"Yes."

"Delilah, this is Dr. Sand." Dr. Sand, of the hesitant smile. He's not smiling now—she can tell even over the phone. "I'm afraid I have some bad news."

Israel has not moved. "Yes?"

"Your mother," he says. "I'm afraid she passed away a few minutes ago. There was nothing we could do."

"I see." She stares at Israel, at the quiet dark of his eyes. He is smiling.

"I'm very sorry," Dr. Sand says. "But we'll need you to come in to sign some papers and inform us as to what needs to be done with the body. Did your mother leave any instructions?"

Roberta is a body now, only that. "I don't know." If she is buried, the worms will eat her. If they burn her, the priests will hesitate to guide her soul.

"We have people here," he says again. Now that it has happened, Dr. Sand is calm and assured. "People who can talk to you. When can you come in?"

"I can be there tomorrow."

"That's good." He pauses. "I really am so sorry."

"That's all right. I'll speak to you in the morning." She hangs up. She hasn't taken her eyes from Israel.

"More time off?" His voice is calm, entirely unsurprised. "Delilah, this is getting to be a habit with you."

"Just a few days." The words are like marbles in her mouth. "My mother is . . . dead."

Debbie gasps. "Oh, Lilah. I'm so sorry."

"Indeed." Israel nods to her. But he does not move. She could be telling him the date, or his own name. Something he's known for ages. "I am also sorry. Take all the time you need, Delilah."

Three times four is twelve. Eight times eight is sixty-four. Her mother and brother are gone now, and she lives in Vancouver alone. "I might need lots of time," she says slowly.

"I have all the time in the world for you," he says, not conscious of Debbie, or not caring. "Surely, Delilah, you know that by now."

TUESDAY

She had planned to take the early ferry; instead, she goes downtown and looks for Timothy. She doesn't find him, which is not surprising. But she walks the daytime streets anyway, and when she asks, no one remembers who Timothy is, or knows where he might have gone. The people who recognized him such a short time ago—these nice people he found on the streets—no longer remember when they look at his picture. She doesn't understand.

"But you sat with him—with both of us—right over there." This to Nadia, the woman in the old mink coat who lives in the alleys of East Hastings. "How can you not remember? We ate olives. You said you loved olives."

"I *do* love olives," Nadia says, and she has that fuzzy smile that Lilah remembers from her travels years ago, when she was speaking a language that no one understood. "I'm sorry. I don't remember."

Or this, from one of the bakery men in the West End. "Him? Nah. I'd remember a face like that. Eyes to break your heart."

Or this, from the cupcake woman. "Poor soul." She is warm and matronly and her hand on Lilah's shoulder is sympathetic, detached. The hand of a stranger. "I'll keep my eye out, dear, and let you know." She asks for Lilah's number. Lilah scrawls it, helplessly, across the back of a cupcake napkin.

"You'll tell me if you find him," Lilah says, echoing her mother. "You'll let me know that he's okay?"

"Of course." The cupcake woman—her name tag says BETH—squeezes her hand. She has already turned back to her icing. "I'm sure he's fine, love. He'll turn up soon enough."

Suddenly she's so angry she could spit—she leaves the bakery instead, and lets the rage carry her right to the office, and when she's through the front door she tells Penny she's leaving.

"I thought you were going to the hospital," says Penny. "Mr. Riviera said you were on leave."

"I *am* on leave," Lilah says. *Mr. Riviera*. But of course—to the unsuspecting Pennys of the world, he will forever be only the boss. "I'm just not coming back."

Penny blinks. And then, "Do you think he'll pay for everything?" Black-haired Penny. "Just because you let him fuck you?"

"This has nothing to do with him." Lilah scowls back at

her and wonders why it has taken her so long to let go. "I don't want to make coffee runs for the rest of my life. That's it."

"Do you have something else lined up?" asks Debbie when Penny stalks out of the room.

"No." There must be more to life than getting coffee, than staring at a screen. Something. She grips the edge of the desk and closes her eyes, overwhelmed by nausea.

"I know it's a shock," Debbie says slowly, "with your mother, and Timothy, and—everything. But please be careful, Lilah. Don't make any rash decisions."

Too late. Panic lodges in her throat. "I'm not, Debbie. Trust me."

"What about your apartment?" Sweet Debbie. "Do you have any savings? What are you going to do?"

Lilah picks through the papers on her desk and takes her mementos—this pen she likes, this stone that Timothy brought her from the shore. Slowly, her composure comes back. Her fingers close around the pebble. It is hard and smooth. "I don't know. I'll figure it out."

"Does Israel know?" Debbie asks. "Did he get you another job?"

"No." She's not sure if this is lying.

Debbie's mouth turns down at the corners, but she nods. "I see." Then, surprisingly, she leans forward and gives Lilah a hug. "I'll miss you," she says. "But I'm sure you'll have a grand adventure. Good luck. Call me?"

"Thank you. And yes, I will." This, now—this is lying. Lilah hugs her back, and then walks out the door. She does not tell Debbie that Israel's number is safe in her phone, that she'll show up for dinner on Thursday, dressed appropriately and exactly on time. She does not admit that she could run away to Victoria and find him there anyway, that the energy between them is intoxicating even in the midst of her grief. Who would understand?

At the hospital, Dr. Sand is all business, efficient and gentle and calm. Suddenly he seems much older. He puts Lilah in the care of Maria, a woman with warm brown eyes and ample breasts. She sits with Lilah in the hall, and moves down her clipboard.

"Did she ever speak about donation, your mother?" They are too late for organs, now, and so Maria is asking about *tissues*. Skin and bone and heart valves—in the end, this is all we leave to the world.

"No," Lilah says. She has Roberta's clothes in her lap, her purse already open. There's no organ donor card. "But she might have wanted to. We didn't talk about things like that."

"What do you think she would want?" Maria asks.

"I think," Lilah says quietly, "she'd want to give. As much as she could." She fights the urge to ask if it is possible to harvest Roberta's faith just like her eyes—if they could take her mother's anger and her will and set it loose in the Vancouver air for Timothy to find.

They tick through all the boxes. Then there are other forms to sign, and crematoriums to call. "We can help you make funeral arrangements," Maria says. "It's a difficult time for everyone involved, we know."

"There is no 'everyone,'" Lilah says. "There's just me." And the church friends—church friends who sent a card, who did not visit. She stares at the floor, at the turned-in peak of her toes. More shoes shuffle past them. More voices rise up and down through the hall. Meetings and family and money and fights—it happens here too. "I just want the ashes," she says. She can sprinkle them in Roberta's garden, or across the water. Or maybe she can toss them out the window as she drives back to the ferry, and let Roberta ride the air, as if on wings.

"All right." Maria stands up, her clipboard in hand. She has seen many faces of death—she's not at all surprised. "We'll call them now."

Lilah signs the rest of the forms and then leaves the hospital. She picks her way slowly along the street. Before long, her footsteps bring her to Roberta's door. Another faded, peeling house in a neighbourhood of faded, peeling houses. She stops with her hand on the doorknob, suddenly afraid. Could Israel be waiting for her on the other side of the door?

She shakes her head and looks around. There is no black car on the street. No unmistakable Emmanuel shadow sitting calm behind the wheel. And the air—the air does not feel as heavy here as it does when Israel is around. No scent of cedar, no tremble of fear in her stomach. She rests her forehead against the wood and pauses anyway, just for a moment. Then she opens the door and walks into the front hall.

The house smells musty, as though it hasn't been opened in years. She drops her bags by the door and this time walks right to Timothy's room. Roberta kept it cleaner than the rest of the house—the bed is made and the clothes are hung neatly. Even his underwear are folded and pressed into place. Only the macramé crafts, which hang untouched on the wall, have begun to gather dust.

She stretches out on the bed and draws the duvet around her, then flips on her side and curls into a ball. The house is empty. The room is empty. The air through her lungs feels empty too.

The crematorium has Roberta's ashes prepared and ready for Lilah by early afternoon. She collects them at two, chooses a plain and practical *carrying container* (no ornate urn for Roberta, whose sole foray into excess ended in the macramé that terrorizes the walls), and heads back to the house.

She cleans for the rest of the afternoon, the music on Roberta's tinny old kitchen radio turned as high as it will go. Beethoven. Mozart. Rachmaninoff. She sweeps up dust from the corners. She scrubs the kitchen sink until it gleams. She heaves the living room furniture against one wall and forces the vacuum across the carpet—the floor was beige when Roberta bought the house all those years ago but now it is an ugly, mottled brown. She takes the plants outside and lines them up on the back porch, then deadheads the flowers until the porch is littered with rusted petals. Her thumbs are slick with grime.

In the bathroom, just about to wash her hands, she notices a line of green under her thumbnails. Chlorophyll. And a clear, sticky residue that has coated the inside of her palms. The plants, it would seem, still harbour secrets. In time they will unfurl, and show their green faces to the rain.

She looks into the mirror, and she is weeping.

She goes to bed, and when she wakes some hours later, the house is enveloped in the hesitant darkness that comes at three a.m. She stands up and drags the duvet with her, out of the bedroom and down the hall. The cover trails behind her.

She walks through the kitchen and lets herself out into the cold, and now she is once more on her mother's back porch, staring up at the stars.

"I hate you," she says. Then she says it again, louder. When she breathes in, it's as though the universe falls all at once into her lungs—she is tiny, she is endless. "I *hate* you!"

Nothing happens. There is nothing above her but empty sky, nothing below her but flowers that wilt and decay and return.

They are, after all, only words.

THURSDAY

When she gets home, she unlocks her door and he's there, in her hallway. Again.

"Delilah," he says. "I've been calling."

"I went to Victoria. Like I said."

He steps closer. "You're avoiding me. That's very rude."

She holds the doorknob to keep from trembling. "You don't have a key. And you say I'm the one who's rude?"

He steps closer still, and touches a wisp of hair by her forehead. She flinches, and he smiles. "How curious, Delilah. One would think that you are almost afraid of me."

"Don't be ridiculous," she snaps.

"You left," he says quietly. "Penny tells me that you gave no notice. Also very rude."

"I want something else," she says.

He laughs at her. "What else, Delilah? What else could there possibly be for you?"

"I don't know." Her mouth is inches from his shoulder. She inhales and closes her eyes. It comes back so easily, like the flowers that even now are recovering on Roberta's porch. Terror, or excitement, or both.

"I've been looking for your brother," he says.

She opens her eyes. The knowledge is sudden, absolute.

"He's gone."

"Yes," he says. "He *is* gone. You are very thorough with your sacrifices." Then he shrugs and moves past her, toward the door. "No matter. Emmanuel will pick you up at seven tonight. You should wear the black dress, perhaps."

She laughs, she's so surprised. "You're fucking kidding me."

"I am not," he says. "We're leaving. This Saturday. We have much to speak of, you and I."

"And if I'm busy?"

He smiles. "Ah, but I have so much to give you, Delilah. You would be foolish to refuse." He opens the door and steps out into the hall. "Seven o' clock. Emmanuel will be waiting. We will go for dinner, and we will eat, and then we will begin to discuss the future."

"The future," she repeats. She speaks slowly, as though the words aren't quite real.

Tonight, at the restaurant, he will be funny and thoughtful and charming. She will drink and laugh, and climb into his car as though she has no clue as to how things will end.

"Everyone else is gone, Delilah." His smile is dark and cruel and endless. "I *am* your future—you have no one left."

He blindfolds her again and binds her so tightly to the bed that it hurts to move her hands. She whimpers and fights the bile rising in her throat. She can hear him moving around the room, taking off his clothes. The air smells of desire and fear.

He kneels at the end of the bed, before her. "You open your hand," he says, "and satisfy the desires of every living thing." Then he slides a finger inside her, and another, and suddenly he thrusts in his hand. She screams. It hurts so much that the world shimmers behind her eyelids.

He laughs. She screams and weeps and please please please stop. She arches her back and shudders, and his hand slides farther inside of her, pushes harder. He could push through and grasp her heart if he wanted, and squeeze it tight between his fingers until it became little more than dust.

He moves to pull out his hand, slowly, and then thrusts it forward, again and again. Her throat is raw. Salt and tears coat her lips. She shuts her eyes behind the blindfold and twists her wrists until they burn, until his laughter is a dark rumble against her abdomen, his mouth low and wet against her thigh.

Then, nothing. A moment, a pocket of calm so deep that her fists fall apart. She stops screaming. She lies silent, waiting, and as he draws his hand out the calm ebbs away and the rest of the world rushes in.

"I am going to make you a queen," he says.

And then his hand is inside her again, and she is praying, actually praying.

FRIDAY

The first priest she's spoken to in years has a beard and looks like a lumberjack. He walks with a peculiar kind of power, as though waiting to burst out from beneath his robes and skewer the world. Yet he seems sad, somehow, and tired. He's speaking to a girl when Lilah first comes into the church—a young woman with red hair that shines in the light from the windows. When the girl moves away from him and lets Lilah move up to take her place, she can see that the girl has been crying. Her eyes are deep and green, and so lonely that for a moment Lilah wants to squeeze her hand.

But the girl shuffles past her, and Lilah turns back to the priest. She sits across from him and shivers, broken and trembling under the weight of her own soul. She tells him her name.

"Delilah," he repeats. "That's lovely."

"Thank you."

He folds his hands across his knee. "What can I do for you?"

"It's been years since my last confession." She blurts the words like a guilty child. "It's been years since I was inside a church."

He nods. "And?"

"And..." And she has come, with the shattered bits of her life held fast between her hands. An offering. "Things are...happening now. I don't know what to do."

"So you came to the church."

"I—yes. Yes." She rubs her hands and blows on them, even though she isn't cold. She cannot stop shaking. "Should I confess?"

"If you think that will give you what you want, then yes." He frowns. "Are you all right?"

She stares at him and then at the stone beneath their feet. "I keep thinking," she says, "that things can't get worse. That I've gone as low as it is possible to go." Her voice is so soft he must bend down to catch the words. "And then I turn around, and I just keep sinking." Into the mattress, or into the plush leather seats of the car, her sobs so hard that it hurt to breathe. Emmanuel, who was silent as he drove her home the night before, had to help her to the door of her apartment as though she was an old lady, tired and infirm. "I don't see a way back now. How do I confess that?"

"Sometimes," the priest says, "it is not about confessing.

If you know what's in your heart, Delilah, and you offer that to God, that should be enough."

She twists her hands. "But what if it's not? What if things are happening to me in spite of my heart?"

"That's how all things happen," he says. "We are here to be pulled out of ourselves. Pulled to God or pulled to other people—it doesn't matter."

She is not prepared for the rush of emptiness this brings. She sits and stares at him, this lumbering man with his beard. "That's it?"

He sighs. "What more do you want me to say?"

"You're supposed to have answers. You're supposed to tell me what to do."

"I can't give you answers," he says. "This isn't about words. This—this isn't *math*, Delilah." He laughs. "If I had a dollar for every time I've said that, I would be a very rich man."

"I can't understand a God," she says, "that hides from me."

"And why shouldn't God hide from you?" the priest asks gently. "Why shouldn't God be deceitful, or unknowable, or terrifying? We betray God all the time. We are unknowable and terrifying to each other. So why not God?"

He is speaking to her, or perhaps to himself. She feels that whisper of doubt along her spine. "Isn't God supposed to be better than we are?" she asks bitterly.

"God is," and his voice is so sure that for a moment, she's almost convinced. Almost.

"I'm afraid," she says, her voice blunt and raw. "Where can I go if God has no answers?"

"Are you in trouble?" says the priest.

She laughs. Israel Riviera, waiting just for her. "You could say that."

"Then you want the police. Don't make the mistake of expecting God to do everything for you—"

"When a restraining order can do just as much?" she says, only half joking. The knowledge lies calm on his face. She wonders how many women have come here, broken and scared. Then she shakes her head. "My brother is gone," she tells him. "My brother is gone, and my mother is dead, and I don't know what to do. I need *something*." A voice. A miracle. God.

He stares at her for so long she begins to squirm. "I thought you looked familiar," he says, finally. "You have the same face. Except his eyes were blue."

If she was empty before, now she is bottomless, a sudden darkened void. "Timothy," she whispers. She reaches forward and clutches at the white folds of his robe. "You know where he is. *Tell me where he is.*"

"I don't," he tells her. "I don't know, Delilah." He covers her hand with his own. "All of this—this is bigger than either of us."

"Will I see him again?" she asks, relentless. "Is he sick? Take me to him. Take me to him, please."

He shakes his head. "I can't."

"He's dead," she says flatly. "He's dead, and you found him." And something, oh wretched, wretched miracle, brought her here.

"He's not dead," the priest says. "That would be easy."

She wants to ask what this means, *easy*. Instead, she lets go, and sits back, and stares at the way his collar catches neatly beneath his chin, at the tired fierceness of his eyes. The lumberjack priest. He reaches over and takes her hands again. They sit. They stare at each other. Outside, people mill about on the street, oblivious. Inside, the great roof of the cathedral rises above their heads, bearing down on them with prayer. The stones are hushed and silent, waiting.

"If he's not dead," says Lilah, "then what happened?"

Unexpectedly, he smiles. "God happened."

"God." Her voice is heavy and flat. Yet even as she says it, the word flows back into her mouth, like water, flows back into her lungs and heart and fills the nothing inside of her. It comes to rest, finally, in her abdomen, a warm golden dot that pulses with life, with possibility. "God," she says again.

And everything changes, and still everything is the same.

SATURDAY

She stays at home, and tries to stand him up, and he comes to find her anyway.

He beats her in the bedroom, in her kitchen, on the floor. He whips her with her own belt, and she feels the pain like coming out of the womb and tasting that first shock of air—clear and cold, infinitely deep. She offers him her shoulders, the mottled expanse of her back. She kneels before him and hides her breasts, her abdomen, the delicate skin of her ribcage. Her neck is bowed and ready.

"Delilah." His voice is so beautiful. "You cannot hide from me. When will you learn?" He cups her face and then slaps her, again, white-hot against the mouth. "We will leave tomorrow, instead. Emmanuel will pick you up at noon. And if you are not there, I will come and find you. I promise."

He leaves her on the bed, curled and shaking, blood at the corners of her mouth. She could not speak even if she wanted to. She watches him walk into the bathroom. Her heart beats very slowly. Caving in on itself, one chamber at a time. The sheets slip to the floor.

Israel dresses in the bathroom and leaves without saying goodbye. Lilah lies alone in a darkened room. Her breath wheezes in and out, like Roberta's. She closes her eyes and listens and yes, it is still there, inside of her, that humming golden dot. Night slides into morning. The shifting shadows across the backs of her eyes tell her that the sun is rising, creeping slowly through the window.

Then she opens her eyes, and it is not the sun, and she lies there and wonders if maybe God has heard her, after all.

SUNDAY

The angel standing in her bedroom doorway is tall and bald with pointed ears. Its lips are thin and pinched and its eyes are blue. The angel is naked, from what she can see, and shaking. It looks like someone's lost child—it could be her brother, except for the wings.

She's dreaming. Or she's been beaten so badly this time that it's a spectacular delusion. How many saints were raped and saw God?

"Can I help you?" Because she can't, on her life, think of what else to say.

The angel shivers. It splays its hands on either side of its face, blue-veined hands with long fingers, no nails. It shakes its head and rocks back and forth, keening in fits and starts. The skin between its legs is wrinkled and blue, a network of veins that congregate where its sex should be and spread outward, fading into white above the pelvis.

There's an angel standing in her doorway.

"Hell-o." The angel has a high voice, almost hysterical. The words are strange and clipped—triangle words coming out of a square mouth. "Hell-o. Li-lah."

"Can I *help* you?" This time, when the angel doesn't answer, Lilah turns and curls her legs over the other side of the bed. She reaches for her ratty bathrobe and places it delicately around her bruises.

"Li-lah," the angel says. "I bring you a message. From God."

So sharp, that spike of fear in her chest. She turns back to the angel. "Is it about Timothy?" she whispers.

"What?" The angel blinks, then shakes its head. "No." It stops and takes a breath. The sound echoes through her room, oddly vast. She blinks and sees air flowing into the angel's mouth—a gaping hole, black, a million stars. "It is not about... Timothy." The angel spreads its hands. "I am a messenger," it says. "I bring you a message from God." Then it frowns. "The message is..." and it brings its hands forward, folds them in a knot against its stomach. "The message is..." The angel stares for a moment, and then bows its head and moans. "I do not know."

Lilah blinks, focuses. The tips of the angel's wings are black, and fine black dust litters the floor around the door. The angel whimpers, shakes its head, draws the wings close around its face like a veil. Then it shuffles out of the room, down the hall.

God happened. God is... happening. God in front of her, around her, everywhere. There is no blue-white energy, no fizzle of electricity in her hands. Just a strange being, shimmering and impotent, passing through her house. By the time she gets to the kitchen, the angel is already sitting down. A bottle of whiskey lies open on the table.

She doesn't laugh. She can't laugh. "Where did you get that?"

The angel looks up, eyes unfocused. Its chest is shadowed,

overcome by ribcage—she sees dips and hollows, a layering of grey on white. "In the stove."

"In the cupboard, you mean."

"Yes. In the cupboard."

She takes two steps and tries to wrestle the glass from the angel's hand. Her skin burns when she touches its fingers—she jerks away and checks for swelling, finds nothing but her own unworthy flesh. Peach-coloured. The angel frowns and holds the glass of whiskey close to its chest.

"No," it says petulantly. "I *like* it." It tilts its hand in the air so that the light—from the angel, from the wings—filters through the glass. "I like the way it—shines." Then it looks away. "I have been waiting for you," it says in a small voice. "I've been waiting for so long."

A dream of a man, the water rising to his hand.

A spear, piercing her shoulder.

A deer, watching its life splinter into shards.

"Have I been waiting for you?" she whispers. "All this time?"

The angel frowns. "I have a message for you, from God."

Lilah sits down at the table—carefully, because it hurts to do anything. She tries to laugh, but her hands are shaking so badly she can't do it. When she speaks, her voice is only a whisper. "I always thought Timothy would bring me one of those."

The angel stares at her. "God," it says, its voice wistful, strange, "is full of surprises."

She sobs, brings a hand to her mouth. And then she looks—they both look—at her coat, crumpled on the floor, the bills hidden and waiting in the cuff of her sleeve. Her voice so calm that night at the restaurant, so apologetic, her fingers so deft and sure as he let her choose the tip. He was right—the service was much better this time around.

"Israel," the angel says.

She takes a breath. "What about him?"

The angel screws up its face. "He's not good for you, Lilah."

This makes her laugh hysterically. She shakes in her seat and wipes the tears from her eyes. "That's not news," she says when she can finally talk.

The angel spreads its hands. "You're wasting so much time."

Days ago she'd have had a retort for this, some kind of smartass remark. Now she opens her mouth and finds nothing. Instead, she clenches her fists and lets her fingers unfurl so that her palms lie open, asking. "Help me," she says finally.

The angel traces circles on the table. "You know," it says. "You know what you have to do." As odd and childlike as it is, the words themselves are deep, certain. Lilah thinks of her own life, and the shape that words can take, what they can do. Golden dot of possibility in her abdomen. Then she thinks of Timothy and Roberta, who are gone.

"How can you be so sure?" she says. The question would be bitter, except that she's not bitter anymore. She's too tired.

"I am not sure." The angel spreads its wings so that the table is blanketed in feathers. "I am only a messenger," it says. Then it shrugs. For a moment it sounds wistful, as though remembering a memory from far away. A memory oddly human, oddly real. "Whatever that means."

Lilah opens her mouth, and something roils up in her stomach. She jumps up from the table and runs to the bathroom, pukes into the toilet. Then she rests her forehead against the gritty tile, too drained to even cry.

"You're bleeding," says the angel, behind her.

"I know." She sobs into the floor, no tears. She will take

the money and leave, today. And Israel will follow, a different kind of angel altogether. He will follow, and she will run, even if it means that they will always be running, even if it means that she has to spend the rest of her life flying away.

"I will come," the angel says softly. "I was meant for you. You, above all others."

She almost laughs. "Doesn't God have better things to do?"

"But Lilah," the angel says, "there's nothing better than you." It places a hand on her back. A sudden warm rush flows from Lilah's spine down to her toes. She jerks up and around in surprise.

The angel smiles with pointed teeth, sharp in the grey light from the street. Lilah closes her eyes. And there it is, again—that golden dot, that pulse of life, deep down inside of her. Waiting. When she opens her eyes, the angel steps forward and bends down, places a hand against her stomach.

"Lilah," it says. "Be not afraid. I bring you a message from God." Then it opens its mouth, and all she sees is light.

NOTES

[Epigraph] "And is it not true in this instance also that one whom God blesses he curses in the same breath?" Søren Kierkegaard, *Fear and Trembling*.

[89] "If wings were not the essential element in determining the difference between a hawk and an airplane, they were even less so in the recognition of angels." Gabriel Garcia Marquez. Published in *Leaf Storm and Other Stories*, Harper-Collins Publishers, 1979.

[181] "Pain is an alchemy that renovates—where is indifference when pain intervenes?" Jalāl al-Dīn Rūmī, *The Sufi Path of Love: The Spiritual Teachings of Rumi*. (MVI 4302-04. Translated by William C. Chittick).

[186] "Once the realization is accepted that even between the closest human beings infinite distances continue, a wonderful living side by side can grow, if they succeed in loving the distance between them which makes it possible for each to see the other whole against the sky." Rainer Maria Rilke, *Letters of Rainer Maria Rilke*. (Trans. Jane Bernard Greene and M.D. Hester Norton. New York: W.W. Norton & Co., 1969).

[225] "O foolish anxiety of wretched man, how inconclusive are the arguments which make thee beat thy wings below!" Dante Alighieri, *The Inferno*, Paradiso, Canto XI.

[253] "Yet in my flesh I shall see God." Book of Job 19:26, Holy Bible, English Standard Version (2001).

[260] "For the Lord disciplines the one He loves, and chastises every son whom He receives." Hebrews 12:6, Holy Bible, English Standard Version (2001).

[293] "All, everything that I understand, I understand only because I love." Leo Tolstoy, *War and Peace, Vol. 2* (Trans. Louise Maude, Aylmer Maude. E-book edition, Digireads Publishing, 2009).

[311] "You open your hand and satisfy the desires of every living thing." Psalm 145:16, Holy Bible, New International Version (1973, 1978, 1984).

ACKNOWLEDGEMENTS

First and foremost to my agent, Samantha Haywood, who pushed this novel to be the best it could be and whose faith never wavered; and to Meghan Macdonald, also at TLA, who was the book's first true champion. This novel would not be where it is today without the help of these two wonderful women, and for that I am so grateful.

To Michael Holmes for his excellent editorial advice; Jenna Illies, my publicist, for her excitement and enthusiasm and for auctioning off a galley copy of *Miracles* in lieu of a Secret Santa gift; and Carolyn McNeillie, Crissy Boylan, Erin Creasey, and all the rest of the lovely folk at ECW.

To John Burnside, Meaghan Delahunt, Oliver De La Fosse, and David MacCormack, teachers and colleagues at the University of St. Andrews back in 2008, who all read and commented on the novel in its embryonic stages. And to John, especially, for bringing Joni Mitchell into the story.

To Natalie Olsen at Kisscut Design, for reaching right into the heart of this novel and giving it the perfect cover.

To Sarah Taggart, who read and commented on the terrible first draft before I sent it off into the world.

To Steph VanderMeulen, copy-editor and friend extraordinaire, who had exactly the kind of ruthless, infinite heart that this book so badly needed.

To Nick and Rhian Wright, who were there with champagne when the journey of this book took a turn for the better.

To Jess DeSanta, who has always known exactly what to say during bad cases of the writerly blues.

To Trevor Cole, for the gift of a jacket photo, and for telling me not to give up right when I needed it the most.

To Mike Cramer and Tricia Sinclair, who talk me up to their accomplished friends even though I don't deserve it, and whose house is still my favourite place to finish writing books.

To my aunt, Virginia Brown, who gave me my first ever Writer's Kit (complete with Skin Thickening Cream!) when I was in my teens. The skin thickener didn't work, but I made good use of those Papermate pens.

I am indebted to a large number of writers and readers who kept me company during the long (and altogether much scarier than I'd imagined) journey to publication. I am going to attempt a list, although I'm most likely forgetting a person or two. I apologize in advance: Angie Abdou, Elissa Bergman, Heidi Bischoff (and the original Chickenhead), Kris Bertin, Trevor Corkum, Clare Coyle, Ally Crockford, Andy Foreman, Krista Foss, Julie Gordon, Steven Heighton, Leigh Hensley, Miranda Hill, Nina Iyer, Will Johnson, Barb and John Jolliffe (a.k.a. the Reverend Mother and Holy Father), Sinéad Keegan, Pamela King, Susan Lewandowski, Sabrina L'Heureux, Maggie MacIntyre, Heather Middlemiss, Troy Palmer, Jessica Rose, Tom-Paul Smith, Sarah-Jane Summers, Ayelet Tsabari, Linda Tuthill, Helen Walton, Liz Windhorst-Harmer, Deborah Willis, Allegra Young, and Vicki Ziegler.

I gratefully acknowledge the assistance of the Ontario Arts Council, whose gift of a Writers' Reserve grant allowed me precious time and space to put the finishing touches on the book.

Lastly, and most importantly, I owe a lifetime's worth of gratitude to my parents, Raymond and Debra Leduc, and my siblings, Allison, Alex, and Aimee Leduc, for believing in this novel and supporting my crazy (and expensive) writer whims. For texting me halfway across the world with title suggestions, fighting over who got to read the manuscript first, and devising master plans to usurp the "Heather's Picks" stickers at Indigo—my love and thanks, forever.

Amanda Leduc was born in British Columbia and grew up in Ontario. She holds a Master's degree in writing from the University of St. Andrews and has published across Canada, the U.S., and the U.K. She lives in Hamilton, Ontario, where she is at work on her next novel.